T0279224

I'd Rather Rather Burn Than Bloom

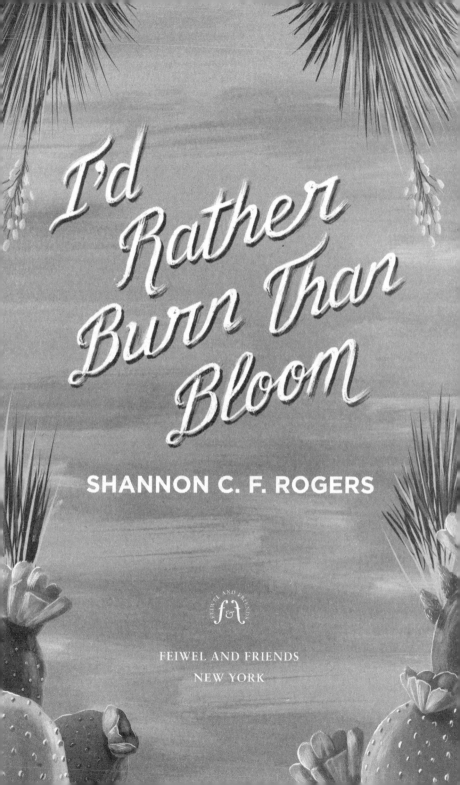

I'd Rather Burn Than Bloom

SHANNON C. F. ROGERS

FEIWEL AND FRIENDS
NEW YORK

A Feiwel and Friends Book
An imprint of Macmillan Publishing Group, LLC
120 Broadway, New York, NY 10271 • fiercereads.com

Our books may be purchased in bulk for promotional, educational,
or business use. Please contact your local bookseller or the Macmillan
Corporate and Premium Sales Department at (800) 221-7945 ext. 5442 or
by email at MacmillanSpecialMarkets@macmillan.com.

Library of Congress Cataloging-in-Publication Data
Names: Rogers, Shannon C. F., author.
Title: I'd rather burn than bloom / Shannon C. F. Rogers.
Other titles: I would rather burn than bloom
Description: First edition. | New York : Feiwel & Friends, 2023. | Audience:
Ages 13 and up. | Audience: Grades 10–12. | Summary: Alternating between
present day and flashbacks, multiracial Filipina-American teen Marisol tries
to figure out who she really is in the wake of her mother's sudden death.
Identifiers: LCCN 2022046368 (print) | LCCN 2022046369 (ebook) |
ISBN 9781250845665 (hardcover) | ISBN 9781250845672 (ebook)
Subjects: CYAC: Grief—Fiction. | Mothers and daughters—Fiction. | Family
life—Fiction. | Interpersonal relations—Fiction. | Schools—Fiction. | Racially
mixed people—Fiction. | Filipino Americans—Fiction.
Classification: LCC PZ7.1.R6626 Id 2023 (print) | LCC PZ7.1.R6626
(ebook) | DDC [Fic]—dc23
LC record available at https://lccn.loc.gov/2022046368
LC ebook record available at https://lccn.loc.gov/2022046369

First edition, July 2023
Book design by Meg Sayre
Feiwel and Friends logo designed by Filomena Tuosto
Printed in the United States of America

ISBN 978-1-250-84566-5
3 5 7 9 10 8 6 4 2

FOR SARAH AND MATT

Prologue

They're not good drawings or anything. Just sketches.

Comics, but not funny.

I can't stop doing them.

Soft pencil scratches across white paper and I've almost got it: my bedroom. The way the fading light leaks through crooked blinds. Me, on one side of the page, screaming so much that everything hurts. Mom, on the other, screaming back, because she's alive. So alive that her face is flushed, her dark eyes bright, and if only I could smell her, hold her close instead of pushing her away, she'd smell like lavender, citrus, and the faint smell of cigarette smoke clinging to her hair.

An impossibility. Rendering smell onto paper. Flattening a sound into two dimensions. Making meaning linear. Mom is dressed to leave for her shift. Not a nurse, but a nursing assistant. Night shifts and night classes and admonitions. *Don't be like me.* Blue medical scrubs. House slippers. Her bun is coming loose. I push the pencil down harder, to capture her tightly knit eyebrows, the muscles in her neck, taut. I can't help feeling like I'm missing something important. Like if I can just get it all down, every detail, the sequence of each event, who said what and when, then, then—what? That I could somehow wrangle it into something that made sense?

Time is all bleeding together, what was then is now.

"You're not wearing it," Mom screams.

She's clutching my favorite T-shirt, the one my best friend Yvonne borrows without asking. It's perfectly faded, worn, a little ripped at the collar. I'm going to Bible study but she'd hate me wearing it anywhere, to bed, even, because *what if the house burned down and you had to run outside looking like that?*

"End of story," she says.

I hate how she says that—end of story. Like she heard it on TV, so she thinks that's what she's supposed to say. Like my next line is, *Fine*, even though it isn't.

I'm sick of all the things I'm supposed to say.

"This shirt has *holes* in it," she says.

Like I'm stupid, like I don't see them.

"You don't get it!" I scream. "What is *wrong* with you?"

On the page in front of me, speech bubbles bloom around our sketched-out faces, freezing these words in time. Pressing them like dead flowers in the book of us. Hers is the only opinion that matters, has ever mattered, even though it's *my* shirt and *my* body and *my* best friend who looks better in it than I do—but it's still *mine*.

Screaming it doesn't make me feel any better, so I scream again.

"Why don't you understand *anything*?"

It's the worst thing I could say to someone who so many people discount on sight—her patients, her doctor, my teacher, speaking slowly and deliberately at parent conferences when I was a kid, glancing at the clock, as if Mom's accent is forcing her to waste precious seconds, as if Mom's accent means she can't understand *English*. As if Mom hadn't been forced to speak English in school since she was a little girl in the Philippines.

As if she weren't sitting there in blue medical scrubs in the first place because the US plopped a bunch of nursing schools there when it was a colony as part of this grand plan to "civilize" its "little brown brother." But instead of telling the teacher off, or telling her to go learn the basic history of her own goddamn imperialist country, Mom does what she always does when this happens. Ducks her head. Smiles a lot. Covers her mouth with her hand. *My accent, I'm sorry, I know, my accent*, as if she were the one who should be ashamed.

The teacher wouldn't talk to my dad that way.

She'd sit up straight. She'd be smiling. She might even be nervous. Having a white dad and a brown mom means we see these things. And when it's my brown mom in her work uniform, the teacher pronounces the words *individualized education plan* slowly, checking Mom's face for signs of understanding, as if *tachycardia* and *cricothyroidotomy* and *embolus* don't regularly roll off her tongue, as if she hadn't shown up for the parent conference bleary-eyed after a twelve-hour night shift, where she saw four people die because the new residents started a month ago, and even though they went to school longer than she ever did, even though they tell her what to do and get paid more than she *ever* will, when the new residents start, that's always when the most people die, *because they don't listen*, she says, shrugging. Just try not to go to the hospital in June.

But it wasn't supposed to be like that with me.

This was her own blood, in her own house. And so, when I hurl each word, they almost seem to hit her, one by one. *Why. Don't. You. Understand. Anything?*

She takes a step back, and then another, back through my doorway and out into the hall. And I still don't feel any better. It didn't work, because I know I wasn't asking the right question, but I still don't know what the right question is.

Mom squares her shoulders. She's small, but solid.

"Why?" she asks, blinking shining eyes. "Why do you talk to me like that?"

I didn't know why then and I still don't.

Why did I? my pencil asks the page. *Why did I?*

"Asawa," Dad shouts from down the hall. "It's just a *shirt*. Jesus. Calm down."

"Yeah, *Mom*."

Dad understands, my triumphant face says, and my voice, venomous, smug, echoes into forever as I snatch my precious, stupid shirt from her hands.

"Why can't you just leave me alone?" I ask.

In my sketchbook, hastily scrawled letters crowd the panel, pressing in on my contorted face, *leave me alone, leave me alone, leave me alone.*

The accident was my fault.

"We gotta go!" Dad calls out, shouting to be heard over us, over the sound of the garage door grinding open, over the thick rage reverberating throughout our home, because of me.

"You know what?" she says. "Fine. I'm done."

I was always telling her, begging her, to just leave me alone. And then she finally did.

Chapter One

"Wake up!"

Mom is yelling at me from the other side of my bedroom door. The New Mexico sun slices its way through the blinds, even with the blades pulled tight.

It's Sunday.

We pile into the car: me, Dad, my brother Bernie, and a million trash bags full of protein bars and toothbrushes and tampons that Mom bought in bulk when she got her check for this pay period. Last night she spread everything out on the table, and we assembled individual gallon-sized ziplock bags, to be distributed today with our neighborhood mutual aid group. We do this once a month instead of going to mass, trading stuffy clothes and organ music for deep blue desert skies and the parking lot by the library, where the group helps keep up a community fridge and pantry.

Mom's driving. Her long black hair is loose and blowing in the breeze. Dad takes her hand at red lights. When she releases his in order to make a turn, he drums his thumbs against the dashboard. He hasn't had time to shave—Mom hustled us out the door too quickly—so he looks somewhat less like a big dorky math teacher today, but only somewhat.

"I love non-church Sundays!" Dad says.

"It's not *non*-church," Mom says.

She changes lanes, glancing at the rearview mirror in movie-star sunglasses.

"Your lola used to say," she says to us in the back seat, "everything is church."

I squint into the sun, coming up over the mountains. *Only church is church.* Long hours listening, and chanting, and praying, and muttering *and also with you*. It's a singularly awkward experience. How is *everything* church?

Bernie is tilting dangerously far over to one side, so I shove him away before he has a chance to drool on me. He's in eighth grade this year, and I'm a sophomore. He's only eighteen months younger than me, but it feels like he's twice as tall; he doesn't need to lean far before he's within drooling range.

"In the Philippines, we had a group like this," Mom is saying. "On Christmas Day we assembled bags and bags of groceries, rice, vegetables, everything, and we'd go door to door, singing, singing—"

"Oh my God," Dad says, turning up the radio. "Remember this one? I haven't heard this in forever."

Mom doesn't talk about her childhood in the Philippines or our lola too much, and whenever she does, Dad finds some way to interrupt her before she gets too sad. Bernie and I were both born here in Albuquerque, and we've never even been to Colorado, let alone Manila, so I wish he'd just let her talk, but now he's *singing* to her, some weird old song, and Bernie pulls his beanie down over his eyes.

"Stop!" Mom says, but she's grinning at Dad.

"Yes, please, stop!" I say.

But they're not listening. They're both singing now, *horribly*, and I kind of want to die, even though no one else can hear them because we're in the car, but then we're pulling into the parking lot of the library, and who is standing there next to the bike racks but Joel Duran.

Looking perfect in the sun.

He's folding an empty tote bag and stuffing it into his backpack.

I feel all the blood drain from my body.

Joel Duran doesn't talk a whole lot in school, and neither do I. So I remember the first time I ever heard his singing voice. Clear and unwavering. And when we sang a duet in "El Burrito Sabanero" at our fifth-grade holiday concert, I was so nervous in front of the crowd, under the hot lights, I was afraid I'd pass out and fall off the back of the risers, but he looked at me and subtly mouthed my part and then I remembered the words. Then there was the time when he told that one teacher how to say my name right, and the time when Bernie tripped on the way into school and Joel grabbed him by the backpack to steady him, *careful, little homie*, and the time last week in geography when he was listening to music with his giant headphones, black hair curling at his ears, and he was twirling his pencil between his fingers and I thought I would *kill* to know what song it was so that I could listen to it over and over.

Dad is begging Mom to leave the car on so we don't miss the best part of the song, and Mom is telling him he's an idiot. I sink down into my seat until only my eyes are visible and peer out the window at Joel.

"Oh, look, who is that?" Mom asks.

I'm screaming internally because it's *Joel Duran*.

"*Mom*," I say. "Please don't talk to him."

She twists around, her brow furrowed in deep confusion at the sight of me all shrunken down below the window. Bernie is snoring against one of the trash bags.

"Why not?" she asks. "He just dropped off something for the fridge."

"Just leave him alone, *please*."

Joel Duran is swinging his leg over his bike and clicking his helmet into place, thank God, but then my mom is rolling down the windows, *no, no, no*.

"Hello," Mom calls out. "Fridge group?"

And now he's coming over here. I can't believe this is happening. *Why is this happening to me?*

I grab one of the bags, shove it in between me and the window, and then I curl forward, folding my arms over my knees and burying my face, trying to keep still.

"Yeah, you too?" Joel is saying, his voice unbearably close. "I'm new. Just dropped off some water and some vegetables."

"God bless you," Mom says, and I cringe. "Temperature was good?"

There's this checklist—when you come, you're supposed to make sure the fridge is still working and the door wasn't left open or anything, so the food won't spoil, and of course Joel Duran wouldn't leave the fridge without checking the temperature.

"Temperature was perfect!" Joel says.

His voice is warm and friendly, and I can't believe he's talking to *my mom*.

I grip my hands more tightly over my elbows.

Bernie snores again, and I kick him in the shin for drawing attention to us.

"Ouch, Mari, *what?*" Bernie groans.

I sit up. And then Joel sees me. *Shit.* Recognition crosses his face. *Shit.* My hair is a rat's nest and my glasses are smudged and I'm wearing a formless T-shirt from church camp three years ago and I'm all scrunched down in my seat like a weirdo.

He adjusts his helmet strap with one hand and raises the other one to greet me.

I freeze.

My mom turns around to look at me.

"Do you two know each other from school?" she asks.

As Joel glances from me to Bernie to my parents and back to me again, my face gets hotter and hotter and my mouth is dry and I can't talk, so I just shrug, willing this moment to be over.

Joel's hand goes to the back of his neck and he clears his throat.

"Anyway," he says. "Take care."

And he doesn't look at me again as he takes off on his bike.

"May God bless you," Mom calls after him.

"You already told God to bless him," I hiss. "He's fully blessed."

I turn my head just enough to see Joel make a left turn out of the parking lot and up the road, getting smaller and smaller and farther and farther away, and suddenly I want to smash something.

"Mom, why did you have to do that?"

Dad jumps out of the car, probably to get out of our way as fast as possible.

"Marisol," Mom says, stuffing her car keys into her purse. "You *have* to learn to talk to people."

Bernie gets out of the car as Dad pulls out the folding table from the trunk.

"I talk to people," I say.

"I don't mean Yvonne," she says. "Or Teresa. And you *barely* talk to them."

She gets out of the car, wrenches open my door, and takes the bag full of supplies from me.

"What do you mean? I'm with them all the time."

"Gallivanting, gallivanting," she says, tutting. "And both of you listening to Yvonne talk the whole time."

"*Mom.* Stop eavesdropping."

"You're just like your father," Mom says, and it isn't a compliment. "You keep everything inside."

"I'm an open book," Dad says. "What are you talking about?"

"Oh yeah?" Mom snaps. "Are you going to go to that grief group?"

He falls silent and struggles with the folding table, his glasses sliding down the bridge of his nose. The sky is filled with white cumulus clouds and airplane contrails crisscrossing overhead.

"What grief group?" I ask.

"The grief group I found online for people who lost a parent as a child," she says.

"Like I said, it was a long time ago, and *I'm fine*."

One of the table legs is stuck, and Dad is trying to force it to be unstuck, the metal rattling under his weight.

Bernie is squinting in the sun, watching him.

You keep everything inside. She's right. About Dad, anyway. In fact, we only ever learn stuff like this about him, important biographical details, in moments when Mom tosses them out in a fight with him in front of us. Like how his mom died when he was a kid, and how his father kicked him out of the house when he wasn't much older than I am now, and how a few years later, after wandering the US, he joined the navy and met Mom at a karaoke party in Manila, where he embarrassed himself to impress her.

I glare at the bike racks where Joel Duran was just standing. There was this one day, in seventh grade, when our English language arts teacher yelled at him and then he flipped his own desk over. I remember the crashing of metal and plastic and the way his hard, ragged breaths punctuated the silence after he'd done it.

The way his jaw set. His eyes flashed.

He'd never done anything like that before, ever. Flipping over a desk. He's usually bent over his pencil like it's broken in half and he's trying to put it back together. Like me, he's quiet. He doesn't give teachers problems, which is something teachers say a lot, like our problems are gifts we lay at their feet but they feel they must refuse—*please, don't give me any problems.*

It was that one teacher who moved here from Fort Worth. She was white, perpetually sunburned, the tip of her nose the same color as her dry strawberry-blond hair. You can always tell they're not from here from the way they pronounce the streets, the mountain ranges, and names from the roll sheet.

"Marisol Martin?" she said.

"It's like mar *y* sol," Joel corrected her.

I remember it exactly. Because he didn't pause or stumble over his words like I would have, overthinking what I wanted to say so much that I'd eventually have just given up and said nothing.

"The sea *and* the sun," Joel said.

I wondered if he thought that I was *from here* from here, like him. People think that sometimes because of how I look. And I like the feeling of belonging. To this place. So I didn't want to tell him that I'm named for my lola, who was born across the Pacific Ocean, in a place I've never seen, a place that my mom carries around with her, heavy and guarded, like she's waiting for someone to take it from her, or maybe to give it to me, but she doesn't know how.

And then, one cold morning, that same sunburned teacher tried to force Joel Duran to take off his cap, but he wouldn't. He said he didn't want to, and pulled the beanie down farther over his ears, and hunched farther over his desk, and she said, *Take it off, Joel, so we can start the class.*

And he said no.

She said, *Now*, and he said no, again and again, and then he flipped his desk over.

The teacher picked up the phone.

His desk, put back upright, sat empty for one week while he was suspended from school.

Everyone was whispering about him.

Did he get kicked out? Did they send him to juvie?

When he showed back up, he stood at the front of the class and gave his presentation on *Animal Farm* by George

Orwell. The teacher was watching him with her arms crossed and nodding like she'd won something. I could barely hear his voice, he was speaking so softly and looking down at his notes, but she didn't tell him to talk any louder, so I couldn't make out what he was saying about the windmill and the barn and what it all meant, and who the pigs were, really.

After class I waited outside, by the chipped turquoise lockers, with my books wrapped tightly into my arms. When Joel came out, he stopped short when he saw me.

"Hey," he said.

He had one hand in his pocket and one on his backpack strap, and he had no cap.

My mouth opened and closed three times. My mouth, a small black hole. It swallowed up everything I needed to ask.

What does the windmill mean?

Who are the pigs, really?

Are you okay?

I had been trying to catch his eye during his presentation. If only I'd caught his eye, maybe he would feel like I did, when he made the teacher say my name right. Maybe I could look at him and he would just *know* what I wanted to tell him, but he never looked up.

My eyes fell on my shoes and I felt him walking away, because I couldn't say the words. I kept them all inside.

"Anak," Mom says, shoving a bag into my arms. "Are you listening?"

I'm back in the parking lot under the hot sun, the car's trunk open next to me.

"How are you going to be part of anything if you make yourself an island?"

"Wow, Mom," I say, carrying the bag over to the table, which Bernie and Dad have finally wrenched open. "That's quite a metaphor."

"Simon and Garfunkel," Dad says.

It was from the song he sang to impress her, that first time.

I am a rock, I am an island.

Chapter Two

THEN

"You're mutilating them," Yvonne says.

She eyes the tattered pile of ruined rice-paper wrappers at my elbow. On the table in front of her, in contrast, a perfect pile of delicate peeled discs grows steadily. Her gold cross necklace seems to shine at the base of her throat, and her dark, gently curled hair falls to her waist. She looks like the patron saint of lumpia. Miss Teen Lumpia USA.

"How are you *not*?" I ask.

We're seated at the end of the table, in our kitchen, the first step of the spring roll assembly line. Bernie and my other best friend, Teresa, are supposed to take from our piles of separated wrappers, add the filling, wet the edges with yolks, roll them, and place them in the tray to be fried, but because Bernie can roll more quickly than I can separate, he's defaulted to leaning back in his chair and scrolling through his phone.

Mom, overseeing our work, pops in and out of the kitchen, frantic, as she gets dressed for tonight's Bible study. She can't always come to Friday night Bible study because she likes to pick up the Friday shift, which pays more. So, when she does come, it's a major social event.

"You're going too slow!" she says.

As she whirls around and marches down the hall, our cat Marty jumps out of her way, a blur of orange. When he stills, he's straight-legged and wide-eyed, watching her until she disappears into her room.

Even he's tense around her when she's like this.

"But you actually should go slowly, if you need to," Tes says to me. "We can't use the ripped ones."

She's pinned her straight black hair back behind her ears with two barrettes. I watch as her manicured fingertips dip into the bowl of egg wash, her fingers flitting and folding and rolling like she was born to do it, born to fill trays and trays of food for Bible studies.

"Asawa!" Mom calls out. "Where are you?"

She reappears, briefly, in the kitchen with half-flat-ironed hair, before continuing her search for my dad from room to room.

He's probably hiding.

"So, party at Jasmine's after?" Yvonne asks, dropping her voice to a whisper.

I can't help but groan.

"Do we have to?" I ask.

One more party at Jasmine Padilla's house and I think I might crack. The sameness of it all. The same people. The same music. The same layout, even, as Yvonne's house and Tes's house. Beige walls and beige counters and a red cooler full of whatever unholy concoction Andrew Padilla came up with today.

"Come on," Yvonne says. "Her brother is making jungle juice."

When she says *come on*, and she smiles that perfectly symmetrical smile, I don't know if she's pushing me because she actually wants me there or if she just needs me there as part of the cover story. I rip a lumpia wrapper in half, just because.

Mom surfaces again, eyeing the debris.

"Marisol," she says. "Why don't you just give those to Yvonne to do?"

I shove my plate of unseparated wrappers at Yvonne and she picks up where I left off, twisting her head so that her long mass of hair moves behind her shoulder.

The bass line of a song spills from the radio of a passing car, drifting through the open window on a warm breeze, and I find myself wishing I could jump into their back seat and go with them, wherever they're going. My mom pulls the window shut, muffling the sound, and now she's coming for me, the next stop on her rampage of straightening and fixing and smoothing out.

I try to lean out of her reach, but it's no use, and when she pulls my hair from my face, I cringe.

"Did you do the reading for tonight?" she asks.

Her nails scratch at my scalp as she wrestles my hair into a bun.

"Why are you only asking *me*?" I ask.

"Because you're the only one who hasn't done it."

Bernie snorts as Tes and Yvonne drop their eyes to their hands. They always do the readings and the associated journaling. Tes has a pink cover for her Bible and a pink highlighter. But I don't understand the point of her highlighting, because when her Bible sits open in her lap, it's almost all pink in there.

"I've read this one a million times," I say.

My mom clicks her tongue, and unable to keep still, ever, she turns to the kitchen counter, her hands attacking a messy pile of mail. She squints at each envelope before placing them into neat stacks.

For tonight, she's done a pretty red lip, but her skin looks dull, and her eyes are tired. Even though she works nights and it's her day off, instead of being asleep when I came home from school today, she was simultaneously making a tray of pancit for the Bible study and cleaning out the hall closet, placing a jacket Bernie had quickly outgrown into a cardboard box.

She's done all that and doesn't look like she slept at all, and I haven't even bothered to read the First Epistle to the Thessalonians.

Yvonne bumps me with her shoulder gently.

"I'll read it again in the car on the way over, Mommy," I say. "Okay?"

Only, she's not listening to me anymore.

"*Where* is your father?"

"Hiding from Jesus in the garage," Bernie mutters.

"What?"

"Probably in the garage."

Mom sweeps into the laundry room, her slippered feet silent on the tile.

"We have to make a pit stop on the way over," Yvonne says. "Just a quick one."

Tes and I already know just what the pit stop will be. My parents and Bernie head over in our car, and I ride with Yvonne and Tes. The sun is going down and it gets in my eyes as Tes navigates the winding neighborhood roads. The desert sky is on fire and the rocky face of the Sandia Mountains glows pink in the east.

Yvonne's secret boyfriend is standing on the curb in front of his house with his hands in the pockets of his jeans. The sprinklers turn on, arcing over a neat square of green grass that shouldn't even be here because it takes too much water, but there are twenty of them anyway, right in a row. Tes hasn't even brought the car to a stop before Yvonne is leaning out the window and pressing her lips to his.

"Hey, beautiful," Nick Barnes says, thumbing the side of her neck. "Hey, Teresa. Marisol."

Tes keeps her eyes on the road and her hands at nine and three.

"Hello," she says.

"You guys coming to Jasmine's later?"

"They're coming," Yvonne says, without taking her brown eyes off his blue ones. Her hair flows down her back in waves.

"If you need a ride, I can come," Tes says to her. "But I need to get my mom's car back to her before nine."

Meaning her curfew is at nine, even though she's too embarrassed to say that in front of Nick, whose parents literally offered to book a hotel room for him and his friends at his junior prom this year.

The lives of white kids are truly unfathomable to me.

"What about you, M?" he asks.

I can't help it, I soften a little when he calls me M. At first, Nick seemed boring, but he's actually cool, sort of, in that he likes to draw and he reads a lot of manga, which Yvonne does not. He tucks Yvonne's hair behind her ear but he keeps his eyes on me.

His eyelashes are long and full.

It's not like I'm in love with Nick Barnes. But unlike Joel Duran, with his soft eyes and his fixed-gear bike and his big headphones, who I watch from across classrooms and hallways and parking lots, Nick is right here, every day. My best friend's boyfriend. He laughs at my dumb jokes and puts his arm around me when we're playing video games on his couch, and sometimes it feels like his love for Yvonne somehow smudges, like pencil on smooth paper, onto me. I wonder what song Joel Duran is listening to, what he's writing in his notebook, where he goes after school when he swings his leg over his bike and glides away, and then I'm sitting on the bus next to Tes and Yvonne, making plans to go to Nick's house.

"I'll be there," I say.

At Bible study, we're seated in a circle in another beige house. Yvonne sits between her mother and my mother. She reads slowly and clearly from the First Epistle of St. Paul the Apostle to the Thessalonians, grasping the golden cross necklace at her throat.

"For we know, brothers and sisters loved by God, that he has chosen you."

My mom pats her on the knee, nodding, like she's listening to her favorite song. My dad is outside, examining the rosebushes in the yard, hiding from Jesus, as he does.

At Jasmine Padilla's party, Tes declines the red Solo cup because she's driving, and I refuse because it smells like robot's blood and I know it must taste worse. Yvonne and Nick make out on the couch. Jasmine is playing music so loudly it makes me want to pluck my eyelashes out one by one.

In the kitchen, Tes drinks from her pink metallic water bottle. It's covered in stickers, just like the case she carries her French horn in. We lean against the counter, reading all the baptism announcements, quince invitations, and wedding save-the-dates magnetized to Jasmine's fridge. I place a magnet of Tweety Bird's head on a bride-to-be's body, but Tes doesn't laugh.

"Do you think Yvonne and Nick will get married?" Tes asks me.

I try not to look over to the couch at Nick, at his hands, at where they are.

"No way."

"Why not?" Tes asks. "I mean after graduation, of course."

"Would *you* get married right after graduation?"

She adjusts her shirt collar.

"After graduation I'm joining the navy."

I look at her, in her matching hair barrettes, and she's serious.

"*What?*" she asks.

Even though I haven't even said anything, she can see it on my face.

"Tes, you can't even swim," I say.

"A barrier, but easily overcome. It's in the blood."

Our dads were in the navy together. He's white, too. They were friends before they met our mothers on a port call one night. It all seems so random. Just because some officers were having a party and somebody invited our dads, and somebody else invited Tes's mom, who invited my mom, now, here we are.

"They'll pay for school," she says, shrugging. "Dad's thrilled."

Tes takes another drink from her water bottle as the party swirls around her. I feel bad for her sometimes. Her house is full of pristine white carpets and rooms you're not allowed to sit in. Her parents don't let her watch R-rated movies or listen to "secular" music. Paying for school is one thing, but I'm sure she could get the lottery scholarship and just go here like everybody else does. She wants to join the navy because she can't wait to get far, far away from them.

"Hey."

Nick's voice is in my ear and his hand is on my waist and I jump.

I swallow hard and put as much space between us as I can. Yvonne's arm appears, snaking around his belly, and she nuzzles her head into his chest.

"Gross," he says. "Your hair smells like those greasy Filipino egg rolls."

She laughs.

Even though I don't know why, I'm laughing, too.

My stomach twists.

"Can we go?" Tes asks Yvonne.

In the car on the way home, I sit in the passenger seat. Yvonne and Nick hold hands in the back. Tes is driving, looking ahead to her future, going all ROTC on me. What if Yvonne and Nick do get married and have a kid, and one day they tell her, *We met in high school, and your Tita Tes used to drive us home from parties*? For some reason, I feel sick.

And as her car is pulling away from my house, the streetlight flickers, and my mom is already pulling the front door open before I can get there, narrowing her eyes at me and sniffing the air.

"You smell like cigarettes," she says.

"Weird," I say, pushing past her into the house.

She's changed into a pajama set that's not so different from the scrubs she wears to the hospital. It's like she has a uniform for everything. Earlier, at Bible study, she was wearing her my-family-is-a-good-family-who-goes-to-Bible-study uniform. Now she wears her waiting-up-for-my-daughter-because-I'm-a-mom-in-a-movie uniform. As background noise completes the scene, the voices of the news anchors follow a familiar cadence.

"Asawa," my mom calls to the next room. "Your daughter smells like cigarettes."

My heart is in my throat because I *didn't* smoke any cigarettes. I've *never* smoked any cigarettes, unlike her, who smokes secretly every day in the thin dawn light before coming inside after work, and when she's watering the roses and thinks we're not looking, and in the ambulance bay with the other women in scrubs. Dad and I drove to the hospital once to bring her wallet when she'd forgotten it, and I saw her stubbing out her cigarette hastily against a trash can when she saw our car approaching.

I hate the smell.

So I've never smoked, or drank, and I've never even made out with a boy on the couch.

And I've never been able to prove it to her.

"Where were you?" Mom asks, blocking my way. "Where were you really?"

"Nowhere," I say, and I wish it were true. Right now, I wish I were nowhere, in a dark void where no one was looking at me or asking me questions like, *Do you think Yvonne and Nick will get married?* and *Why not join the navy?* and *Did you do the assigned reading?* and *Why don't you just let Yvonne do the lumpia wrappers?*

"Who were you with?"

"Who am I always with, Mom?"

She expels a puff of air like she's really sick of me. Well, I'm sick of me, too. I'm sick of all of it.

I slam the door to my bedroom closed.

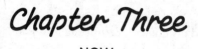

Chapter Three

NOW

It's Monday morning, three months since Mom died.
My sketchbook slips from my lap, and when I grab it, my pencil falls from my hand and rolls away down the center aisle of the school bus.

I can't tell if I'm hungover or still drunk.

I can't remember if I slept.

My body lurches forward as the bus churns around the corner, my cheek pressing up against the cracked leather seat in front of me. It smells like old vomit and something chemical masking it. Choking down a gag, I squint into the sun and tuck my sketchbook away into my backpack.

Every day, Monday to Friday, we crawl down this same bumpy dirt road together, so I can recognize each person here, even from the back of their head.

And two are missing.

My thoughts feel distant, muffled, like I'm overhearing a conversation from another room down the hall. Maybe I should text Yvonne. Sometimes she oversleeps. She can sleep and sleep for days if you let her, and she'd be mad if I let her. But Tes never oversleeps, and Tes isn't here either.

What if Yvonne knows what happened yesterday?

It was raining. Nick pulled the car over. It was raining so hard. His arm was already draped over the back of my seat. And when he leaned toward me—

It's fine, I say to myself.

Erasing the scene from my mind.

But even if I believed that it was fine, my body has moved to a place beyond my control. Breath shallow. Palms slick. And at the back of the bus, Alyssa Lujan keeps *laughing*. Her teeth are too white. She steps on a crinkled-up water bottle on the floor and it's the loudest sound in the world and I have to pinch the bridge of my nose to keep my skull from exploding, sloshing blood and brain matter across the windowpane.

Why aren't Yvonne and Tes here?

I stumble off the bus, across the dusty parking lot, and it's when I'm on the concourse on the way to homeroom that the notification comes through on my phone.

YVONNE MORALES HAS POSTED A NEW PHOTO OF YOU.
slut slut slut slut slut slut slut

My phone dings and dings. Each ding is like hearing the word:

slut slut slut slut slut slut slut

It's not a new photo of me, it's an old photo of me. From Yvonne's birthday last year. Her arm is draped around my shoulders, but she's cropped herself out. Her arm is just there, disembodied.

He told her. Or she just knew. Or somebody saw.

I'm still as a stone against the tide of backpacks and sneakers squeaking on the linoleum. They slide over me like I'm not

even there. The clock over the trophy case—GO, PUMAS!—
says it's one minute to the late bell, and I have to get out of
here.

Now.

Scanning for the red block letters, EXIT, I risk a pull from my
water bottle.

It isn't water.

"Marisol!"

Her voice cuts through the crowd. It parts to reveal her
standing there. The concourse is Yvonne's stage now. I push
the hair from my face, which is wet, salty.

"Are you crying?" she asks, rushing me. "Are you crying?"

She grabs my jean jacket into her fist.

We're five years old. I'm pretending to be asleep on her bedroom floor, sandwiched between two of her cousins. I want to
go home, but I'm too embarrassed to say it: I hate sleepovers.

I miss my mom.

Yvonne slips out of her bed and peers down at me, pushing
the hair from my face.

"Marisol," she whispers. "Are you crying?"

But we're not five years old anymore. We're sixteen, and I've
fucked her boyfriend, and now she's going to kick my ass.

I've been waiting for this moment, really. It feels right, her
anger crackling in the air, finally. Finally, we're doing this.

I am crying now, and Yvonne pushes me, her brown eyes
aflame, her face beautiful, even when twisted with rage. *She
could be on TV, you know?* My mom's voice, in my head,
always her voice in my head. *Yvonne could move to Manila
and be on TV in a second.*

Yvonne pushes me, again, open-palmed.

I stumble, tripping on my own feet.

"Fight!" somebody screams from the crowd.

"Slut," Yvonne says, spitting the word.

She grabs my arm and smacks me across the head, hard, with her other hand.

Where are my glasses? My hands are covering my head, and then they're pulling her hair. The rising sun cuts across the concourse; it's in my eyes and bouncing off Yvonne's glossy hair and the glass doors of the trophy case and everything is noise.

Nick was *my* friend, too.

He was always bringing new manga to show me at lunchtime.

"Check this out, M," he'd say.

"Nerds," Yvonne would say, and he'd grin at her across the table as he drew her face on a napkin in steady strokes of a felt-tip pen, the napkin version of Yvonne rolling her eyes up toward the sky.

My sketchbook: It *had* to have come from Nick. The one that Dad pressed into my hands after Mom's funeral. I asked him where it came from as he peered down through heavy-lidded eyes, straightening his only tie. He shrugged. It was wrapped neatly, in a brown grocery bag, and tied with a string. It felt weighty, solid, like the only real thing left in this world.

With Nick Barnes, I found out that kissing is like drinking too much. Oblivion. Everything is quiet. He kissed me, and for once, I didn't think. Not about Yvonne declining my phone calls, or Joel Duran swinging his leg over his bike and gliding away, or Mom smoking at dawn by the rosebushes—or anything at all.

He didn't *say* the sketchbook was from him.

He didn't ask me if it was my first time.

It was.

"Stop it!" someone shouts.

A teacher. The crackle of a radio.

"Security? We have an altercation in Concourse B."

Yvonne takes a swing at me and misses.

"Why *you*?" she snarls.

In her voice, I hear the hurt and the confusion—how could he do this to her? With me?

Why don't you go to Bible study with Yvonne? my mom asks from the dead. *She's such a good girl.*

I take a swing at Yvonne and I don't miss.

Chapter Four

There's a name for this place, but everybody just calls it juvie. A squat, concrete box of a building surrounded by gravel and twiggy trees, where they send you to take classes on a computer when you've been kicked out of your own school, either for a little while, or forever.

Yvonne isn't here, because she didn't have a water bottle full of vodka in her backpack, for the second time. But I did.

It's not so bad. Even though I can barely complete the assignments, and I have to read paragraphs over and over and I still don't understand them, and I'm so tired all the time and I don't know what's wrong with me. But there's this one girl, Ella, who has a streak of blue hair behind her ear and is at least seven months pregnant, who gives me a piece of gum every day. She doesn't even say anything when she does it, just twists around backward in the metal chair and offers it, the foil wrapper catching the fluorescent light. She makes me feel like I don't even have to say anything back.

It's nice.

Nothing else is, of course. Mrs. Mirsky isn't nice. She says we engage in *high-risk behaviors* because we're *troubled*, and we're *troubled*—she mutters this part—because we haven't accepted Jesus Christ into our hearts. She says this while looking pointedly at Ella and crossing her arms across her chest in her ugly, drapey blouse, which makes her look like a bat.

I'm pretty sure Mirsky's not supposed to say stuff like that to us, and anyway, Ella's just sitting here, being totally nice, sharing her gum, and here's Mirsky, narrowing her eyes at Ella like she's the Antichrist.

If I told my dad about the "accepting Jesus" comment, he'd be pissed—and he's white, so he's not afraid to yell at teachers. My mom never yelled at teachers; she just yelled at me.

Dad is famously a raging atheist, and a jerk about it, too. Mom was a Catholic, raised that way in the Philippines, but Dad has always refused to show his face at Our Lady of Guadalupe, not even on *Easter*, which was super embarrassing for Mom, because everyone goes to church on Easter, at least. She wore him down one time, just one time, and then he took Communion even though he wasn't supposed to, and then, as if that wasn't bad enough, he said, "Mmm, savior flavor!" when he returned to our pew, which made Bernie snort-laugh super loud and made Mom whack both of them in the arm with her hymnal.

She was trying not to laugh. Or, maybe, she was trying not to cry.

I don't know. It's like I have two copies of every memory, and they keep spawning and making more and more copies every time I turn them over in my mind, multiplying and multiplying until I can't remember. Until I can't draw them fast enough. Until I can't get back there, to how it was, to how we were. Until I can't see a way to undo what was done.

And unfortunately, one cannot simply unpunch Yvonne Morales in the face, so here I am.

When I got suspended from La Manzanita High, Principal Peña told me the first step toward getting better was to recognize that I have a *problem*. But by the time she told me that, I already knew. I knew that getting drunk at school, spending my fourth period with my cheek pressed against a disgusting bathroom floor haunted by the ghosts of Sharpie penises past, was what she'd call a *problem*. I wouldn't call it that. Problems can be solved, but my mom is gone. As in, nowhere. She doesn't *exist* anymore. And no matter how many bathroom tiles I press my cheek to, she'll never be here to yell at me about it.

How can that be, when I catch her scent in coat closets, when I thought I saw her at the grocery store yesterday?

Sometimes, in fact, my mom isn't actually dead. Not to me. If I close my eyes very hard and my mind is just blurry enough from the watery beers Dad keeps in the fridge, I can trick myself into believing that she just moved away, maybe. She lives on Bainbridge Island, in Puget Sound, in Washington, where my parents lived before I was born. It's green as hell there because it's always raining. She even has a vegetable garden. And lawn furniture. And a big-ass deck, where she watches the sun go down over the water, like a Popsicle melting into a sticky, golden sea. I make up this whole backstory about how she got sick of the desert. She was done with stepping in cacti and pulling bloody spines out of the bottoms of her feet. She said it wasn't my fault. She quit smoking. Started a collection of little silk fans from

Chinatown, lining them up on windowsills, row upon row: turquoise, marigold, and rose.

I save a picture from a magazine that looks exactly like the house she wanted. I Scotch tape it to the wall next to my bed. Squeeze my eyes tighter and it's real now, it's real. During Christmas break, after I take my last midterm, I fly into the Seattle airport by myself to visit her. I take a taxi to the ferry with my backpack in my lap. It's raining and my shoes are wet. The Sound is the same slate gray as the sky, and the city lights are a smudge in the mist. I shake out my umbrella on the front porch and find the key under the flowerpot. Peel off my damp socks, lie down on her couch, wrap myself in a warm red blanket. Close my eyes. She'll be home soon.

But this I don't draw, because this didn't happen.

"Okay, remember, the first thing you have to do is check your mirrors," Dad says.

He pulls the passenger-side seat belt across his checkered flannel shirt, the one that makes him look like a lumberjack. A nearsighted lumberjack who teaches math. In my drawings, his glasses come out bigger than they are in real life.

I've had my learner's permit for a year. Since before Mom died. I'd already learned most of the basics and Dad even let me drive home from dropping Mom off at the hospital one night—on the surface streets, not the freeway. But after her accident we dropped it completely. I never asked to drive anywhere, and Dad never brought it up. Now, all of a sudden, Dad's completely obsessed with "getting me back out on the road."

I've tried to get out of it every way I can think of. Trapped in an enclosed space, with no escape? What if he tries to talk to me about how my *grieving process* is going? Listening to him run through this checklist like we're on some sad mission to nowhere is even more mortifying than I'd imagined.

"Now, adjust the seat, if you have to," Dad says. "There's no shame in being a short stack, Short Stack."

"I *know*."

I shift the seat forward to get closer to the steering wheel.

Short Stack, just one of the many Dad nicknames. Bernie is Flubs and our cat, Marty, is Furmaster Flex. The church we used to attend is affectionately known as Our Lady of Endless Guilt and Shame.

Dad has many nicknames for me. His use of this particular nickname, at this particular moment, is a sign that he's trying to keep it light.

Knowing that just makes it all worse.

My phone buzzes in my pocket. I snatch it out, hoping it might be—but no, it's just a stupid alert from this astrology app Yvonne made me download. We used to laugh about the word salad it serves up every day, and this one's a classic word salad:

Both your expanse and your limit are invented in the prison of your mind.

"Hey," Dad says. "We're in the middle of something important here."

I tuck my phone away and stare ahead.

"I thought it was Yvonne," I say quietly. "Maybe."

He shifts in his seat uncomfortably.

"Oh," he says.

If Mom were here, at least she'd have something to say besides *oh*. At least she'd scream at me that I needed to ask God to forgive me, that she raised me better than to be a girl like *that*, and that I'd made it so she'd never be able to show her face at Our Lady of Endless Guilt and Shame again.

Or maybe she wouldn't do that. Maybe she wouldn't say those things. Maybe she'd let me crawl into bed with her, and cry and cry my eyes out, her fingers smoothing down the little hairs at my crown, saying, *Shh, shh*.

I'll never know.

"Dad," I say, my voice thick. "What if she never talks to me again?"

He clears his throat, looks around the garage, his hands resting on his knees. "You'll make new friends."

Right. Easy. Like I'm in kindergarten. Like Yvonne was just *some friend*. My knuckles turn white against the steering wheel.

"Listen . . . ," he says, his tone shifting.

Every muscle in my shoulders tightens, every fiber, every molecule.

"This reluctance around driving . . . is it because you're scared of . . . ?"

He gets quiet, like he can barely get the words out.

I hate this, I hate this, I hate this.

"Because of what happened to—?"

"No," I snap. "I'm not scared."

"Marisol . . ."

"I *said* I'm not scared. Jesus."

The air is thick in my lungs. I force it out through my nose.

"Okay then," Dad says.

He clears his throat again, and we're back to Alpha, Bravo, Charlie.

"Sit back in the seat so that you're comfortable yet able to remain alert."

He pushes up his glasses with his knuckle. I copy him, reflexively, with my own. We're both so myopic that the only letter on the eye chart we can read is the *E*. On that drive home from the optometrist, the day I got glasses, in third grade when a teacher finally noticed I couldn't see the board, everything sharpened, everything cleared, and things that I thought were one thing were actually something else. The white smudge hanging low in the sky was not a cloud, but the moon, and my mom had a birthmark on the back of her neck in the exact shape of the state of Nevada. She turned around and smiled at me, in the back seat of this car, which sometimes still smells like her.

Or maybe I'm just imagining it.

"You okay?" he asks.

"I'm *fine*," I say because he's looking at me that way, and I need him to stop looking at me that way. I feel like all he does is stare at me now, studying me, prodding me, asking me, *Did you meet anyone nice today? Did you have anything good for lunch? Did you drink enough water?*—until I'm so tired that I want to fall into a hole because, *no*, *no*, and *no*.

He pushes the button on the garage door opener and the machine screams to life.

I wish there were an eject button, for him or for me, I don't really care which at this point. The garage door slowly grinds open and the afternoon light floods in.

The key turns in my hand, and the wheel hums as the engine comes to life.

"Check the rearview."

Another car rolls down the street behind us.

"Whenever you're ready, go ahead and back up."

Our neighbor across the street is putting out the trash. Her kid is riding a bike in circles in the driveway, the silver streamers on the handlebars moving in the wind.

"Whenever you're ready."

My eyes flick to the Virgin Mary air freshener dangling in front of me. *Sorry.*

I shift the car into drive, stomp on the gas pedal hard, and we smash forward into a shelving unit, which collapses in a dusty cascade onto the hood of the car. I slam the brake as two cardboard boxes full of Christmas ornaments, an old sled, a pair of Rollerblades, and a telescope all rain down on us, thumping one by one onto the hood and the windshield.

"Jesus, Marisol!"

Dad unbuckles himself and jumps out of the car. He coughs and waves the dust away from his face, inspecting the damage.

"Turn off the engine! Turn. It. Off."

We have passed over a dozen other weird nicknames and gone straight to "Marisol."

My hands release the steering wheel as the dust settles into the slanted sunbeams now streaming in through the open garage. My dad pulls the telescope out of the box by its legs and flips it over to check if the lens is broken. I wonder if he can see my face at the other end—really tiny. Really relieved.

Dad gave that telescope to Bernie and me for Christmas last year, after Mom's accident. Even though it was too late. Even though she hadn't been gone that long, only a month, which simultaneously felt like ten months and only ten seconds. Even though everything felt strange and raw and fake. Even though we both knew the telescope was actually supposed to be for her, because she was always dragging us to Family Fridays at the planetarium. She said she loved it because it reminded her of how small she was. I told her that maybe she had a contact high from all the UNM kids around us who were totally blazed. She was pissed. *How do you know what a contact high is?* But now I know what she meant.

We're all really tiny and insignificant, and it's actually really crushing to think about. When I sketch the planetarium, I black out the paper around one billion little points of light. I start at the corner of the page and I don't stop until I fill up every inch. Hours have passed and it doesn't matter at all. I'm the same as those little points of light, as the shavings from my eraser.

Dust.

It took Dad all Christmas Day to put that telescope together. Crouching on the green shag carpet, squinting at the small print in front of him, insert *A* into *B*. Lifting his chin as his glasses slid down the bridge of his nose. The afternoon stretched out, long and tired. The house was quiet. Bernie and I went outside and stomped our boots into the muddy slush that had once been snow, but Dad stayed in there, his hands cradling all the little pieces.

Later, when we were both asleep on the couch in front of the TV, he shook our shoulders gently.

"Coats," he said.

The two of us padded over to the hall closet and reached for big winter coats to be pulled over pajamas, moving silently in the moonlit entryway. Outside, Dad stuck the telescope's legs onto the icy sidewalk. We could see our breath, and the faint outline of the mountains' ridges in the dark. Hear the cars in the distance. Feel the faraway heat of ten thousand suns. See Jupiter's moons. Feel everything.

It was too much.

The crushing weight of all that emptiness and she wasn't there.

She wasn't there.

Bernie turned toward the house and made his way back up the driveway.

"Where are you going, Flubs?"

"She asked you and asked you," Bernie said without turning around.

"What?" Dad asked, almost as quiet as the traffic light changing.

Bernie's sweet little-kid face seemed to melt away right in front of me. His eyes narrowed, his features hardened. It felt like another death.

"Mom was the one who wanted to see the stupid planets, Dad," he said. "Not me."

I looked at Dad, but he was staring at the crack in the driveway, maybe because he knew it was too late.

Bernie pulled the door shut behind him when he went inside.

"It's okay," I said, because it seemed like something I *should* say. It seemed like that was what I was supposed to do, not because it felt true or real, because nothing did.

When we went inside, he put the telescope back in the box and slid it onto the highest shelf in the garage. I think he meant to leave it there forever. But now I've knocked it loose with the car, and we all have to look at it again, this thing that we shoved aside.

"Today we have a treat," Mrs. Mirsky is saying.

I gaze out the window into the dirt lot outside the classroom. It's late spring, and with the school year almost over, my time at juvie is almost complete. Already the heat is radiating from the dusty earth in shiny, pink-white waves.

Somehow I think roasting alive in the desert would be preferable to whatever Mirsky considers a treat.

Dad has cleared the entire house of any and all alcohol so that I can't sneak it into my water bottle anymore, and everything looks and feels too sharp, too loud, and too clear.

Mrs. Mirsky leads us in pushing all our desks to the side, *to make room*. For what, I don't know, but neither do I particularly care.

There are ten of us today, from schools across the city. That number has been fluctuating as lengths of suspensions vary *depending on the severity of the infraction*, per the student handbook. Expulsions are also possible. Principal Peña said I was lucky for not getting that when she suspended me for the remainder of the year.

Lucky.

We all move sluggishly until the chairs and desks are put away, leaving everyone standing awkwardly, exposed, with nowhere to slump, nothing to lay our heads on top of.

"We have a student here to do an activity with you," Mirsky says.

She reads from a creased sheet of paper in her hand.

"A *movement* activity. She's from La Manzanita High."

I flinch at the name of my school and drop my eyes to the floor when I see the aforementioned student standing in the doorway. Elizabeth Parker. I know her. She's the one with the best grade in every class, destroying the curve, making her the number one enemy of Andrea Flores, who's been gunning for valedictorian pretty hard since we were, like, five.

What's she *doing* here?

"Hi, everyone," she says, moving her long dark braid from one shoulder to the other.

Elizabeth Parker is wearing yoga pants and an overlarge sweater, like a ballet dancer in a movie. Like me, she has a white last name but she isn't white. Her features are soft in places and sharp in others, thick dark hair and light brown skin. She ushers us into a circle, and everyone is doing everything to keep from looking at each other, or at her, because she's being so earnest, and it's embarrassing.

"Thanks for having me here in your space," she says, flicking off the overhead lights. "I'm practicing for an independent study about the psychology of character work in theater. So we're going to go ahead and settle into our bodies here."

Ella can't do all the stretches or the movements. She hinges at the waist but she can't touch her toes, and she reaches for me to help hoist her back upright afterward.

"Now I want you to connect with your breath," Elizabeth says.

Someone in the corner has slumped over and fallen asleep, and Mirsky is sitting behind her desk, scrolling on her cell phone, but Elizabeth is closing her eyes and showing us how to breathe with our bellies instead of our chests, and suddenly I'm aware of my own lungs.

The air as I breathe in and out.

The sound of her voice.

My eyes flutter closed.

"Now," Elizabeth says, "I want you to turn to the person next to you."

It's Ella, thank God. We turn to one another.

"And look into their eyes."

We both snort a little, roll our eyes.

Then we look at each other.

Her eyes are a very deep brown.

"And maybe ask yourself, what's the worst thing that's ever happened to this person?"

Ella touches the blue streak in her hair. What's the worst

thing that's ever happened to Ella? Maybe being here at juvie? Maybe she saw something really horrible happen once. Maybe she saw somebody die.

Her eyes soften. Can she tell?

Can she tell the worst thing that's ever happened to me?

"Try not to look away."

I swallow hard and squirm, but Ella isn't looking away, and I feel like she can see it, the worst thing that ever happened to me, right there on my face. How Mrs. Trujillo from the neighborhood mutual aid group had to pick me up at school and drive me to the hospital because Mom was there and our car was smashed on the side of the highway on that bright November morning. It was the same hospital where she worked. The hospital with the break room where I sat on a plastic chair, coloring in worksheets, on Take Your Child to Work Day. The hospital where, once, a patient grabbed Mom's arm so hard, using her small body to pull himself up from bed, that her shoulder got dislocated. She'd said, *Wait, let me call someone else to help*, but he hadn't waited. *He was in pain*, Mom said. *He didn't mean to.* But that hardly seemed to matter. This was the same hospital where she sat, at the nurses' station, answering the phone with the wrong hand, her dominant arm in a sling, after it happened. It was in that hospital where nobody ever said sorry to her, about that, or anything else, where everybody took her and her body for granted, grinding her down, night shift after night shift. It was in that hospital where she never woke up, where the nurse said to talk to her because supposedly she could hear me, but I wasn't able to say anything, I couldn't, or wouldn't, because I was just like everybody else. It was in that hospital where she died with all those tubes in her, that day.

Elizabeth weaves through the bodies in the crowded, darkened classroom.

"Now, I want you to imagine," she says, "that this thing, whatever it was, is now a sticky ball that fits in your palm."

I close my hand around it, this imaginary sticky ball.

It's warm.

"Now place it somewhere on your body. Behind your knee, or on your left shoulder, or between two ribs."

She's lost some people, drifting to the corners or staring at the ceiling. But there's a quiet shuffling of sweatshirts and sneakers as some of us place our sticky balls. Like I'm in some kind of trance, I place this imaginary object at the base of my throat where the clavicle meets the sternum.

"Now, let's move through the room. Just walk. But as you move, notice how you move differently, knowing that sticky ball is there."

Because of where I've placed it, I notice that when I walk, my arms sway a little, even just walking, and so my shoulders move back and forth, forcing that sticky ball to rub into my flesh, and the more I move, the more it burrows down, into bone, splintering it open, all from just walking, from moving through the world.

"Are you okay?" Ella whispers to me.

"Yeah," I say. "Why?"

"You're crying."

The sticky ball's burn has spread into my throat and my chest cavity, and my eyes ache. My breath catches.

"Oh," I say, wiping tears away.

Ella grips my arm, holds me up, and I rub the place over my heart with my palm, the place where my sticky ball has been all along, without my knowing.

Chapter Five

NOW

That night, I'm in bed but not asleep. I can't sleep no matter how tired I am. I keep thinking about the hospital, the machines beeping, about Mom clutching that T-shirt, and how if only I hadn't said what I said, then she wouldn't have been so mad, she wouldn't have waved Dad away, saying, *I'm driving myself*, and then she wouldn't have—

There's a tap at my bedroom window.

For a second, I hope that it's Yvonne out there, even though I know that's stupid. I hope for it anyway. Her head cocked to one side, *let's go to Jasmine's*, like none of it ever happened. But by the time I've crossed my bedroom, passed the photo collage of us pinned to my corkboard, baptisms to birthdays, I know that it's Nick at my window.

I part the broken blinds that have been mangled by Marty, who likes to sit on the sill in a sunbeam, exposing his orange-white belly to the sky.

Nick. In a tuxedo. With a white flower pinned on the lapel. The streetlight playing in his thick brown hair. His car parked on the other side of the street. I shake my head and I'm about to turn away when he produces a metal flask from his pocket and dangles it before me, grinning.

The house, of course, is dry now. So I open the window, pop the screen, and climb out, my naked feet landing in dirt. As with just about everything these days, I find I don't really care.

It's a warm, late-spring night, the sky full of stars, crickets chirping in the trees.

I accept the flask. The metal is cool in my palm.

"It was prom?" I ask, realizing it must have been.

I didn't even realize it was that time of year. Every day in juvie felt the same until Elizabeth came. But time keeps moving forward. It seems cruel.

Nick nods, leaning on the rough adobe wall next to me and tilting his head toward my window.

"I see your dad didn't put bars on your window yet."

I can smell his soap. My heart tightens, to recognize it.

"Not yet."

Nick drew a picture of me once, his elbow grazing mine, in the cafeteria at lunch. I leaned forward to watch his hands moving the pencil, gliding across the sheet of notebook paper, tracing the curves of my face.

I could smell his soap then, too.

I take a swig, gagging a little, because whatever is in here is terrible, and I feel him staring at me in the dark. I grip the flask because it feels good to hold, but suddenly I don't want any more of what's inside it.

Why is he here?

We haven't even talked or texted since . . . since.

"How was the dance?" I ask, even though it's a dumb question, and I don't care how the dance was.

"It was whatever," he says, looking out across the street, at the rows of square houses, the glowing windows in the dark. "You weren't there."

He's drunk, I realize. His words are pushed together, lips soft, even when tugged smugly to one side like they are now.

His long eyelashes point downward. He leans toward me.

As he closes the space between us, my mouth goes dry, and for some reason all I can think about is Yvonne's secret tattoo. Nick's last name is Barnes, and for that reason, she has a secret tattoo of a barn on her hip.

"It's like a secret code," she said when she showed it to me, a small red box with a pitched roof.

"That is so dumb," I said, laughing.

"Why?"

"It doesn't matter what the tattoo is *of*, Yvonne!" I said. "Your mom will kill you just because it's *a tattoo*!"

"RIP me, then," she said, her eyes sparkling. "Love makes you do dumb things."

Love.

It had been raining that day. I left my house because my dad was crying. He was crying because some people from the mutual aid group were boxing up Mom's shoes and clothes, her church dresses and her medical scrubs. He was the one who told them they could come and that it was time. But when they asked him if he wanted to keep the hangers, he said he didn't know. And then he started crying. And I didn't know what to do.

Yvonne didn't respond to my first text or my second. So I texted Nick. Maybe he was with her. Maybe he wasn't. It didn't matter. I needed to get out.

Can you come get me, please?

We were driving around with no destination at all. The air smelled clean, sharp.

He was driving with his arm draped over the passenger seat, behind my shoulders. It was raining so hard it was coming down in sheets, like a waterfall over all the windows, and he couldn't see, so he pulled over. We were on a dirt road at the edge of town.

He turned to look at me. He really looked at me. Just me.

And when he pulled me close to him, everything else disappeared.

Afterward, when I got home, I started picturing what would happen when Yvonne found out. How I would tell her. The words I would use. The look on her face.

How she would hate me.

My fingers turned to ice. I couldn't get warm no matter what I did. I told my dad I wasn't hungry for dinner. I put on two pairs of socks and got under my winter blanket even though it was 8:00 p.m. I turned off the light, trying to shut out every sound and every thought. When that didn't work, I pulled the bottle of vodka out from underneath my bed and drank until it didn't matter what time it was, until time itself stopped jumping around, like it had been. Then and now all mixed up.

And then:

YVONNE MORALES HAS POSTED A NEW PHOTO OF YOU.
Slut slut slut slut slut slut slut slut

But here is Nick, again, leaning toward me under the street-light.

Our lips connect. His palm goes to the back of my neck. I

wait for my mind to quiet, like it did that day in his car when it was raining.

I wait to disappear, I wait for oblivion.

But instead, I think of the sticky ball, lodged at the base of my throat. The closer his body gets to mine, the hotter it burns, and the hotter it burns, the more it hurts.

I push the flask into his chest and hold him away from me at arm's length. I just hold him there, trying to catch my breath, staring at the flower pinned on his lapel.

It's crushed.

The white petals are browning at the tips.

Yvonne's stupid tattoo. My mom's shoes, going into boxes. The sound of Dad crying.

"You just went to the dance," I say. "With Yvonne, right?"

I look up into his eyes. Blue and gray, flat, like the bottom of a storm cloud. Yvonne told me he never asks her what she's thinking. He never asks me either.

Silence.

"Yeah, but . . . ," he says, shrugging, smiling, as if we have some kind of shared knowledge of what's going on here, like it's all fine, like I already agreed to something a long time ago, don't I remember?

He tries to pull me back into him, but I don't let him.

"She must have been really upset," I say to the flower at his lapel. "When you told her about what happened."

He expels a puff of air. He looks around, frustrated for a moment, but then recovers himself and comes up smiling.

"Why do you want to talk about that now?"

"You didn't even tell her, did you?" I say, laughing suddenly, because it's all so ridiculous. "Of course not. You're *far* too chickenshit. She figured it out somehow on her own. She forced it out of you."

His face twists in disgust or maybe shame, I don't care which.

"Did you tell her it was my fault?" I ask.

He tucks the flask into his jacket pocket, and he doesn't have to say anything. I know he did.

"Can you leave?" I say.

I'm not sure I said the words out loud for a full minute, because he doesn't move.

Then he puts his hands into his pockets.

"Yeah, okay, M," he says. "I'm gone."

I watch until he disappears into the darkness beyond the streetlight's reach.

Chapter Six

NOW

"Why is it so oppressively, miserably hot?"

"Because we live in the desert," Bernie says.

I roll my eyes and plunge my head back into the freezer in the frozen foods aisle.

Bernie, fourteen, precocious, and prematurely cool, leans on the front of our shopping cart. He'll be joining me at La Manzanita when I go back this fall, but we look like we've each been cast in an entirely different movie about high school. He's wearing crisp black denim, leather shoes, and his hair in a pompadour like it's the 1950s. I'm wearing pajama pants and slides. In my defense, we are standing in a Family Dollar, in New Mexico, in the summer, not on the set of *Grease*.

"Shouldn't we be eating more vegetables?" he asks, gazing out the window at the end of the aisle into the parking lot.

I hold up a bag of frozen peas.

"What do you call these?"

"Small spheres of negligible nutritional value. I'm a growing boy, for peas' sake."

At this point, our conversations are limited to banter. Which feels good, in some ways. Normal. But sometimes when we're joking around, I feel like we're walking single file on a tightrope, arms wide, afraid to look down.

The cart is packed full of TV dinners and freezer bags.

We're definitely going to have to hustle back to the house before everything thaws out under the sun. If we miss the bus, we'll have to walk; it'll be too long until another one comes. But Dad has the car, and he's been so overwhelmed that we have no food to speak of in the house, so I offered to go shopping today while he's at his summer teaching seminar.

I check each item off the list I made on my phone. *Good.* We're under budget, and everything is microwavable and from a box, which is best for everyone. Cooking just isn't the man's calling. Or mine. I will burn 100 percent of the brownies in these TV dinners, because I refuse to pause the microwave at the halfway mark to take them out. In my opinion, that is actual *cooking*, and if I *knew* how to cook, I wouldn't be eating this Hungry Man Classic Fried Chicken—Now with Accidental Corn in the Brownie!

"Hey, man, sweet shoes."

I stiffen at the sound of the familiar voice behind me. Hope and fear bloom in my chest at the same time. It can't be him.

Joel Duran.

No. Not when I'm wearing these ancient Hello Kitty pajama pants and yet another wrinkled T-shirt.

Joel Duran. Standing in front of me. In the frozen food aisle. Complimenting my little brother's shoes.

The cloudy freezer door shuts with a snap. The mountains rise behind him in the big glass window at the end of the aisle. Warm brown skin and slow, deliberate smile. Just like I remember.

Like nothing bad ever happened. Like good things are still possible.

"Thanks," Bernie says, turning his heel out a little so that Joel can get a better look at his fancy dress shoes. "I got 'em at Revolver."

A vintage store. How is my little brother so much cooler than I am? How is this happening right now? I step in front of our grocery cart full of frozen food, embarrassed by its contents.

Joel smiles at me.

"Haven't seen you in a while," he says.

I try to smile back, but suddenly my face won't work right.

"Man, I love those," he says, gesturing to the Hungry Man dinners I have stacked in the cart behind me.

Say something. Anything.

"I hate that you have to hit pause at the midpoint to take out the brownie," I blurt out. "I can't cook, that's why I'm eating a TV dinner!"

"Here comes Marisol with the sharp commentary, as always," Joel says with a laugh, shifting his messenger bag across his broad chest. "Anyway, catch you later. Nice specs, by the way."

As always?

Nice specs?

What is he talking about?

I can't speak anymore, so I just nod and adjust my new glasses, the only pair in the entire Walmart Vision Center that even approached the realm of cool. He retreats down the frozen food aisle, his right pant leg still cuffed from having ridden his bike here. It's a yellow bike, which he built himself at the bike shop where he works downtown. He posted a picture of it three weeks ago.

And he's noticed things about me. But has he noticed things about me like I've noticed things about him?

"Careful, Mari. You're melting the egg rolls," Bernie whispers.

"Shut up, *Bernardo*," I hiss at him, pushing him out of the way and taking over steering the shopping cart. "How do you even know that vintage store exists?"

"Al Gore's internet," he says simply, patting the top of his pompadour.

Joel Duran is gone, just as quickly as he appeared.

Maybe going back to school won't be so bad.

❁ ✳ ❁

Of course it will be bad.

"Bernie, you're gonna be late!" I warn the giant lump under the plaid comforter as I pass by the open door of Bernie's room. "Dad's getting ready to leave!"

"'Kay," is the giant lump's lackluster response.

Since the day we ran into Joel Duran at the grocery store, I've revised my first-day-of-junior-year outfit three times. I have finally landed on a printed shift dress over jeans, cowboy boots, and a giant sweater. The dress is a hot-dog print, with perfect tiny mustard squiggles on each one.

My mom hated this dress. I know just what she would say if she were here.

Do you have to dress so crazy crazy? On the first day?

Bernie has zero hour because he's in the orchestra, so Dad's going to have to drop him off before he goes to our old middle school, where he teaches. When we were both in middle school at the same time, the commute was much less complicated, but much more embarrassing. Even worse than the basic embarrassment of having a teacher for a parent are the surprised looks when anybody sees us and our dad together for the first time:

"Oh—are *these* your kids?"

I stop to smooth down the front of my dress as I pass by the hallway mirror.

Such a pretty girl.

In her voice there was regret and something else I couldn't name. I can almost feel her fingers trying to smooth down the small, frizzy curls on my crown, on some first day of school long ago.

When will it stop feeling like this?

I wish someone could tell me.

In the kitchen, I put on a pot of coffee and stare out the window at the dirt lot on the corner, where I'll continue to wait for the bus to pick me up in the morning before school—until such time that I am able to prove my grasp on the concepts of *drive* and *reverse*.

Which might be never.

"Short Stack?" Dad calls from down the hallway.

"Bernardo's awake!"

I dig in the cupboard for my favorite mug. The big one that holds more coffee than is necessary.

Dad walks into the kitchen in his nerdy first-day-of-school sweater. He doesn't even register my outfit. I wonder if it's just because he's a dad or specifically because he's a white dad that these are not things he pays attention to: how I dress, what my hair is doing, how any of it reflects on him, on us, as a family.

"What do you think?" I ask, posing with outstretched arms.

"About what?" he asks.

I drop my arms.

"Nothing."

He takes an apple out of the bowl. He rolls it around in his hand and stares at it like he's never seen an apple before.

"Dad," I say.

It's an accusation. He looks guilty.

"I signed you up for driver's ed."

Shit.

I try to stay very still. Not give anything away. He completely dropped the issue after the failed attempt last time. I thought I'd gotten away with it.

"But," I say slowly, "isn't it expensive?"

He shakes his head and reaches over me to close the cupboard that I've left open.

"There's a free class at your school. It covers all the same stuff. It'll be after school, three times a week, for a semester. And you can take the bus home."

Driver's ed. After school. Three times a week. Why can't I come up with any plausible excuses? Maybe I could suddenly develop a passion for a conflicting after-school activity. Basketball. Yearbook. Anything.

"But, Dad—"

"What?" he asks.

That look. I can't take it. My dad looks scared, actually scared, of what I'm going to say. Like he already knows what

I want to say, that I'm irreparably damaged, that there's something wrong with me, and he has no idea how he's going to deal with it, and if we just get through this somehow, he'll never have to.

I've seen that look once before and I never want to see it again.

"Nothing," I say, pulling all my particles back together. "That's fine."

He claps his hands.

"Great!" he says too loudly. "It starts in September."

"Great," I say, even as tears begin to well up in my eyes.

He can't see this, I can't let him, so I duck into the fridge for some creamer and I blink and blink and hope they dry. *Don't be ridiculous*. It's just a stupid class. They probably won't even make us drive for at least a few weeks. There'll be a slideshow, guaranteed, a shitty PowerPoint, and an ancient workbook that ten other kids wrote in already and it'll be fine.

"Marisol?"

I can't let him see me like this. Not after that cold winter night when he found me on the front porch, on the cool concrete. When I couldn't even stand. My arms were slick with sweat, but I was cold. Behind his terrified face, the porch light was flickering. It was covered in large brown moths, their papery wings beating in slow motion.

"Marisol," he said.

Maybe he had been saying it for a few minutes, panicked. Disbelieving. Desperate. Holding me like he hadn't done since I was a little girl.

"Marisol, are you drunk?" he'd asked me.

In the brightness of the kitchen, I finally blink my tears away, grab the cream for my coffee, turn around, and look him straight in the eye.

"Great," I say again.

I smile until I mean it or almost mean it.

He smiles back and reaches over to give me an awkward pat on the shoulder. But as he zips up his work bag, his bushy brown eyebrows get all furrowed together.

"What?" I ask.

What is it now?

"You can always step outside the classroom if you need to. Will you do that?"

My shoulders tense up, but Bernie saves me from responding as he emerges with his book bag and violin case.

"Are you wearing suspenders right now?" I ask.

"Your dress is covered in tiny hot dogs," he says, snapping a suspender.

"Fair enough."

"How's it going, Flubs?" Dad asks.

"Can we go?" Bernie grumbles, not a morning person, and yet he signed up voluntarily for orchestra at dawn.

Dad gives me one more unbearable, concerned look before they head out the door.

I trudge to the bus stop, squinting into the sun as it breaks over the top of the mountains, the sky overhead a thin blue, almost white. Feeling like all my atoms could fly apart any second. Yvonne and Tes will be on the bus, and I have no idea how they'll react when they see me, but I don't think it'll be by asking to braid my hair and go ride bikes.

But I'll see Joel Duran later, too. If we have a class together, this time I'll talk to him. This time.

I know he went on a family vacation to Denver this summer, because after I saw him at the Family Dollar and he said *nice specs*, I spent the bulk of July listlessly stalking him online so I could find something to talk to him about. I could probably find a way to mention Colorado without sounding like a stalker.

Right.

Scraping some mud from the bottom of my boot onto the edge of the curb, I imagine him with a cool girlfriend who he probably met at a cool place I've never heard of. She can probably fix a bike when the chain falls off its track, or play the harmonica or some shit.

The corner lot where I wait for my bus is full of prairie-dog holes and clumps of cattails, cacti, and remnants of last night's hail storm, little white balls of ice still clumping beneath the bright pink cactus flowers that got caught up in the surprise of a late-summer bombardment last night. Weather is like that here. Sudden. Severe. Then so quiet that it's referred to as the absence of weather, as in, *I heard we were going to get some weather later in the week.* Mom never got used to it and acted surprised every year, covering her mouth and staring out the window as the streets filled with silty water and the white hail knocked petals from the roses. But this is where Dad is from—this desert, in the shadow of a mountain, where the seasons come on like lightning and roll out in a creep.

I hear the bus churning around the corner before I see it, and my stomach drops at the familiar sound. Everything is just the same as last year: same bus, same bus driver, wearing the same faded blue L.A. Dodgers cap.

Walking down the aisle of the bus, I pass by some freshmen I don't know, nervously clutching their book bags. Next, Tyler Paulson, who punches J.J. Jimenez in the arm when he sees me.

"Nice wiener dress, Mary," Tyler says, showing all his teeth.

At some point last year, they made an unspoken agreement that it would be *hilarious* to call me Mary. I ignore them and continue down the aisle toward the main event.

Tes and Yvonne stop mid-conversation when we lock eyes. Yvonne's mouth forms a tiny little O for just one moment before she glares at me like I slept with her boyfriend and then punched her in the face.

Tes stares into her lap. Her eyelashes are so delicate that you almost can't see them against her cheek. Yvonne looks different, too. As I get closer, her new blond highlights come into focus. It feels so automatic to compliment a girl on her appearance that I almost tell her I like them.

"What are you looking at?" Yvonne hisses, her chin jutting out.

My eyes drift downward, to her shirt, and my heart jumps. She's wearing it.

The T-shirt. The one Mom tried to throw in the trash. The one Yvonne said looked better on her, anyway, and that I should just give it to her because her tits are nicer. Not that she'd ever use the word *tits*, but that's what she meant. Her blond-black curls are tumbling at her collarbone, framing her gold cross necklace, and she's not breaking eye contact with me, daring me, daring me to do it, and I want to grab a handful of her hair and tear it out, but when I make a fist, something catches at the hollow space at my clavicle, radiating a searing pain that spreads through my chest.

It's that goddamn sticky ball again. My throat begins to close up.

"Nothing," I choke out.

I stumble all the way to the back of the bus and slide into a seat by myself, trying to *breathe, breathe*, into my belly instead of my chest, but I can't tell if it's working. I slump forward and watch as Yvonne leans her head on Tes's shoulder.

"Bitch," Yvonne says, loudly enough for me to hear all the way in the back.

So she still hates me. Of course.

I should just drop out. I'll take correspondence courses online and then I'll never have to learn to drive, because I'll never have to leave the house and never have to deal with anyone, ever again. I tug at the bottom of my sweater, turn away, and press my forehead against the cool glass window, rubbing the base of my throat with my palm. *Breathe, breathe.*

The bus lurches forward and a new resolution crystallizes.

I need to find Elizabeth Parker and find out what the hell she did to me.

Chapter Seven

NOW

She isn't in any of my classes so far. I look over my shoulder for her in hallways that smell like stale air-conditioning. The building feels enormous to me now, full of echoes. Tennis shoes squeak on linoleum as the crush of bodies lurches from class to class.

I don't remember it being so big. Juvie is contained within one square building and three portable trailers, sharing a parking lot with a nondenominational church and a Blake's Lotaburger. I'd gotten used to that snug little world, where everything smelled like oil from the fryer at Blake's and almost everybody was just as over it as I was.

When I walk into third period, geometry, Tes and Yvonne are there, already sitting together. Yvonne snaps her compact closed and glares at me again. Tes places her backpack in the empty chair next to her and looks down at the floor.

As if I'd *want* to sit with them. I need to find a seat as far away from them as possible. I just need to get through today.

I can't think about the next day and the next day and the next, so I try not to.

It's too crushing.

The seats are filling up fast as bodies stream into the room. I scan quickly and *no, no, no*, the only empty seats left are with Tyler Paulson and J.J. Jimenez.

The bell rings.

"I'm Ms. Valdez," the teacher says. "As you can see, I've arranged your desks in groups of four."

This is, supposedly, so that we can "peer-tutor" each other this semester, but given the fact that as Ms. Valdez passes out the knowledge-based assessment we're meant to complete together, Tyler and J.J. begin talking animatedly about each other's thrilling summer vacation activities—doing whip-its and racing shopping carts in the arroyo behind the Super Walmart—I think I'll be on my own with geometry. The peers at my table would be unfit to peer-tutor a soft cheese.

Then she walks in.

Elizabeth Parker.

Why is she even here? She's on the Honors track and she should be in some advanced math class that I'll never touch.

She places a stack of copies in front of Ms. Valdez on her desk.

"Thank you, Elizabeth," Ms. Valdez says. "Maybe you can fill in somewhere and see if anyone has questions about the directions."

Ah, once again, she's just here to help the mortals. As she takes the empty seat next to me, my heart begins to race. I feel her looking at me but I can't meet her eyes. *Ask her, ask her.* I don't feel anything right now; my body feels normal, numb even, but I know that the sticky ball is there and I need to know how to get rid of it.

"Hey, Liz," J.J. says, leaning back in his chair and tilting his chin up at her.

J.J. Jimenez.

Elizabeth's eyes go unfocused, as if there's an annoying

sound coming from somewhere but she can't pinpoint the source.

"You look nice today," he says, grinning.

He rubs his hands together, and it's like he's smiling because he's pleased with himself for being bold enough to say so, or because Tyler is now elbowing him and snickering, or an endless loop of both.

"Do you have any questions about the directions?" Elizabeth asks, all neutral.

Tyler catches me watching them.

"You look nice, too, Mary," he says.

I bite the inside of my cheek.

Elizabeth slides the paper closer to herself so she can read it. It's blank.

"You haven't determined any of the values of the points on the coordinate plane," she says.

"Mary won't talk to us," J.J. says.

Tyler claps me on the back of the shoulder. "She always hates being in our group."

I flinch and make my face a stone. I missed so much school last year, but we had English together, briefly, after I got demoted from Honors English for not turning in any of the weekly assignments on Greek roots. Also, I didn't read *Catch-22*. Or *Catcher in the Rye*. Or any of the creased paperbacks with the destroyed spines that Mr. Napoli put in front of me.

These books all sat in my backpack untouched until the day of discussion, where I stared blankly when he called on me. He finally pulled me aside after class and suggested, gently, in his crooked tie stained with soup, that the course *might be too demanding* for me, and there was nothing to be ashamed of for admitting it. I remember feeling like I should care, like I should be ashamed, but I wasn't. I used to love reading. It was like some other girl was embarrassed by what was happening. But I didn't know her anymore.

I need to be away from here.

I'm halfway into my proof, which I'm pretty sure I'm doing all wrong, but my pencil needs to be sharpened, so I get up. Before I'm too far away, I hear Tyler's voice.

"Oh man, is that Hello Kitty? *Meow!*"

A hot redness crawls up my neck as I turn around.

Tyler has gone into my backpack—*what the fuck*—and taken out my spare glasses case, which is covered in Hello Kitty stickers. He opens it with a click and puts on my dorky second pair of glasses. I've always kept a spare with me since the time in sixth grade when I took a soccer ball to the face in gym class. My glasses broke and nobody could come pick me up. I spent the whole day totally lost, with a pounding headache from straining to see.

Tyler cocks my frames to the side in a comically crooked way. Of course, J.J. finds this to be top-tier prop comedy.

"Meow, good little pussy!" Tyler says. "I heard Mary's pussy's pretty tight."

Cold prickles wash all over my body.

Mary's pussy's pretty tight. Mary's pussy's pretty tight.

He laughs hard, shaking J.J. by the shoulders. Ms. Valdez is all the way across the room, helping someone, so she's not listening over the dull hum of people talking and working.

Tyler looks over at Yvonne across the room and calls to her.

"Oh, sorry, Yvonne!"

Slut slut slut slut slut slut slut.

My head snaps in Yvonne's direction, but if she hears him, she doesn't let on. Her long hair is hanging over her face.

Is she making a fist?

"Hey, too much noise over there!" Ms. Valdez shouts.

"Yeah, Tyler, shut up!" some guy from the baseball team says.

Elizabeth puts her pencil down and reaches for my Hello Kitty glasses case. She slides it slowly toward my empty seat. She stares at Tyler, cold and hard, and she doesn't stop until he finally shrugs, takes my glasses off, and puts them back.

I turn away from them and shove my pencil into the sharpener, trying to let the loud electric whir drown out everything.

Then an alarm goes off. Half my pencil breaks off in the sharpener as I jump. It's not the fire alarm—it's three quick pulses and a pause. Three. Quick. Pulses. A pause. It means we're on lockdown.

We've had this drill since we were kids. Chairs push back, bodies fold under desks. A light flashes at quick intervals from a small red box near the top of the propped-open door. But I just stand there, stuck, until Ms. Valdez pulls me by the sleeve.

"Get away from the door," she says quietly as she guides me toward her desk by my arm.

"Is this a drill?" I ask her.

She purses her lips. Her eyes are telling me that she doesn't know. She starts to say something, then starts to say something else, then just pushes me beneath her desk. Then she stands with her back pressed against the dry-erase board, flicks the light switch off, and pulls the door closed. Curled into a little ball, I stare at her boots. The right toe is scuffed.

What if it's real this time? I can see it, my dad racing to get here. In my mind it looks like news footage. Speeding. Getting turned away at a police barricade. He gets out of the car. He puts his hands on the top of his head like he does when he's completely overwhelmed, like when Bernie started a grease fire in the kitchen last month. *Holy hell, Bern!* he'd said.

Now he's standing out there in the middle of the street, looking at our school, the big concrete cube, Bernie and I trapped inside with some dumb kid with a gun and a hole in his heart.

And he's afraid that now he'll be alone forever.

Then the alarm changes. It only takes a few seconds until there's nothing but the sound, a slow, long pulse you feel in your chest.

This one means evacuate.

"Let's go, let's go," Ms. Valdez yells, beckoning us toward the exit.

I bump my head as I crawl up and out from underneath her desk and move through the classroom door out into the hallway with the rest of the class. The alarm pulses through me and it feels like I'm moving in slow motion.

Yvonne bumps into me as she passes by me.

Suddenly everything speeds up again.

"Hey!" I say.

"Hey, what?"

She turns around, getting in my face. Her eyes are hard. There's a drop of spit on her lip. The alarm is still blaring and somebody else rushes past me, shoving me into her.

"Get off me!" she grunts.

And then she pushes me. Pushes me. Wearing my fucking favorite shirt. And when she pushes me, something inside knocks loose and I'm pulling a fist back to take a swing at her. But then Elizabeth Parker is there, too, and she's pushing us apart.

"Hey, relax!"

She's yelling to be heard over the sound of the alarm.

Looking at me with cool eyes that say, *Not worth it.*

Yvonne steps back. She glares at me, then at Elizabeth, and then backs off down the hallway, Tes tugging at her arm.

"Come on," Tes says.

"Move, ladies!" Ms. Valdez is yelling from somewhere behind me.

After a moment, I follow, my breathing shallow, my nerves frayed, the place at my throat burning, burning.

What were you thinking? My dad's voice from that cold night. His face, ashen, next to me as I came into consciousness in a hospital bed after having my stomach pumped. *What have you done?*

Our pace is slowed by the mass of kids as they flow toward the exit, out into the brightness of the parking lot.

A thousand hands brush the cold metal door open as we leave.

❊ ✺ ❊

I'm pacing the asphalt. I feel totally exposed.

My eyes search the crowd for Yvonne and Tes, but they're nowhere.

We have all been standing out in the school parking lot for almost twenty minutes, and the alarm stopped, but nobody has said to go back inside yet.

The teachers are now helpfully clumped together underneath the lone piñon tree. There's a couple of seniors sitting in their cars with the doors hanging open, legs sticking out, like they're at a tailgate or something. But you can tell that people are nervous.

I pull my cell phone out of my pocket to text Bernie to make sure he's okay.

It's dead. Shit.

I'm sure I have millions of text messages from Dad, too. Billions. If this is a real lockdown situation, parents will be notified. I look around to see if there's anybody I know whose phone I can borrow.

A beach ball drifts lazily over the crowd. Hands pop up from the masses to keep the colorful orb afloat. It doesn't seem like it should be there.

It gives me an eerie feeling.

"Am I having a stroke or is that a beach ball?" somebody says.

I look over my shoulder, and Elizabeth Parker appears, her soft sweater slouching gracefully, her long hair moving slightly in the breeze.

I don't know what to say to her now. Why did she have to insert herself between me and Yvonne like that? It was none of her business.

I put my hand to my forehead to see her through the glare.

"I didn't need you to do that," I say. "In there."

She's applying some rose-colored lip balm with her ring finger.

"Looked like you did."

Wow.

"Listen," she says. "Ethan Peña has some Oreos in his car over there, if you want some. I had to walk away because I already ate, like, five of them."

She points with her chin at Ethan Peña's car.

I narrow my eyes at her.

"Is that, like, *a lot* of Oreos in your book or something?"

"What, five?" she says, laughing.

"Whenever Oreos are around, I have to eat a whole row of them. Pretty sure Oreos are measured in terms of rows."

"Oh, this is very good news," she says. "So when they say 'serving size' . . . ?"

"Yeah, it's totally a *row*. A gaggle of geese, a row of Oreos."

She laughs.

"My mom buys those cardboard ones, though, from the health food store," she says, wrinkling her nose.

"Oh no, the one that sells crystals and incense and no good chips? Their cookies are bullshit."

"Yes, I'm very deprived," she says dryly.

She obviously isn't. Her boots look new, shiny, and not from Payless, like mine, which are definitely flammable. Honestly, this girl *bugs* me. She's always showing up, and getting involved, and doing weird, messed-up theater shit. My hand goes involuntarily to the base of my throat.

Nothing tender now. Just bone.

"You okay?" she asks.

God, what does she *care*? If I tell her I'm basically hallucinating from her little movement exercise, she'll probably turn me in to the guidance counselor, and then it's back to staring out the window to run out the clock in therapy, and another pamphlet with a sad font and stock photos from the nineties to add to my collection: *Your Grief Journey: Teen Edition*.

"I didn't need your help with J.J. and Tyler either," I say.

Her eyebrows come together.

"Oh, that? I just couldn't take it anymore. Didn't mean to, like, overstep."

She shrugs, and I realize I've been squeezing my shoulder blades together so tight I could have held a pencil back there. Like I've been holding my breath since the alarm went off.

I expel a puff of air.

"I just want this day to be over," I say. "Really bad."

She tilts her head to the side, studying me. I hate being studied. I don't know why I said that.

"So, let's go," she says with conviction, putting on a pair of large sunglasses.

"What? Go where?"

"We should leave. The first day is always a wash anyway."

She gestures toward the street. I eye her suspiciously.

"Come on. I got my driver's license yesterday."

"Really? Oh. I don't know," I say, looking around the dusty parking lot.

Elizabeth raises her dark eyebrows at me over her sunglasses, her car keys dangling from her hand, like she's busted out of school a thousand times. Something tells me that if I don't go with her, I'm stupid. That if I go now, something will be different. I don't know what, but something.

"Yeah, okay," I say.

"Great," Elizabeth says. "Let's blow this joint."

Who talks like that? I suppress a smile. She almost got me that time.

Nobody even tries to stop us. But as we're walking toward Sombra del Monte Street, where Elizabeth says her car is parked, a familiar figure striding across the school parking lot in the distance catches my eye. In suspenders. With a violin case.

What the hell?

"Hey," I say softly.

I put my hand on Elizabeth's shoulder to stop her walking.

"What?"

"That's my little brother. Where the hell does he think he's going?"

"Umbers. Intrigue—let's tail him!" she says.

Like she's in an old-timey detective movie.

She takes off in a jog and I follow. As we cut across the huge parking lot, Bernie disappears over the top of the hill, so we speed up even more.

When we get to the street at the top of the hill, Bernie is already getting into the passenger side of a green car stopped at the corner.

Who does he even know with a car?

My heart speeds up remembering his little-kid face, now gone forever, scrunching up in laughter as Mom folded him into her arms, *ang gwapo kong, baby boy*, even when he wasn't a baby anymore. He still let her.

"Where's your car?" I ask urgently.

"There!"

She steers me toward an old Subaru parked next to a particularly gnarly cactus and shoves the key into the door.

"Mind the cactus. There's always a spot here. I'm not paying those assholes seventy-five clams for a parking spot. I wasn't born yesterday!"

She pulls her seat belt down to her hip, and I successfully navigate the cactus spines without getting stabbed and jump in as she starts the engine.

The green car turns the corner and we pursue.

"Okay, so, where's this kid going?" Elizabeth murmurs, rolling the windows down to let some air in. "This is all crazy. We're in hot pursuit."

She sits casually at the steering wheel, as if she didn't actually get her driver's license yesterday, but ten years ago, or in a previous life.

I chew on my thumbnail and try to get a clear view of the back of Bernie's head. Bernie, who is suddenly going to vintage stores on the other side of town to buy shoes; Bernie, who disappears into strange cars in the middle of the school day. Elizabeth's long hair whips all around her as she drives, following the green car at a safe distance. She doesn't ask me to explain, just lifts her chin, gesturing toward the green car.

"You know what?" she says, slapping the steering wheel with her palm. "I bet they're going to Charlie's."

I don't know what—or who—she's talking about, but I'm too embarrassed to say, so I don't say anything. *Great.* Elizabeth will now assume that I *do* know what Charlie's is, since I didn't ask, and as a result, she's probably going to continue to talk about it. Then, when I have nothing to say, she will discover that I am a complete idiot.

"It's a record store," she says, saving me from myself. "And a café. Like ice cream and coffee and stuff. A bunch of those little crust-punk kids from orchestra hang out there."

That seems innocent enough. Records. Ice cream. It's a regular after-school special. I'll give Bernie a little lecture about skipping school and then that will be that. Dad doesn't even have to know.

The sun makes everything in the car turn golden, even the hair on my arms. I pull my sleeves down.

"I knew it," Elizabeth says. "It's Charlie's! Damn, I'm good."

The green car swings behind a row of flat-roofed adobe buildings under an old neon sign. Route 66.

I duck down low as we turn in to follow them, and Elizabeth laughs at me.

"Such intrigue," she says, grinning.

As she pulls into a parking spot, the gravel crunches beneath the tires. When I sit up again, we both look around.

"Wait, shit, where did they go?"

The green car is gone.

"Damn these crafty crust punks," Elizabeth says. "They must have just cut through and gone out that way." She points to the other exit at the opposite end of the parking lot. "I'm sorry, should we give chase?"

My heart falls.

Bernie, I think helplessly. *What are you up to?*

"It's okay," I tell Elizabeth, who is looking at me with concern. "Forget it."

"Come on, let me buy you a coffee."

✻ ✱ ✻

Inside Charlie's, Elizabeth buys us both lattes with dark chocolate and red chile flakes. The buckets of ice cream under the glass are swirled with caramel and dusted with pistachios and crushed candy bars. Every inch of the walls is covered with concert posters, the dates and times long past, and the music is loud, and the singer is screaming.

Drifting through the aisles, we riffle through records, albums, and tapes, even though I don't have a way to play any of these things. Elizabeth says her mom has a record player and a laptop that plays CDs, and that she would rip the album she was getting and send it to me.

I keep checking my watch to make sure I'll be back home on time.

"You're the oldest, aren't you?"

She asks this knowingly, pointing at me with a perfectly manicured finger.

"I am. So?"

She shakes her head at me and comes to a stop beneath a giant poster of Björk. Elizabeth crosses her arms just like Björk in the poster.

"I knew it. You're just like my older sister. You can relax. You didn't, like, invent everything. He can skip school, too. He's fine."

I chew on the inside of my cheek. I hope it's true. That he's fine. I want to believe it's possible to be fine again.

Elizabeth talks a lot. She talks about bands she knows and who last came to town and when, and she talks to me about her sisters and how annoying they are, and how she wants to be an actor, but she asks me questions, too, like, *What kind of music do you listen to?* and *Where did you get the hot-dog dress?* After a while, we settle into the quiet and just stand there, listening to the music and the soft shuffle of the records passing beneath our hands.

I feel like I'm just being myself and it's nice.

The coffee is bitter and sweet in the best way and I'm wondering why she's doing this, if now maybe she's my friend, or what.

After Elizabeth drops me off in my driveway, my heart sinks. I've stayed out way later than I meant to. After Charlie's, Elizabeth drove us around to some more of her favorite spots, and we kept talking, and all of a sudden the sunset had gone all orange, with a few strands of pink woven in. Soon it will collapse into inky night all at once, and my dad is probably losing his mind that I went AWOL.

Elizabeth's car is only about halfway down the block when my dad comes running out of the house, with the screen door slamming closed behind him. I hope she doesn't see him in her rearview mirror.

I try to walk swiftly past him, but he blocks me.

"Where the hell were you?"

Bernie appears in the window at the front of the house. He gives me a little wave with his skinny arm. So he beat me home, that crafty little crust punk.

"Why is your phone off?"

"It died."

"Jesus, Marisol, I got you that phone so that I'll know where you are at all times! You have to plug it in every night before you go to bed."

"Okay, okay! I'm sorry."

I duck under his arm and run into the house before the neighbors start poking their heads outside to see what the hell is going on. He follows me inside and almost trips over me as I untie my shoes in the entryway.

"Well?" he asks, still yelling. "Where the hell did you go?"

"I just went with my friend Elizabeth to a record store to look at tapes and stuff."

My dad does a double take.

"Your school was on *lockdown*! You just left? And *who* is Elizabeth?"

"I said I'm sorry—"

"We don't even have a tape player! Or a record player! There's a store that still sells records and tapes? *Where?*"

"I'm *sorry*," I repeat helplessly, not sure if these are real questions.

Maybe if I just keep saying I'm sorry, he'll eventually stop freaking out. Mom isn't here to click her tongue, tilt her head to one side, and give him that look. *Asawa, calm down.* So Dad keeps shaking his head over and over, spiraling continuously, a human ball of anxiety.

"I'm going to sue the school district for just letting you leave like that," he says as he shuts the door behind us. "Some lockdown!"

"Dad, you work for the district."

"Screw the district!"

He tells Bernie to put the news on, and we sit silently on the couch next to each other, listening to the sound of Dad slamming metal trays in the kitchen while he puts in a frozen pizza for dinner.

While we're all eating pizza in front of the TV, which Mom would never have allowed, we find out that the reason for my school's lockdown was that somebody had left a duffel bag in the cafeteria and the teachers thought it was a bomb, but really it was just a bag of gym clothes.

"I am suing the district," Dad says again.

Bernie and I exchange a look.

"So litigious all of a sudden," Bernie says.

Dad puts his plate down on the coffee table and crumples up the paper towel he was using as a napkin, sighing.

He pushes his glasses up the bridge of his nose and puts his hand at the back of Bernie's neck, gently.

This is his version of a hug. He does it with Bernie only.

We both stare at him warily.

"Just keep your phones charged. And don't go anywhere without telling me."

I'm waiting for Bernie to say okay, but then I remember I'm the one Dad is talking to, really.

"Okay," I mutter.

"Good."

Dad pats Bernie on the back before getting up to get another slice of pizza from the kitchen. I watch Bernie closely as he pulls out his cell phone and begins tapping away on it. Who is he texting? Is Elizabeth right? Am I being a total big sister by worrying just because he did the same thing I did? I mean, he *is* in high school now.

"What?"

He's caught me staring at him.

"Nothing," I say.

I push him away from me with my foot.

"Just be good."

He flashes a smile.

"I'm always good."

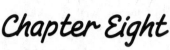

Chapter Eight

THEN

It's been three weeks since Mom died. Yesterday I went back to school. I said I was fine, and that I could handle it, when the family grief counselor the school helped us find asked. And Bernie said so, too. We both nodded. *Yes.* Shrugged. *Fine.* Dad was twisting a shiny pamphlet in his hands.

But just as I'm supposed to leave now, for the bus, to do another day, I can't.

I stand in the entry of the silent house.

Yesterday, I was late to chemistry because I thought it was in B Hall when all along it was in C Hall. I kept pacing back and forth over and over, looking for the room where it never was.

Then somehow I'm walking down the street, one foot in front of the other, because I'm fine, toward the mountains in the east. I stop when I see that the mailbox that sits in front of the house on the corner has been knocked over, clear to the ground, a dusty hole in the earth where it used to stand.

I walk right past the bus stop. I just keep going. The morning sun climbs higher and higher from behind the mountains. I cut through the park and over the bridge, the concrete arroyo beneath it bone-dry and waiting, waiting for a flash flood. Little brown finches flit between desert salt grass and cholla and bottlebrush squirreltail. *Ditches are deadly, stay away*, I think to myself reflexively. *Find safer places to swim and play.*

I can't stop thinking about how one day in middle school Yvonne told me her mom let her stay home from school because she wasn't feeling well, and she stayed home from work too, and they made cookies together and watched TV, and then suddenly I'm ringing the doorbell to Yvonne's house, even though I know she isn't there because she would have left for school already.

Her mom, my tita Violeta, opens the door, and I'm surprised at how good it feels to see her, because since Mom died I've felt tired, or angry, but mostly I've felt nothing, just blank nothing, even when I've tried to feel something.

Tita Violeta is wearing her work clothes. An oversized blazer and slacks. The same house slippers that my mom had. She's a paralegal, and for a year she'd been trying to convince my mom to become one too, whispering to her urgently in the kitchen at Bible study.

You could take the classes online, like I did.

The money is better.

You're working too much.

Tita Violeta's eyes are sad when she sees me standing there with my backpack. She doesn't ask me why I'm here or what's wrong. She doesn't ask me any questions. She opens her arms and pulls me close to her. She smells like a heavy floral perfume that makes me want to gag, but I don't care. I let her hug me.

"Come in," she says.

I'm hunched over the coffee table, pushing pancit around on my plate, when Yvonne comes home. She walks in and removes her backpack, her eyes darting from me on the couch, to her mom hovering over me, to the TV. We're marathoning a home renovation show. Her mom spoons more food onto my plate.

"Hi," Yvonne says.

She sits down on the couch next to me, and even though I see all the questions written on her face, like *What are you doing here?* and *What am I supposed to do?* and *Why won't you talk to me?* I don't have any answers to them, so I just stare at the TV.

"They're going to find mold in the bathroom," I say.

"It'll be termites," Tita Violeta says.

"Do you want to come upstairs?" Yvonne asks me quietly.

Yvonne has tried talking to me about it all. She's said I can call her even if it's the middle of the night. She asked me lots of questions. But I feel like I'm underneath glass, and her questions can't get through. I feel like I'm under water, and she wants to drag me up to the surface, but the harder she pulls me, the more I'm just sinking deeper and deeper into myself.

Tita Violeta carries over a plate for Yvonne, her house slippers swishing on the carpet. Steam rises from the heap of white rice, and as she sets the plate down in front of Yvonne, she blows on it gently.

"Be careful," she says to Yvonne. "It's hot."

And it's absolutely excruciating.

That tiny moment of care is unbearable.

"I have to go, actually," I say.

I'm gathering my things and sweeping out the door before they can say anything, ask me anything, try to drag me to shore.

❊ ✳ ❊

Two months since Mom died. The house is quiet. I haven't showered in three days.

The doorbell rings.

I don't know where Bernie is, or Dad, but nobody answers it. It's a rare cloudy day, and I have no idea what time it is.

The doorbell rings again, and I drag myself out of bed to answer.

It's Yvonne and Tes with more food. They're still bringing stuff. Plates covered in tinfoil from their parents, plastic trays of biscochitos from the grocery store.

"Hey," I say.

I move away from the door and brace myself for more questions. *How are you doing?* and *Is there anything you need?* and *Do you want to talk about it?*

But in the doorway, they hesitate. And this time, they don't breeze in like it's their own house, like they usually do. They don't throw their jackets over the back of the couch or kick off their shoes into the waiting basket.

"We can't stay," Yvonne says.

Tes is reading the ingredients on the biscochito tray like it's real fucking interesting. Anise seed, sugar, shortening, beef fat, cinnamon, salt—where is the fucking mystery?

I accept the plates and the cookies and they both mumble, *Text us if you need us* and *See you at school*, and I watch the red taillights on Tes's mom's car sweep around the corner and disappear.

That night, I wake up suddenly in the dark, my breath shallow, my face wet.

My eyes dart around the room, translating shadows, *that's my desk, that's my dresser, I'm in my room.* Another nightmare, the same one I've had every night. Her in the hospital bed. Tubes in her. Eyes swollen shut. I feel someone's hand around my throat and I can't speak. It's my hand.

Just a dream, I tell myself, *just a dream,* but it isn't.

My heart is pounding and I can't breathe.

I grab my phone off my nightstand, clutch my phone to my chest, and then, using every ounce of will I have left in my body, I call Yvonne. From the background noise, I can tell she's at a party. She probably didn't mean to pick up at all, but maybe she was in the middle of taking a selfie or something and answered by mistake.

"Shit," she says. "Hey, Mari, what's up?"

Her voice is thin. The bass line of a familiar song thrums beneath it.

"Where are you?" I choke out.

"Just some party," she says. "With Nick's friends."

Like it's no big deal. And it isn't. I don't even want to be there. Some beige party somewhere. And yet.

"Is Tes there, too?"

She pauses for a second.

Then, Tes laughing.

"Yeah, she's here."

"So you just didn't invite me?"

"I didn't think you'd want to come," she said. "I thought maybe you were still too sad for parties."

Sad. Smoothing out the rumpled blanket on my unmade bed, I listen to the song in the background, at the party. To the laughter and the words blurring together in the unknown beige house. *Still too sad.* I picture Yvonne's annoyed face on the other end, impatient for the conversation to end, and then, again, my mom's face, *no*, no, no, I don't want to remember it like that, that's not what she looked like, and my throat is closing up and it takes everything I have to force out the words—

"Well, I *am* sad."

It feels true and untrue at the same time, but honest, at least, if not totally accurate, and I want her to know that I'm being honest with her now, and that I need her, I need her.

But I can't say it.

"Let's go to the movies or something this weekend, okay? Nick can drive us. I'll talk to you later."

She hangs up.

Our moms dressed us up to match for photos at First Communion. The same ruffled white dresses. The same bows, the same lace. At confirmation, we picked saint names. We accepted the wine and the body of Christ side by side. There never seemed to be any space between us at all. In the pictures, that's how it looks anyway.

Chapter Nine

NOW

I clutch the printout that Dad gave me as I move against the tide of bodies exiting the school building and make my way to Room 406 for the first day of driver's ed.

It's late September and the leaves on the aspens that line the mountains' ridges have begun to turn. I've been flying completely under the radar at school but every night at dinner, Dad is tense, like he's just waiting for me to mess up.

School is a minefield, but I've observed Yvonne's schedule, and by now I know which hallways to go down in order to avoid her. I'm taking the long way to Room 406 for that reason, telling myself that everything is fine, and the class will be fine, but then I see Nick Barnes in the crowd—that thick brown hair, those broad shoulders. He's walking right toward me, and with Tyler Paulson and J.J. Jimenez, too, a total nightmare combination. Nick laughs about something Tyler says as they jostle each other, Nick cuffing up the sleeves of his button-down shirt as he walks.

I duck into the library and pull the heavy metal door closed behind me.

Pressing myself flat against the flyers and library event schedules and thumbtacks, I wait for them to pass.

But then Nick pulls open the door to the library.

"Oh," he says.

His smile fades as he walks through, seeing me there.

J.J. and Tyler shove him forward.

"Hey, it's Mary," Tyler says.

I move my backpack from one shoulder to the other and push my hair from my face. Looking anywhere, and everywhere, but at them.

"How's it going?" Nick asks as they pass by.

His voice sounds different. It's hard at the edges.

Not the same as the voice he uses with Yvonne, not the voice he uses with me when no one else is there, or at least, used to, before I told him off and laughed in his face. Their eyes are burning holes into me, the three of them. I fight competing urges to make myself seem small and unimportant or mean and not worth the trouble.

I tug at my backpack straps.

"Later, Mary," J.J. says.

I stare at their backs until they disappear around the corner into the stacks, and humiliation gnaws at me, but why?

What did *I* do?

Nick glances back at me, and somehow him looking at me is worse than him pretending he doesn't know who I am, and it's not fair, no matter which hallway I go down, it's the same, I'm trapped, there's nowhere I can go where I can just be.

My stomach twists and I turn to the bulletin board behind me, grabbing at flyers at random and tearing them down, the paper ripping and shredding. I gulp air and place my palms flat against the bulletin board, taking in the shredded, crumpled mess at my feet.

Breathe in. Breathe out. *Breathe into your belly.*

When I raise my head, there's one flyer left, still neatly pinned, with today's date:

LA MANZANITA AZN CLUB!
Room 305, 2:30 p.m.
There will be lumpia!

After my mom's funeral, Yvonne's mom sent her over to my house with trays and trays of uncooked lumpia to keep in the freezer. But they were short and skinny, not fat, like my mom's, with different filling, with cheese, which is fine, but because that wasn't how my mom did it, I couldn't even look at them. Dad doesn't even know how to cook them, so they are still in the freezer, pale and collecting white crystals.

An Asian Club. That's new. Yvonne and Tes will be there, if *there will be lumpia!*

Nick doesn't even like lumpia, or as he called them, *greasy Filipino egg rolls.*

What an asshole, I think, *what an enormous asshole,* and then, before I know what I'm doing, I find myself standing outside Room 305 instead of Room 406.

The door is shut. My palm presses the handle.

Inside Room 305, the art room, a bunch of Asian kids from all grades sit in and on top of desks. Mr. Hoang, the art teacher, sits in the back of the room organizing supplies into bins. Yvonne and Tes stand in front of the room, where they've apparently just written on the whiteboard:

IDEAS FOR THE CULTURAL ASSEMBLY

And now, everyone is looking at me.

"Sorry," I say, for no reason.

Yvonne's eyes are hard as I slide into a desk in the back of the classroom. She's wearing one of Nick's hoodies. I imagine her pulling it over her head at the end of the school day and giving it back to him, him pulling it over his own head, still warm, and suddenly I want to hit something very hard.

Tes puts a hand on Yvonne's arm. Tes is wearing a floral dress over tights, and the effect is that she looks much younger than she actually is. Her jet-black hair is neatly parted down the center of her head.

"So," Tes says, clapping her hands together and drawing the attention back to the front of the room. "Cultural assembly ideas?"

Sloan Nguyen, a cheerleader, raises her hand, her many bracelets jingling.

"A dance routine?"

Yvonne takes a break from glaring at me to roll her eyes at Sloan. "Everybody does a dance routine."

"Well, maybe because they're *fun*?" Sloan says.

She leans back in her chair and kicks her white sneakers on top of her desk. Tes dutifully writes *DANCE ROUTINE* on the whiteboard in dry-erase marker.

"I could do a martial arts demonstration," Kyle Holtzman, who is white, says.

Tes hesitates for a fraction of a second with her marker. "I'm sure that's something that we could incorporate."

Tes is probably going to be president one day or something. She is very diplomatic. But I guess Yvonne has forbidden her from talking to me, because she hasn't. Our group text is dead.

"We could do a cooking demo."

"Karaoke contest?"

Tes neatly logs the ideas on the whiteboard as the group chats excitedly, until she notices that Yvonne and I are locked in a staring contest. Our bodies are mirrors, arms crossed and eyes filling up.

"Um—" Tes says brightly, her eyes darting between us. "Why don't we take a break and have some lumpia?"

She holds up a stack of paper plates.

"Yvonne's mom made them."

Tita Violeta was the default party host. Fried drumsticks and glassy noodles piled high in warming trays, rice cookers lined up along the counter, shoes piled by the door. The three of us squeezed into the love seat, laughing our bellies sore as our moms belted out Mariah Carey on the Magic Sing, Yvonne leaning her head on my shoulder.

These were parties where our moms all made food like one hundred more people were coming, like they expected their whole families to show, the ones they'd been separated from, the ones they pack boxes and boxes for every Christmas, full of candy and towels and things that their families asked for, and sent them over the ocean in place of themselves.

I swipe at the corners of my eyes as everybody in the classroom crowds around the food. My arms close tightly around my backpack, hugging it to my chest, as the sounds in the room blur together.

A white paper plate appears in front of me. Attached to it is Tes. I take it. Stare into its blank flatness. Am I even Filipino anymore, without them?

Without Mom?

Yvonne appears at Tes's side.

"I think you should go," she says.

She has pulled herself together again. Tucked in all the corners and pulled up all the walls.

"Make me," I say.

Her nostrils flare.

"Come on," Tes says. "She's obviously upset."

"Shocking," Yvonne says. "Marisol is having a feeling again."

I flinch. I'm five years old, crying in her bedroom in the middle of the night. She is soothing me, telling me that everything is okay. She is walking gracefully across the stage at confirmation, in the dress her mom picked out for her, that she wore without complaint, that fit her, suited her. I'm frozen in the wings, unable to move, because I know I'm going to say the wrong thing, but Yvonne is looking at me like *you can do it, it will be okay*, and she keeps looking until I walk out after her, into the light.

"Can we talk?" I ask. "Somewhere else."

Yvonne marches over to the door, and I follow her out of the classroom and down the empty, echoing hallway until she finally turns around to face me in front of a giant poster of Malala Yousafzai.

"What do you want?" she asks.

I don't know what I want, I don't know why I came here, I don't know anything. The way she looks me up and down, it's like she's disgusted by every single inch of what she sees, *Marisol is having a feeling again*, crossing her arms in Nick Barnes's hoodie, and it's like he's always, *always* here, even now.

"Are you seriously wearing that asshole's hoodie?" I ask.

Her eye twitches, wing-tipped lid crinkling.

"Are you kidding me? *That's* what you want to say?"

No. It isn't. It's not coming out right.

How do I even say this? Nick was outside *my* bedroom window. The three of us, when we were sitting at lunch, Nick sat in the middle and we both faced *him*, like he was the sun. At Bible study, my mom sat next to *her*, patting *her* on her knee while she read out loud. And all these things feel important in a way that I can't explain.

Yvonne crosses her arms and tucks a long blond tendril behind her ear expectantly.

"That day with Nick," I say, trying again. "That morning, remember, the people from the mutual aid were coming to get her stuff, finally?"

My voice is like glass breaking, and I hate the sound of it, but when I see her nod, almost imperceptibly, I go on.

"And my dad was—he was crying, and you didn't—"

I feel her looking at me, knowing she's watching me, but I can't look at her anymore. Not while I say this.

"You didn't answer your phone. And when Nick—kissed me," I say, "it was all erased. It was like it was all gone."

I bring my hand to the base of my throat, which aches from the remembering. The knocking at the door. Dad's face twisted up. The boxes. The air in the house, thick. The blue-black storm clouds gathering like bruises in the sky. The rain. Nick pulling the car over.

My whole body feels scooped out, raw.

"You fucked my boyfriend because I missed your call," she says.

The words are heavy in her mouth.

She moves closer to me, knitting her brows together, narrowing her eyes.

"Aren't you listening?" I say, frustrated, not backing down. "He kissed *me* first."

"And you didn't stop him. Because you were punishing me."

My mouth opens and closes.

"For what?" I ask.

And she barks out a bitter laugh, and she doesn't say, but it wasn't that I was punishing her, at all. No. The rain was falling down in sheets. Nick was there. She wasn't. But that didn't seem important. Not really.

Because nothing did. I was blank. I was numb. I was a void.

"Yvonne," I say helplessly. "I was just really sad."

Again, it's all I can find the words for. And again, it sounds so stupid I'm not even surprised when she laughs at it this time.

She's shaking her head.

"I know! I know you were. And I wanted to help, but I didn't know how and you wouldn't let me. You *never* could, even before that. Because you're *always* sad, Marisol, and negative, you're always pissed off, about what your mom was making you wear to the Fil-Am dinner, or church, or whatever. Big fucking deal."

God, she makes it sound so silly and insignificant, when it wasn't. Yes, those things made me mad, but it was also something else, something much harder to figure out, that was making me mad, too, and yes, yes, I was always mad, and I still am, so what?

"It *is* a big deal," I say. "That *nothing* I ever did was good enough. And she was always comparing me to you, because you're so perfect and you don't even try."

Her eyes flash.

"I try incredibly hard," she says. "I try *every day* to make my parents happy. It's literally the least we can do, and it's not like some huge burden. And if you had just stopped *resenting* it and just accepted it for what it is, maybe you wouldn't have been such a bitch to her. She didn't deserve it."

It's like she hit me, again.

But she didn't have to. This is worse. Much worse.

"Fuck *you*," I say, and I want it to sound cutting, but it doesn't.

"At least now you can stop feeling sorry for yourself," she snaps. "It's not like your dad will force you to go to church or hang out with us anymore."

"What?"

"Oh, shut up. I know you always thought you were so much better than us. Well, congratulations, you're free."

She turns away, as if she hasn't just stopped my heart cold, and the sound of her heels on the linoleum reverberates up and down the hallway. She leaves me in the over-air-conditioned chill, her words echoing in my ears, in my bones.

Chapter Ten

NOW

Congratulations, you're free.

My vision blurs as I rest my hand on the rusty old dumpster behind the school to steady myself. The metal is warm from the sun. I'm crying so hard over what Yvonne said that snot drips down my face, and I can't wipe it away fast enough. Now my shirtsleeves are soaked in snot, and this is so gross that I just cry harder.

You know what? I'm done, Mom is saying from the dead.

It's as if she's right here next to me, despite the finality of those words, as if we're picking up again in the middle of the fight that will never end, because why couldn't I just do what she wanted? Why couldn't I just be a good daughter, like Yvonne and Tes?

If I could do it all over, I would, I'd do anything.

My face is hot, and oh my God, *I'm horrible,* I'm so horrible.

"Holy shit. Marisol?"

I look up and across the bumpy pavement. Elizabeth Parker is peering at me from her car, from behind her movie-star sunglasses.

"What's wrong? Get in."

She leans over and pushes the passenger-side door open.

Just ignore her and walk away. I just want to be alone. I *need* to be alone. And then I almost laugh, because that's just what Yvonne said. *Congratulations, you're free.* I am alone. Completely.

"Come on, little girl," Elizabeth calls in a singsong voice. "I have candy."

In spite of myself, I'm laughing through my snot.

"Get out of here, you creep!" I shout at her. "Stranger danger!"

At the steering wheel, she raises her dark eyebrows expectantly, just like that day in the parking lot after the bomb scare.

Like, *So? Are you coming or not?*

Dragging my feet a little, I trudge over to her car and get in, taking a few deep breaths.

"Jesus," she says, handing me a pack of tissues from the glove compartment.

As the school shrinks into the distance behind us, Elizabeth turns up the volume on the radio.

"What the hell happened?" she asks.

"Just the consequences of my actions," I say, sucking in air, still not breathing normally.

She knits her eyebrows together.

"Do you want to talk about it?"

My shoulders tense.

"No," I say, pressing the heels of my palms into my eye sockets.

"Okay, well, do you want to come over?"

I let out a puff of air and shake my head.

"Why are you so *nice* to me?" I ask.

She glances my way, her eyebrows arched, amused.

"You say it like you're so disgusted. Do I need a reason?"

I continue shaking my head and staring out the window

at the dusty mesa and yellow flowering shrubs rolling by. Elizabeth Parker has her perfect GPA and her independent study. Her weird theater shit and her nice boots and a thoroughly disarming level of confidence. What could she possibly want to hang out with me for?

"I don't have any friends," I say.

She stares straight ahead, one hand on the steering wheel, the other bent, resting in the window.

"Me neither," she says.

Her dark hair moves in the breeze. I watch her closely. And I guess that's true. Despite how comfortable she seems everywhere she goes, aside from school projects and with teachers, she's never talking to anyone, not really.

"So," she says, "are you coming over or what?"

I shrug, but when I feel she's still freaking looking at me, I nod just so that she'll keep her eyes on the damn road.

"Okay, we have a nod, people!" she yells out the window. "As we all know, nods are legally binding!"

I stick my head out the passenger-side window.

"We do not all know that," I scream into the wind. "That is false information!"

My laughter falls away into the sunlight and the sagebrush dotting the mesa.

"You've already agreed to come over, and there's no backing out now. So let me lay out the cast of characters for you," she says, making a left turn. "As you may recall, I have three sisters, all witches."

"Like literally?"

"You'll see."

As we approach her place, she elaborates—there's Karina

and Janelle, the twins, who are freshmen, and Rebecca, who is a senior.

"Then there's my parents," she says. "Dad's an engineer. Mom's a lawyer."

Parents. Fancy parents. Looking at the damp, eyeliner-smeared cuffs on my sleeves, suddenly I'm not so sure this is a good idea.

"I'll only stay a little while."

"Oh, come on. You can stay as long as you want. I want my parents to meet you."

I look at her in total bewilderment.

"Why?"

"Because you're cool and interesting," she says, as if this were obvious. "You're like, I'm Marisol Martin and I'm wearing a hot-dog dress, sue me."

Nobody's ever said the hot-dog dress was cool. Yvonne specifically requested at one point that I not wear it anymore. At least not in pictures.

"I'm not in a presentable state right now."

"Relax, they're cool. They'll probably hand you a glass of red wine like it's nothing, try to shock you by dropping an F-bomb at the dinner table, and then somehow work the *New York Times* crossword puzzle into the conversation. They're all about being the hip, cultured parents, and as long as you can keep up, they'll like you."

I shrug and hug my backpack to my chest and try not to look intimidated.

"Wow, you look *all* nervous," she asks. "Don't be. You're a shoo-in."

"As long as you're not one of those girls who's like, 'my mom is my *best friend*,' because I can't take that right now."

"Of course not," Elizabeth scoffs. "Are you kidding? That's absolutely psychotic."

Thank God.

"Sometimes, though," she says, letting her left hand float in the breeze out the driver's-side window, "I think she wants us to be like that. But she doesn't know how, exactly. She says she had this really strict immigrant parent upbringing and that she's really relaxed compared to that, right? But it doesn't feel that way to me."

I sit up a little. "Where did they come from? Your grandparents?"

"Mexico," she says. "Chihuahua. They both passed away when we were young. Karina and Janelle don't even remember them."

So Elizabeth's mom had immigrant parents, and they were strict, and she's told Elizabeth about that and how she wants their relationship to be different. But it's not? How so? I tug on the ends of my sleeves. I think of Mom and Tita Violeta having a secret smoke and a conversation in Tagalog outside the Christmas party, their heads bent together, their body language changing, becoming whole different people who I could never fully know.

"Do you speak Spanish?"

"Mom does, Dad doesn't really, so we didn't use it much growing up, but I did study abroad last summer and I got pretty good—my mom came to visit me and we went down to Mexico City and it was *amazing*. I'm dying to go back."

My cheeks burn. She's done *study abroad* and she speaks Spanish and I've never even left the country and I'll never get to go to Manila with Mom. And it's a thought that's never occurred to me before, but it's not a good thought to be thinking or a good time to be thinking it, so I squeeze my hands into fists and stare out the window until I don't think it anymore.

The Parkers don't live far from me, but in a different neighborhood, which is nicer than mine. The houses are bigger.

A lot bigger.

Even though there is a four-car garage, Elizabeth parks her car on the street.

"In the getaway position," she says.

A yucca tree towers in the middle of an elaborately xeriscaped yard. I run my hand over the smooth metal doorframe on the eerily clean, modern porch, while Elizabeth pauses with her keys in the door.

Inside the house, a dog is barking.

"You're not scared of dogs, are you?" she asks.

"I *like* dogs," I say, and when she looks unconvinced, I go on. "It's just, the way they make hard eye contact with you when they bring you those sad, soggy little chewed-up balls and stuff? It's kind of like they can see into your soul, and they know you're a bad person for not wanting to touch their slobbery ball."

"I know. We do not deserve dogs."

"Typical dog person's answer."

The barking intensifies as Elizabeth pushes the door open just enough for me to glimpse a big snout and hear claws skittering on the linoleum.

"Hey, hey!" Elizabeth says forcefully. "Down. Down, Cash!"

I am actually kind of scared of dogs, so I cower against the doorframe. I don't know what kind of dog Cash is, but he's like a cross between a black bear and a lowrider. He has short little legs connected to a thick body covered with coarse black fur.

Elizabeth forces her way in by pulling Cash by his collar, wordless from the effort of wrenching him with all her body weight, and beckons for me to follow her inside. I slide into the house behind her, and the screen door slams shut.

Cash is scuttling and sliding all over the place and barking at me as I remove my shoes.

"CASH!" she says. "Sit. Sit."

A smaller version of Elizabeth comes down the stairs in a pair of big, fluffy slippers.

"Hey, what are you doing to the dog?" she asks.

"I am trying to keep him from eating my friend! He's acting like a wild animal! You monster, Cash, let's go outside. Go outside!"

Elizabeth tries to tug him deeper into the house and toward the back door, but he wrenches free of her and begins to run around me in circles.

"Okay, let's just ignore him," she says, tossing her long hair over one shoulder and gesturing to the younger girl on the stairs. "That's my sister Karina. She's busy stinking up my slippers with her sweaty feet."

Elizabeth leads me into the kitchen.

"I'm right *here*, you know!" Karina says, stomping a slippered—sweaty?—foot.

Cash follows us into the kitchen, breathing audibly with his tongue hanging out, his tags jangling as he waddles, where another mini-Elizabeth is standing in front of an open refrigerator.

"Pick something, all the cold air is getting out!" Elizabeth shouts at the small version of herself.

"I'm *picking* something! Calm yourself."

"That's Janelle," Elizabeth tells me quietly, as if referring to an unsavory person just out of earshot.

She shoves past Janelle and pulls two cream sodas out of the fridge door.

Their giant refrigerator is completely stocked with sodas and yogurts and sparkling water and neat plastic bins filled with who knows what else.

Karina, who is Janelle's twin, slides into the kitchen across the linoleum in big, long lunges, as if she has invisible skis strapped to her slippers. I mean, Elizabeth's slippers.

"Why are you being weird? I have a *guest*!"

Elizabeth smacks Karina on the butt, hard.

"Ouch! You are SUCH a WITCH!" Karina screams, rubbing her butt cheek.

I have no idea what's going on. Maybe this is what sisters do.

"You're the witch," Elizabeth shoots back, in a weird voice that resembles a vaguely British cave troll. "I'm going to burn you at the stake, because you're such a witch!"

She grabs me by my sleeve and pulls me toward the stairs.

"Well," Karina shouts after us in her own version of the troll voice, "I'm going to throw you in a lake to see if you float, because you're such a witch!"

"I'm going to cook some turkey bacon," Janelle announces, not participating in the bit.

Elizabeth whirls around.

"If you eat all the turkey bacon, I am going to STONE you to death because you. Are. Such. A. WITCH!"

She takes my arm and we run away from them.

"That was completely *unhinged*," I say.

"I know, huh?" she says breathlessly, laughing, back to her normal voice.

At the bottom of the stairs, there's an ofrenda. It matches the house, in a way, with clean lines and a curated color palette. Each tier is covered in red cloth. Neatly arranged black-and-white photos sit in matching frames, marigolds burst from little glass vases grouped in threes. At the base, a bowl of water.

As we pass, Elizabeth stops to light a candle.

"These are my mom's parents," she says, gesturing to the couple in a wedding photo.

The dark-haired, round-faced bride looks serious in a wedding dress with puffy white sleeves, her groom smiling beneath a thick mustache.

Elizabeth gestures to the remaining photos on the altar and lights another candle.

"This is my aunt Joy. She wanted to be an actor, like me. And this is my tío Gabe. He was really good at Pictionary and liked to scare us with stories about El Cucuy when we went camping."

I grip my elbows and look at Tío Gabe's smiling face as I imagine him telling a story by the fireside in the mountains, leaning close to the crackling fire. Something about the ofrenda shames me, seeing her ancestors together like that, like the first-grade family tree project that caused such a fight between my parents when I brought it home.

I gave her their names and I helped her glue on all the stupid leaves. What more do you want?

Pete, we're supposed to talk to her about them. That's the point of the project.

The candles flicker as Elizabeth leads me up the stairs to a photo hanging in a frame on the wall, a brown woman with her same cheekbones and a white guy in a bolo tie.

"These are my other grandparents, the Parkers. My dad's mom is from here, and his dad is from Ohio."

The walls in the stairway are lined with more family photos and individual portraits of Elizabeth and her sisters holding up awards—trophies, certificates, medals around their necks. The higher I climb, the older the girls get, and the more awarded.

My stomach twists at the thought of Elizabeth coming over to *my* house one day. The empty fridge. The piles of unopened mail and overflowing laundry baskets. No medals. No ancestors.

When we get to the top of the stairs, Elizabeth bursts into the first door on the right. The strings of beads that hang in her doorway clatter as she flies through them and plops facedown on her bed. She lets one shoe drop off onto the carpet, plop. Then the other, plop.

"What, pray tell, should we listen to?"

Elizabeth picks up her phone and taps away on it, and after a moment music begins to spill out of a white speaker on her vanity, which is littered with makeup brushes, nail polish, and earrings with lost partners.

Unlike the pristine decor downstairs, Elizabeth's room is beautiful chaos, and here, I begin to relax. Every inch, except for the ceiling, is covered with some scrap of paper, or a pile of change, or a stack of books, tilting over. Crumpled T-shirts and jeans lie at the foot of the bed. On the walls, concert posters and flyers for plays and bicycle maps are pinned up neatly, with clear plastic thumbtacks. I sit down on the edge of her bed and find my reflection looking back at me in her vanity mirror, which is partially covered in a collage of artfully ripped pictures from magazine pages and a photo-booth series of Elizabeth laughing with, and kissing, someone I've never seen.

"Who is that?" I ask.

"My girlfriend," she says. "Tara. She's a freshman in premed at UNM."

Of course Elizabeth Parker is dating somebody in *college*. No wonder she doesn't bother with anyone at LMHS. This girl is too cool for school.

"Here," she says, pulling out her phone and showing me her lock screen.

A photo of Tara is set as the wallpaper, the sun glowing over the mesa behind her, a halo around her darkly freckled face, short dark hair curling at her ears.

"Wow, she's dreamy," I say.

"Right?" Elizabeth says, rolling over and tapping away on her phone. "I'm telling her you said that."

My cheeks burn a little, but I don't stop her.

"Are you talking to anybody?" she asks.

Yeah, right. I shake my head and get up again, pacing back and forth in front of her desk, which is covered in notebooks, metallic lipstick tubes, and markers with mixed-up caps: blue on green, green on yellow, and the yellow cap missing altogether.

Janelle and Karina run past the door, shrieking and stomping the whole way.

"Your house is loud," I say.

"Wait until my parents get home," Elizabeth says, stretching.

"What's it like having *three* sisters?"

"A living nightmare," she says. But she is laughing.

All these sisters, crowding everything, wrestling over the snacks. Shared sweaters being scooped up and pulled over different heads of dark hair, their sleeves tugged long from being fought over. I think of Bernie reading a book silently by the front window. Bernie turning his back after the telescope. Bernie disappearing into the green car. There's a rock in my stomach.

"At least you talk."

"If yelling and doing bits is talking," she says.

I flinch. Maybe yelling isn't really talking.

"Actually," Elizabeth says, sitting up and crossing her legs into a pretzel, "Karina and Janelle ask me for advice."

Not Bernie. And we certainly don't ask each other, *Where did you go when you left school that day?* or, God forbid, *Are you doing okay?* We ask each other stuff like, *Do you want any of these frozen taquitos I just microwaved?* or *Do you want to watch this weird old kung fu movie with me and Dad?*

I look at my face in the mirror, framed by magazine cutouts of flowers and bicycles and girls with tattoos, my hair a half-fuzzy, half-curly crown, and rest my hand on a stack of thin books on the desk. Plays by Migdalia Cruz, Ntozake Shange.

Swallowing, I pick up one of the slim books and turn it over in my hands.

I clear my throat.

"That sticky ball thing you did," I say. "You said it was a theater thing?"

"A character exercise. To help you live in the mind and body of someone else. The character you're embodying."

I rub the place over my heart with my palm.

"Do you think that's what makes a person who they are?" I ask. "The bad things that happen to them?"

She watches me in the mirror.

"No," she says. "Not at all. I just think our experiences affect us. Change how we see things. What we do."

I adjust my glasses.

"The things we do seem more important," I say. "Like, that really, who you are is what you do. That's when you really show who you are."

"That's why I love theater so much and character work so much, though. Because as an actor, you have to try to figure out *why* people do the things they do. There's always a reason, and sometimes it's not an obvious one."

"Isn't that just kind of like an excuse? Like, I choose to do the things I do."

I chose to get drunk at school, to fight with Yvonne. I did those things. I slept with Nick. I screamed at my mom. I walked away from her, in her hospital bed, when she was—

"But trauma does literally live in your body."

She jumps up and hops over to her bookshelf.

"I have a book about this. Let me find it."

As she turns away, my breath catches and I rest my palm again over the hollow spot at the bottom of my throat. My eyes close. *It's okay, it's okay.* I settle back onto her bed, slowly, and the music fills the room, some acoustic guitar and an electronic beat. A little piano.

Trauma lives in your body.

"This band is so good, right?" Elizabeth asks. "I'll make you a playlist."

I nod, my mind turning, about bad things and bad thoughts and where they go and what happens to them, but really, if I do bad things and I have bad thoughts, then doesn't that just mean that I'm . . . ?

"So how do you get rid of it?" I ask.

"What, trauma?" Elizabeth says. "There are things you can do. To heal."

"You mean like therapy?" I ask, disappointed.

"Yeah, that's one."

She's humming softly, running her finger along the spines of all her books. They are organized by color, the only thing in the room arranged by any discernible system that I can detect.

Well, I already tried doing that. And it didn't work. Nothing works. I lean back against the wall, my head heavy. I'm so tired today. I'm always tired, actually. I hardly sleep at all. I stay up, drawing, to avoid thinking about the nightmare that chokes me awake each night. And then, when I finally fall asleep, I have the nightmare, and I wake up, and I don't want to go back to sleep, because I don't want to have the nightmare.

This band is good.

Acoustic guitar, a little piano.

My eyes droop. Something in here smells like lavender.

There's a blanket over me, and my neck hurts from spending too long slumped over to the side. From downstairs, the smell of something savory rises, along with the clanking of silverware being picked out of drawers, the sound of plates sliding onto a tabletop.

I sit up abruptly.

A voice drifts in from down the hallway.

"You should go wake her up. Her parents might be wondering where she is."

That must be Elizabeth's mom.

I slide off the bed and pick up my jacket.

Another voice.

"Isn't that the girl who . . . ?"

I freeze, hunched over with my jacket in my hand. I don't recognize the second voice. It must be Elizabeth's older sister, who wasn't here earlier, and I can't make out what she's saying, but I'm guessing it's not *Isn't that the girl who loves completing the* New York Times *crossword puzzle?*

"Rebecca, go see if your dad needs help," says Elizabeth's mom. "Why don't you invite her to stay?"

"Sure, Mami," Elizabeth says.

"Mira, mi cielo, I think it's great that you're being friendly with this girl," her mother says, her voice dropping low. I lean toward the door to hear better. "But remember what we talked about? About making friends who aren't—"

Friends who aren't what? I'm screaming in my head.

"*Mami!*" Elizabeth says.

"I'm just saying. You know what I mean."

My heart is thrumming in my ears as I drop my stuff and crawl back onto the bed. I try to rearrange the blanket back just how it was and close my eyes.

I'm so embarrassed I wish I could just evaporate.

After a minute, Elizabeth opens the door slowly, creakily, and knocks softly on the doorframe.

"Hey, Marisol? You awake?"

I stretch my neck and turn my face away so that she doesn't see it.

"Yeah. Sorry, I didn't know I was so tired."

"No worries. My mom wants to know if you want to stay for dinner?"

I pull my cell phone out of my pocket, expecting to find a text from my dad reminding me of our strict 6:00 p.m. home-for-dinner policy.

DAD: Guys, I am still in a mandatory PD. Running late. TV dinner night? Home about 8 pm.

BERNIE: Can I stay for dinner at Scotty's?

DAD: If Scotty's mom says it's okay. M, where are you?

Where I am is at my new friend's perfect house with her perfect family. And I don't belong here. I should just go home to eat a TV dinner by myself.

"Come on, stay," Elizabeth says. "Please? My dad made posole."

My stomach growls at the thought of food that isn't processed chicken with soggy, unseasoned breading. Karina's and

Janelle's shrieking laughter drifts up the stairs. Dinner in a house that isn't quiet and dark.

Elizabeth grabs my shoulders and shakes me gently.

"Posole, posole, posole," she chants.

Maybe it won't be so bad.

"Sure," I tell her before I can change my mind.

I type out a response to my dad on my phone.

Was invited to my friend Elizabeth's house for dinner. Will be home by 8.

His reply text comes in faster than seems possible.

No. I've never met her or her parents.

I feel Elizabeth's eyes on me, so I smile at her.

"Great, I can stay," I say.

I shut my phone off.

The weight of my decision settles over me almost immediately.

As long as you can keep up.

Friends who aren't what?

The downstairs hallway to the dining room is lined with large framed art prints, which I recognize: Diego Rivera and José Clemente Orozco and Georgia O'Keeffe. The candles on the ofrenda are flickering wildly, and I notice what I hadn't the first time: a liquor cabinet. As we pass, my eyes linger a moment too long on a tall, slick-looking bottle of vodka. It's a label that I've never seen. The colors on the label swirl like the shadows in the Orozco painting.

"Marisol?" Elizabeth asks from the doorway to the dining room.

I blink.

"Coming."

When I take a seat at the table, I immediately feel something nudge my shin. Cash, prowling for scraps under the table, his tail slapping loudly against the legs of all the chairs.

"Cash, get out from under there, buddy," Mr. Parker says, plopping a pot holder onto the table and setting a pot onto it. "Human food does not agree with you."

"It's true," Mrs. Parker says, pulling the cork out of a bottle of white wine. "He always regrets it afterward."

Mr. and Mrs. Parker are both maybe a little older than my dad, their dark hair streaked with gray at the temples, and like him, they both wear glasses. Mrs. Parker's hang from a string of beads around her neck. *I'll never see Mom with gray hair*, I realize; she was only thirty-eight when she died. This realization hurts and takes my breath away, and now I have to have a normal social interaction anyway.

"Anyway, welcome, Marisol," Mrs. Parker says, putting on her glasses.

"Thank you for having me," I say, not quite sure where to look.

Mrs. Parker is arranging little ceramic bowls with sliced limes, radishes, and little cubes of white onion on the table. Should I offer to help with something? Her words, both the ones I heard and the ones I couldn't hear, play over and over in my mind. *Friends who aren't . . . friends who aren't . . .*

My mouth is dry.

"We're happy to have you," Mrs. Parker says. "Call me Juana. This is Daniel. You've met Janelle and Karina, our youngest two. Have you met Becca?"

She gestures toward the kitchen dramatically.

"She's our eldest, our firstborn child."

Becca walks into the room, carrying the same tortilla warmer that we have at our house. Unlike her younger sisters, she seems quiet and serious, nodding at me but not saying anything as she sets it on the table.

"Hi," I say.

"I hope you're not shocked," Mrs. Parker says. "We're a wine-drinking family. Would you like a glass? Daniel, pour her a glass."

Elizabeth looks at me knowingly. The wine, the first names? So far they are exactly on brand, as described.

"No, thank you," I say, too quickly, because I don't want to seem like I *drink* drink, because of whatever Becca said about me. But then I regret it, because it looks like a fancy bottle, just like the fancy bottles in the hallway cabinet. I've never tried wine before, let alone fancy wine. Dad's more of a light-beer kind of guy.

Elizabeth pours herself a small glass.

"You can try mine," she says, and winks.

The Parkers have put out all the food on the table, but I wait to serve myself anything in case they are a wine-drinking family *and* a praying family as well. Bowing my head at Yvonne's house, I'd try not to laugh as Tita Violeta asked Jesus to bless everything and everyone in sight, and my dad would do an impression of her in the car on the way home to make Mom laugh. *Dear Lord, we ask you to bless this food before us, bless cousin CJ who has mono, bless Brother Danilo's car, which is in the shop again, bless my air fryer, which isn't working right and is no longer under warranty . . .*

The Parkers are not a praying family, apparently, because Janelle begins ladling herself some soup, with Karina snatching the serving spoon from her impatiently soon after. The steam rises from the pot of posole rojo and when my stomach rumbles, audibly, I flush with embarrassment again.

"So," Mr. Parker says to me, "Elizabeth tells us that you two sit next to each other in a few classes."

"Yes." I search for something more elaborate to say.

Mrs. Parker glances at Elizabeth, and I feel a heat creeping up my neck. I can't believe I'm already bombing this. Mrs. Parker's fingers are tented in front of her, her glasses perched on the tip of her nose. *If you're smart, they'll like you.* It feels just like being under the fluorescent lights and giving a presentation.

"In math," I say.

I stare at the place mat, wishing I had never said yes to this, that I was home alone microwaving my plastic dinner tray, when Janelle and Karina start fighting over something under the table.

"Girls, cut it out with the grab-ass at the table," Mr. Parker says evenly.

"Karina is trying to read stuff on my phone!" Janelle accuses.

"Put the phone up, Janelle," Mrs. Parker says. "And put it on silent."

"Good posole, Padre," Elizabeth says, dipping a tortilla into the red broth.

She's pronounced *padre* like a white cowboy in an old Western would, but it seems to be a joke between them. He winks at her and offers the tortillas to me. I wish *my* dad could cook. He loves posole as much as anyone, but he's afraid of the pressure cooker. We should just sell it, because I am, too. I sprinkle a few radishes and a pinch of cilantro into my bowl, trying to remember the last time I ate a fresh vegetable.

"So, girls," Mrs. Parker says, in a tone that makes each one of us sit up a little straighter, even me.

She turns to Janelle and Karina first.

"What's going on with the soccer league? We're doing it, we're not doing it? I need a decision by Thursday."

"Okay," they say in unison.

"Elizabeth," Mrs. Parker prompts.

Elizabeth gives her mother a salute.

"Ma'am."

"Update me on the situation at the Little Theater."

"They're doing *Romeo and Juliet* this season, and the first audition is in two weeks," Elizabeth says, passing me her wineglass. "I want to play Mercutio."

"Mercutio is hot," Karina says.

"Very," Mrs. Parker agrees.

I smile into the wineglass, holding it up to my nose and smelling it like they do in the movies. I take a sip; the liquid is tart and dry on my tongue.

Mrs. Parker is staring at me.

"It's nice," I squeak out.

I give the glass back to Elizabeth quickly. Mrs. Parker turns her attention away from me.

"It'll look good to law schools, if you can stick with it," she says. "They love theater majors, actually. They can command a room."

Elizabeth swirls the liquid in her glass. She didn't say she wanted to be a lawyer. She said she wanted to be an actor. But I see, now, how Mrs. Parker is okay with it only because it's in service of something else. Elizabeth sits up straighter in her chair, holding her head high. The same way she does as she walks down the halls of LMHS. The way she walks into any room. But now I know. It's because she's carefully balancing a heavy weight.

Meanwhile, Mrs. Parker has moved on down the line.

"Eldest daughter, did you submit any applications today?"

"Two, actually," Becca says, taking an elegant bite.

"Which, pray tell?" Mrs. Parker asks.

Becca chews slowly before speaking.

"Brown and Caltech."

Apparently, Becca is the sort of person who speaks sparingly. I guess she's saving all her energy for applying to colleges I've never heard of but I suspect are really good.

"I went to Brown," Mrs. Parker says to me, as an aside.

Mr. Parker clears his throat.

"And Daniel went to Caltech," she adds, rolling her eyes.

"And there will be no posole at Brown, Becca," Mr. Parker says. "Not a tortilla in sight. Just remember that."

The Parkers start arguing about where the best tortillas are from and whether they could ship them to Becca at Brown. I just listen to them talking back and forth and for a second, it feels like if I don't make any sudden movements, or say anything stupid, maybe I will blend in.

"*Anyway*," Mrs. Parker says. "Have your parents started bullying you about college yet, Marisol?"

I fumble to dab the corner of my mouth with one of the Parkers' nice cloth napkins. The heat from the chile has left tingling remnants on my lips. My mind is screaming, *Say something*, but I don't know what to say. The cuffs of my sweatshirt are smudged with eyeliner from when I was crying before. They look so dirty. My parents. My parents. My cheeks grow hotter and hotter the longer I stay silent. Adrenaline courses through my veins. Elizabeth invited me here. She said she wanted me to meet her parents. Why? She wanted me to impress them? Suddenly it makes me furious. I think of those photos lining the stairway, ancestors at the bottom, and the higher you climb, the more and more medals appear around the necks of daughters. *You know what I always say about making friends who aren't* . . .

"My mom is dead," I say flatly. "And she didn't go to college."

Mrs. Parker's mouth drops into the shape of the letter O. Both Becca and Mr. Parker clear their throats and stare into their soup.

I glance at Elizabeth, expecting her to be mad that I'm not playing the parents game. But her face is even and unreadable.

"I'm so sorry," Mrs. Parker says, faltering. "I didn't know."

Which part? I almost blurt, but then I chew the inside of my cheek. I watch as Mrs. Parker removes her glasses, and as if to buy time to recover herself, she cleans a smudge from the lens with the bottom of her shirt. And seeing her brown eyes exposed like that softens something inside me, for just a second.

"It's okay," I mutter.

"How did she die?" Janelle asks.

"*Janelle*," Elizabeth says, kicking her under the table.

"In a car accident."

The sound of spoons scraping at the bottom of bowls. The words come out detached, devoid of any meaning, like I could have said *in a mailbox* or *on the moon*. I don't feel like I'm inside my body at all anymore. I don't cry.

"Your brother is Bernardo Martin, right?" Karina asks.

"Yes."

"He's in our gym class," Janelle says. "He's really tall."

Karina and Janelle are both giggling and blushing, and then the awkward moment has passed. Elizabeth and I look at each other like, *Oh my God, the witches are in love with Bernie.*

"But I haven't seen him this week," Karina says, with her mouth full. "Is he sick?"

"What?" I ask. "No."

That can't be right. My dad has been taking Bernie to school early every day for orchestra. Like normal.

"Karina, chew your food, please," Mrs. Parker says pointedly.

Her glasses are back in place. She's eyeing me closely, and my heart rate spikes again, my muscles tensing, but what does Karina Parker know?

Bernie is fine. Bernie is good.

"Maybe you just haven't noticed him."

And when I hear my voice, it sounds too defensive, and even

I know that it makes no sense. Bernie is extremely noticeable, especially because he probably wears suspenders in gym class.

Karina shrugs.

Mrs. Parker cuts her eyes to Elizabeth.

Elizabeth raises her eyebrows in a look that says, *Drop it*, and chews exaggeratedly when she sees me looking. It seems they can communicate without speaking, and the thing they're communicating about right now is me, the weird friend, and I'm frozen in place, holding a torn tortilla in my hand.

"Straw poll," Elizabeth says. "Do you think that *Romeo and Juliet* is Shakespeare's best play or his worst play?"

"Worst," Mr. Parker says. "Definitely."

"You're just a Mercutio hater," Karina says.

"May I be excused for a second?" I ask.

I push myself away from the table a little too forcefully and make my way down the hallway toward the bathroom. I pass the altar, the ghostly faces dancing in candlelight, and then, the liquor cabinet. My eyes are stinging.

I am fine, I am okay, Bernie is fine, Bernie is okay.

In her wedding photo, Elizabeth's grandmother's dark eyes look out at me from across time and space, and I wonder how she was with her daughter, if they had their own secret language or if all they did was scream at each other until she died.

The door to the liquor cabinet slides open noiselessly. The neck of the vodka bottle fits neatly into my palm. I glance both ways down the hall before taking a gulp, and another. My eyes water. I can't tell if it's from the liquor burning my throat or from something else, something less manageable, so I take a gulp again.

I twist the cap back onto the bottle and shove it back into the cabinet too quickly.

The bottle clangs against another one and teeters for one heart-stopping moment until I grab it and set it right.

"Hey, M?"

I slide the cabinet closed and spin around just as Elizabeth comes around the corner.

My heart is in my throat.

"What's wrong?" she asks.

Can she tell? Did she hear?

"Nothing, it's just—"

I swipe at the corners of my eyes, where tears are springing up, my body betraying me again.

"What is it?" she says.

Her brow is knitted with concern.

"Your mom hates me," I say.

"No, she doesn't," Elizabeth says. "I'm sorry. She's just kind of intense, that's all."

I tug at the ends of my sleeves.

"I'll talk to her," she says. "Okay?"

"Can you take me home?"

Just then, the doorbell rings and Cash explodes into the front room, a tornado of wild barking and claws skittering on tile.

"Cash, cool it!" Elizabeth's mom yells from the other room.

Elizabeth grabs his collar and pulls him away from the front door as her mom appears, hurries down the hallway, and pulls the door open.

Dad's on the doorstep, hands in his front pockets, and

because Mrs. Parker is peering at him through her designer glasses, I see him the way she does. His old, faded jeans. An even older jean jacket. Our old, dusty car parked on the street behind him.

"Can I help you?" she asks.

"Just here to collect my daughter," he says, not warm but not cold, either, gesturing at me with his chin. "She's gone rogue."

My eyes fall to the floor.

How did you even find me? I want to scream.

Everybody is staring at me.

"Mr. Martin, it's so nice to meet you," Elizabeth says, sticking out one hand to shake his while holding Cash back with the other. "Marisol has been letting me pick her brain about our next English essay. Hers are always the best."

He raises his eyebrows.

"Well, maybe they'll let you stay in Honors this time after all, Short Stack. Let's go."

Elizabeth blinks.

Suddenly seeing red, I snatch up my backpack from where I'd dropped it on the floor.

"Thank you for dinner," I mutter in the direction of Mrs. Parker as I brush past my dad on the way outside.

"Good night!" Elizabeth calls out to my back as I march toward the car.

The sun has just slipped beyond the horizon, the sky is inflamed with twisting clouds, orange and red formations churning and raging against the deepening black. I try to open the car door but it's locked, so I pull on the handle again and again.

"Hold your horses," my dad says, trotting over and unlocking it with the clicker.

I get in and slam the door behind me.

"*What* is with you?" he asks as he gets in.

I hug my backpack to my chest and swallow the red-hot ball of anger that pulses there.

"Do you have one of those apps where you can track me or something?" I ask.

"Of course I do."

I press my palms into my eye sockets to keep from crying. I hate that he's come to get me like I'm five years old. I hated the way Mrs. Parker looked at him. I can't stop picturing her face when he made that comment about the Honors program. If she didn't already, she definitely thinks I'm stupid now.

"I'm sorry, did I embarrass you in front of your fancy new friend?" he asks.

I stare straight ahead down the street, lined with neat, two-story houses, and say nothing. This is why Elizabeth is wrong about psychology and people and why they do stuff and *character work*. He knows he embarrassed me. He did it on purpose because he hates people who live in neighborhoods like this one, who have four-car garages, who he imagines are looking down on him all the time, and they are, Mrs. Parker definitely was, but who cares why he did it? It was mean and he shouldn't have done it.

"I wasn't doing anything wrong," I shout. "We were just eating posole and it was delicious!"

"Hey, calm down, will you?"

He starts the car, shaking his head like he's so goddamn

rational all the time. He's the one who *tracked* me and raced over here like I was fucking kidnapped just because I didn't text him back. Always telling Mom to *relax* and *just chill* when we were fighting, like he was some kind of sage peacemaker, but it was just because he couldn't deal with it. He just wanted us to pretend like everything was fine. *Asawa, it's just a shirt. Jesus. Calm down.* Always taking my side, even. And I just *let* him. This is his fault. If only he had told me to stop being such a brat, if only he'd stopped me from acting like a total monster, then I wouldn't have exhausted Mom so much to the point of—

I can't even breathe now, but I'm okay, *I'm okay.* If I just keep staring hard out the window, I'll be okay. I start counting mailboxes, *five, six, seven,* until I stop thinking about that night and what I said to her and everything that happened after. Until it's just the darkened road, and the houses passing by.

"You had posole for dinner at the fancy house? Who made it?"

The questions, the incessant, probing questions. He hates when *I* ask *him* anything. He likes things quiet. When I was a kid, if I was quiet enough, he'd let me sit next to him and watch him while he was cleaning out his tackle box or rewinding his fishing line, and we'd just sit there in an easy rhythm, nobody asking or answering any unnecessary questions.

I set my jaw.

The stoplight changes.

"How was driver's ed?" he asks.

But this, he asks so gently that it nearly crumbles me.

I close my eyes, breathe in a slow breath, and rest my forehead on the cool glass of the window.

"They didn't show the movie," I say.

I'm surprised at how easily the lie comes.

"Good," Dad says. "You're grounded for a week."

I open my eyes and watch the world roll by.

Chapter Eleven

When I sketch this one out, I try to capture the fine dirt under our feet first. How it rises in plumes under my dad's sneakers. We're playing softball in the mountains. He throws the faded ball to me, but I'm not quick enough to catch it and it hits me square in the chest.

It's like the stuff that holds me together evaporates, like somebody cut all my strings. All I see is pink, dusty sky, and all I feel is the hard-packed dirt at my back.

I hear my dad running up, sliding in the dust.

"Why don't you watch what you're doing?"

Concern and guilt and blame all intertwined.

My mom appears, leaning over me, in bright blue and white. The sun is sharp and bright behind her face as I try to force the air back into my lungs.

Her hands, always cold, cradle my head and brush the hair from my forehead.

"It will come back," she tells me. "The breath will come back, you just have to wait a second."

She's gone again. Why is it getting harder and harder to picture her face?

My pencil can't move fast enough. *No, no, no, no.*

I'm pulling on my shoes by the front door while Dad hovers over me like he wishes he could have grounded me for life.

"Are you sure you're not imposing on the Parkers too much?" Dad asks. "You were just there."

My eyes flick to Elizabeth's car pulling into the driveway. It's Friday, and Dad has given his okay for me to sleep over.

"Dad, they invited me," I say to my shoelaces. "I'll text you, okay?"

He nods, but I feel him watching as I run down my driveway before Dad can change his mind and rescind his permission.

The sky is a swirl of pink and purple, with just a few stars peeking through, and one bold yellow airplane contrail that looks like it took a dive straight down into the red sun's face.

Once Dad grounded me for having dinner at her house a few weeks ago, Elizabeth went on the offensive and launched a respectability campaign with my dad. She knocked on the door with fresh tortillas, which she said were from her mom, who, according to Elizabeth, won't even cook eggs, let alone a freaking tortilla. After witnessing her dropping off her Lit textbook to lend me after I forgot mine at school, he said he had forgiven her for kidnapping me during the lockdown and that she seemed like *a responsible, together young lady.*

Unlike me, I guess.

Still, I kept my expectations low when I told my dad I'd be staying over at Elizabeth's house tonight—but it actually worked. I would *never* have tried to pull that with my mom. She was telepathic. She would have immediately known I was lying and that I was actually trying to go to a party, *with boys,* and then I wouldn't be allowed to go anywhere but church and Bible study for a month.

"It's nice that you've made a new friend," he said in his gruff way.

Maybe I should feel bad about lying to him, but I don't.

I want to keep things for myself. All the things I'm doing instead of going to the driving class. Answers to the questions he doesn't know to ask. Driving aimlessly with Elizabeth. Wandering the stacks in the library. Flipping through boxes of records at Charlie's.

I pull open the door to Elizabeth's car. I wave goodbye to Dad with my backpack over my shoulder. Smile.

We aren't going to the Parkers' for a sleepover.

We're going to a party.

Elizabeth has told her parents she's sleeping at my house just as I told my dad I'm sleeping at hers, but we're actually sleeping at her girlfriend Tara's, at the house she rents with three roommates near the university.

As Dad pulls the front door shut, Bernie's also waving goodbye to me from the window at the front of the house, holding this little paperback book in his hand. He's framed like a picture in the Christmas lights that Dad puts up way too damn early every year. He looks kind of like a Filipino James Dean, with a pompadour and a black leather jacket and everything. How? How is he so cool, and I'm not?

He's dressed to go out. I wonder if he's planning to sneak out later. I didn't know how to ask him whether he is, so I didn't.

The car doors slamming behind us do nothing to change

how cold we are. In fact, it's getting colder by the second as we lose the sun in the west.

"Jesus, Jesus, Jesus!" Elizabeth bounces up and down in the driver's seat as she starts the car, the keys jangling. "Damn this weather! Damn climate change!"

I blast the heater, and then the radio, and I feel myself smiling. A college party. A neighborhood with little brown adobe houses and yards full of yucca and cholla cactus.

Elizabeth has assured me that Yvonne Morales will most definitely not be there.

We park the car, and the sound of our heels punching the sidewalk echoes down the street.

I know the party house by the people drinking beers in the driveway, perched in the bed of a truck. Jupiter is bright, hanging low in the sky, and the tip of my nose is cold. There's a hum of anticipation in my chest. Elizabeth links arms with me as we walk through the creaky blue door into the house, the music swelling as she pulls the front door open.

The furniture has been pushed to the walls to make room for the people dancing on the scratched wood floor. A row of bikes hangs from a rack in the ceiling by the front window. Fluttering overhead, papel picado on strings: green, orange, and purple. As we push through the dancing bodies, I scan the old black-and-white photographs in frames that line the walls.

"What did you say your girlfriend's name was again?" I shout to be heard over the music.

"Tara," she shouts back. "Tara Duran. You know Joel Duran? Like, the only remotely cool guy in our class? Tara is his sister."

Joel Duran.

No. No, no, no.

I swallow hard. What if he's *here*?

I quickly take stock of my outfit, and my hands fly up to assess the state of my hair. I regret everything. I regret every single choice that led up to my physical appearance at this moment. Obviously, I would have been a bit more selective had I known that I would be attending a party with Joel Freaking Duran.

"What?" Elizabeth asks. It's like she can smell fear.

"Nothing!" I say, way too loudly, and shake my head. I am not going to tell Elizabeth Parker, who has miraculously taken me under her cool-ass wing for no good reason, about my dumb, middle-school-level crush. It's just too embarrassing.

Joel and I are in Anatomy and Physiology together this year. He sits two rows in front of me and three desks to the right. I watch the back of his head. His soft black hair grazing the top of his shirt collar. That's the only anatomy I'm interested in.

I wish I could tell Elizabeth that corny joke, but if I told her about my crush on Joel Duran, she'd totally encourage me to talk to him, and I absolutely cannot talk to him. This crush has gone on for so ridiculously long that I'm sure he'll know it instantly, as soon as I open my mouth. Or I'll blurt out something insane like, *That shirt you wore last Thursday is my favorite*, and then I will have to drop out of school and get my GED online after all.

I scan the party but I don't see him anywhere. There's incense and weed smoke in the air. My mouth is dry.

"Let's get a drink," Elizabeth says, reading my mind again

and yet oblivious to the source of my inner turmoil. She pulls me by the hand into the kitchen.

Strangers link arms and dance around us, telling stories and passing joints from hand to hand. They look relaxed and cool. I'm positive everybody thinks I look about twelve years old in this stupid shirt. Elizabeth seems unfazed by being at a college party, so I try to follow her lead. Her thick braid falls over her shoulder as she leans into the fridge.

There's an impossible amount of beer in there.

I don't recognize any labels, so I don't know what's good and what's not; I don't know what to reach for, or whether I even should. I went from turning my nose up at the jungle juice at Jasmine Padilla's stupid parties to drinking vodka by myself in the morning before school. Dad hasn't brought any alcohol into the house since he found out about my *high-risk behaviors*. Before all that, though, when Bernie and I were kids, he used to bring cans of Miller Lite in a red plastic cooler when we went camping up in the Jemez. He let me try a sip as we sat by the campfire, and he laughed when I said it tasted like watery old bread, and then we sat there together until the fire turned to embers, not talking, just looking up at the sky above the ponderosa pines, lit up with more stars than I had ever seen.

I'm sure he didn't tell Mom about the sip of beer. I wonder what she would have said. I wonder what she would have said if she had been the one to find me blacked out on the front porch, in need of a stomach pump, instead of Dad. Actually, I don't need to wonder. I know exactly what she would have said.

I stare at the racks and racks of beer inside Tara's fridge.

"You like La Cumbre?" Elizabeth asks me. "IPA or red ale?"

I shrug because I don't know what any of that means. She presses a dark brown bottle into my hand, takes one for herself, and we clink them together.

"Salud," she says, winking at me.

I close my eyes and take a drink. It's cold.

"Salud," I say back.

I'll just have one. It'll be fine.

We find Joel Duran by the fire in the backyard.

The air smells like pine needles, smoke, and dry leaves. He's sitting in a camping chair with a beanie pulled down over his ears and his pant legs cuffed up, showing his ankles. He's talking with a petite girl wrapped in an orange quilt. She laughs in the yellow light of the fire. When she spots Elizabeth and me approaching, she jumps up and grins, draping the quilt over the back of her chair.

"Hey," Elizabeth says, kisses her, and then picks her up and spins her around.

"Put me down!" Tara shrieks.

"But you're just so tiny, I want to carry you around in my freaking pocket!"

But she puts Tara down.

With her feet firmly on the ground again, Tara tucks her close-cropped hair behind her ears. In the crackling glow of the fire, a red rose tattoo peeks out from under the collar of her T-shirt.

"It's freezing," Elizabeth says, turning to Joel. "You can't give your sister your coat, Duran?"

"She didn't want it," he says, smiling, and I see it now, how similar they look.

They both have heavy, dark eyebrows and warm brown eyes. But where Joel is tall, Tara is, well, freaking tiny.

Joel and I make eye contact for half a heartbeat before he picks up a stick to poke the fire. My heart is hammering.

I feel so drawn to him that I have to force myself to stay still, I have to force my eyes away from his. It's like there's a magnet in my chest and he's got the other one.

Elizabeth puts her hand on my back and gently pushes me toward Tara.

"This is my friend Marisol," Elizabeth says.

Tara pulls me into a tight hug and then holds me out at arm's length to look at me.

"I love your glasses."

Her hands are warm, despite the chilly night.

"Oh, thank you." I push them up with my knuckle. "Elizabeth said you're at UNM?"

"I also work at Fix, the bike shop on Coal and Columbia? With Joel—do you know my brother, Joel?"

She jumps back into the chair next to him, wrapping herself up and reaching for a cigarette.

"Yeah," I say. "Hey."

I'm trying to sound totally casual, trying not to stare at how the light dances on his face in the glow of the flickering fire.

"Hey," Joel says. "Never seen you at one of these before."

My heart is in my ears. *Never seen you.* Does that mean he's looked for me? Or that he didn't think I'd be cool enough to come? Or—

"So," he says. "Are you ready to dissect a cow eyeball next week in A and P?"

I run my tongue over my teeth nervously in case something is stuck there. I clear my throat.

"How can one ever truly prepare for such an ordeal?"

The thought of the impending cow eyeball dissection in Anatomy and Physiology class has been filling me with dread and disgust. *Almost enough to offset the thrill I get from staring at the back of your head*, I think.

I glance around, hoping I look cool and aloof, while Elizabeth and Joel start talking about a band they want to go see next weekend. My eyes trace the circle of cinder blocks that surround the fire pit and land on Joel Duran's shoes. Here we are. Talking. I've imagined this moment tons of times, but I'm coming up short on witty things to say.

"I want to see your new bike," Elizabeth says to Tara.

"Oh great! Yeah, let's go."

Tara hands her cigarette off to Joel and hops up. Before I even have time to react, Elizabeth steers me back inside the house, the screen door slamming shut behind us. I take a deep gulp of my beer. I try to get a grip. Tara leads us to her bedroom. The walls of the hallway, like those of the living room, are lined with old black-and-white photos in picture frames.

"Tara?" I ask, pausing in front of the photo wall. "Who are all these people?"

"In the pictures? They're cool, huh? Old-timey," she says, putting her hands on her hips and smiling crookedly at her gallery. "Ancestors, mostly. Some family friends. They were my grandmother's photos. She passed away last year."

"Oh," I say. "I'm sorry."

"Thanks. She was great. When we were going through her things, we found boxes and boxes of these old photo albums, and I framed some of my favorites."

She searches the wall and points to the large photo in the center, while running her other hand through her hair.

"That's her."

It's the one that caught my eye. There's her grandmother, as a young woman, against a dust-gray sky, her dark hair swirling in the wind, like the arm of a galaxy cupping her smiling face. In a pair of blue jeans and boots, she poses with one foot propped up on the bumper of a truck, her hands pulling up the collar of her plaid shirt to frame her round face, with that same Duran dimple.

She's looking right at me, I swear.

"Whoa. Her power."

"I know, huh?" Tara says, grinning.

I trace the frame with my finger.

Dad's father sends a neatly signed birthday card to both me and Bernie every year. Dad tries to throw them in the trash before we see them, but I know he sends them because once I got to the mailbox first and found my birthday card, and I kept it. So all I know about my grandfather is that he kicked Dad out of the house when he turned eighteen, he knows that Bernie and I exist, and our birthdays, and he lives in Tucson, Arizona, now. He didn't write anything inside the card, just signed his name, so I also know that, too. But there are no clues or hints as to why they don't talk, or what he's like or anything, just Dad's silent moods and long drives in the desert.

"Tara, your bike!" Elizabeth calls from Tara's room.

We follow her in and Elizabeth whoops with delight as Tara pulls her new bike down from the wall rack. She rolls it a few feet across the hardwood floor of her bedroom.

I lean against the doorframe and admire it.

"You built that thing?" I ask, impressed.

"I did," Tara says. "My brother helped a little. I keep telling Elizabeth I'll build her one, too. Just come by the shop and pick some shit out."

Elizabeth reclines, catlike, back on the bed, which is littered with what I would call an excessive number of decorative pillows.

"I already have wheels. And I refuse to have helmet hair."

"Do you have a bike, Marisol?" Tara asks me.

"Me? A really old one."

"Is it a fixed gear?"

"I think it's a Huffy?"

"Okaaaay," Tara says, making a face.

"Hey, I also have a pink Barbie helmet to go with it—you can't say I'm not consistent."

She laughs and snorts, a big, room-filling laugh from a tiny person.

"No shame in your game," she says, pointing at me.

Someone turns up the volume on the stereo out in the living room. Elizabeth and Tara share a look.

"I think we should dance," Elizabeth says.

Her eyes are literally twinkling.

I wouldn't say I'm into dancing. The homecoming dance freshman year was terrible. I went with Yvonne and Tes, and our parents said no dates. So we met our dates at dinner. Mine was my lab partner from biology, who I didn't even really like, but Nick had asked Yvonne, and somebody from band had asked Tes. I think he also played the French horn, because they were all talking about some big trip to Los Alamos they had coming up. So I just had to endure an awkward conversation with Dave from bio over endless bread at Casa Pasta, followed by a long night of being crushed in a sea of sweaty people unabashedly grinding to Top 40 hits. Dancing raises so many questions. *Where do I look? Do I look at this dude?* I don't even really like looking at this dude, not even in biology, when he's wearing normal clothes, and even less so now that he's wearing this ridiculous jewel-toned cummerbund.

Dancing at the party at Tara's house isn't like that at all. It's fun.

Somebody's laptop is connected to two giant speakers stacked up on top of each other and jammed in next to the couch. Just like at my house, there are Christmas lights strung up in the windows, blinking. The music is so loud I feel it in my chest.

At first, it's hard to get into it, because I'm too nervous, and what if Joel Duran is looking at me, and maybe I should grab a second beer from the fridge. Then I realize he isn't looking at me, or I stop caring, because Elizabeth and Tara are laughing and being silly, shaking their hair and waving their arms and stomping their feet, and then so am I, and it's so much fun. The full moon can be seen in the big window of this little house, and the tissue-paper squares hanging from the ceiling sway and move along with us.

I forget about time. I feel free.

And just as soon as I stop caring that Joel might be looking at me, he is. He's right there dancing with us. He moves his shoulders up and down, just so. I try to wipe a stupid grin off my face, but I can't because Joel Duran is just so unbelievably cool, and I start laughing. My favorite song comes on and I freak out and pump my fist in the air.

"Oh, this is your jam, huh?" he asks.

"Totally!" I shout over the music.

"Me too!" he says, leaning forward so I can hear him.

And then he starts singing the lyrics, and he nails every word. Tara is clapping. Then I jump in with the next verse, perfect. Joel gives me a little bow, in deference. Then all of us are belting out the chorus at the top of our lungs and jumping up and down.

I can't remember the last time I felt like this.

Light.

After we dance for I don't know how long, my legs need a break and I'm breathless, so I plop down onto the couch. Suddenly it's late and I realize how sleepy I am. We planned on sleeping over here, since we can't go home because of the alibi. I'm content to sit on the couch for now, just watching everybody. An old slow song comes on, sounding of tin and plucky guitar. Some people are still dancing, like Elizabeth and Tara, who are twirling each other around.

Some are singing along. Others are pulling on their coats and hats, hugging at the door, and the cold leaks in, a crisp and sharp scent in my nose.

The orange couch sinks and creaks a bit as somebody sits next to me. I realize it's Joel, and I feel so at peace that I'm not even nervous, until I get a good look at him in the twinkly Christmas lights, of course. He's taken off his sweater and is down to a T-shirt, and I can barely look at him for two seconds before my cheeks are burning.

He smiles at me. He's got this smile that tugs up a little, but then goes back down again, just on the left side. I don't know what to do with my hands. My face. My heart.

"I heard you helped Tara build her bike," I say.

"Yeah, I work with her at the bike shop some afternoons." He points up at one of the bicycles hanging from the rack on the ceiling, a bright yellow one. "That one's mine."

I already knew that from being a weird internet stalker, but there's no way to say that without revealing myself as one.

"It's very . . . visible," I say.

He laughs.

"Yeah, exactly, you wanna be visible on a bike. Visibility is pretty much key."

"I saw the picture of your grandmother on the wall."

I don't know what made me say it, or where I was even going with that, but he just nods, as if waiting for me to finish my thought.

"She looks badass."

"Oh yeah. She was."

He leans back into the overstuffed couch and looks out across the room full of dancing people, his hands in his lap.

"She was very hard-core," he says. "She fixed cars. Taught me how to cook. She lived with us. We were close."

He taps the rhythm of the song against the arm of the couch.

"My mom died."

I don't know why I just said that. Just came out and said it.

But Joel Duran doesn't even blink. He just nods a few times, acknowledging it.

"What's the space that she left?" he asks.

"What do you mean?"

He tilts his head toward his sister, who sways side to side to the music under the twinkling lights.

"So this is something that Tara and I do. It's kind of dumb, but it helps. Almost like a game. We're making a list to quantify the space she left. The exact grandma-shaped space. Like the radio presets she programmed in the truck. The spot in the cabinet where this very specific brand of bulk cornmeal she always bought used to be . . ."

"The space that she left," I say, trying out the words.

It's kind of like my drawings. Sometimes when I'm doing them, it feels like I'm trying to figure something out, to solve an equation, to, how did Joel Duran just say it? To quantify. An accounting of what happened and what it meant.

He's nodding, watching me think.

"Her voice," I say, realizing it. "My mom's, I mean. It's quiet in the house now."

Me and Bernie and my dad sitting in separate rooms, looking out of windows. I turn toward Joel on the couch.

"Because she talked on the phone a lot," I say, and tuck my legs underneath myself. "To her family overseas. She talked so much to so many people. I could picture them on the other end, passing the phone around, and she would have to tell the same story ten times. I was always listening and trying to figure it out, because I don't speak her language."

"Spanish?"

"No. Tagalog."

"Oh, no way, I didn't know you were Filipino. And your dad?"

"He's white."

I've heard people say they hate the "Where are you from?" question, because it's kind of like the other person is asking you what makes you different from them. But right now, it's not like that. It's like Joel is trying to figure out how we're the same, and I don't hate it at all, the way he's nodding with his head bent slightly to one side, showing his perfect jawline, and actually talking to me. To *me*.

"So," he goes on. "Her voice."

"When she was on the phone, she would lean on the counter and twirl her hair in this, like, really girlish way. It was like watching her change into somebody else or travel through time or something."

It was a side of her that I could never know, even though I wanted to. I just wanted to understand her. And I just wanted her to understand me back. That's all.

"Well." Joel claps his hands together. "Listen. We're basically cousins."

"Um, what?"

"Okay, not cousins," he says, and winks. "But we do share a colonizer."

I snort, because it's kind of a weird thing to say, he's kind of weird, and supersmart, and he freaking winked at me.

"So you don't speak any Tagalog? Or Ilocano?"

My face burns. I wish I did.

"She spoke Tagalog, but no. Only some words here and there."

He swings around so that he's sitting cross-legged on the

couch, facing me. My heart is racing in my ears as I twist to look at him, straight on. Straight in the eye.

"Okay, which words?" he asks.

I tuck a stray bit of hair behind my ear, flushing.

"Uh, like, table?"

"Mesa?" he asks.

"Mesa, yep, same as Spanish."

"What else you got?"

I can't help but smile. I can only hope it doesn't look as dopey as it feels. I nod my chin at a pair of Tara's house slippers tucked beneath a bookshelf.

"Tsinelas."

"Chinelas," he says.

"Really?" I ask, laughing. "I didn't know it was the same. Um, okay . . ."

I try to pick something harder, something more abstract.

"How about tsismis?"

His whole face lights up.

"Chisme? What, like gossip? Es lo mismo."

"For real? Okay, here's an important one: arroz."

He laughs, a deep sound, and my chest is warmed by hearing it. He rests his arm on the back of the couch, and I do the same, the space between us closing, slowly, my fingertips almost grazing his.

"Hell yeah, rice! *Arroz!* I think that's Arabic, actually."

"No shit?"

Thinking about how far and how long this word has gone changes something in my brain, and the words are tumbling out of me now.

"Can I tell you something?" I ask. "It's really embarrassing."

"Of course."

"The first time I tried to make rice by myself, after my mom died, I had to Google it. I felt like a total fraud."

He leans against the back of the couch and lets out a low whistle.

"Oof—this is awkward. I'm going to have to report this matter to the rice board."

"I'm serious," I say, laughing, with tears in my eyes. "I felt so *sad*!"

"I'm serious, too! Please, turn in your rice card."

I whack him with a pillow.

"I must call them," he says. "Right now!"

He wrestles the pillow from me and holds it out of my reach when I grab for it, finding our bodies much closer than they were a moment ago.

His eyes are soft, and there's a whisper of a smile on his mouth.

The force of gravity is pulling me closer, closer to him—but something holds me back.

I break eye contact and scoot over.

Putting space between us again.

Joel takes the pillow and hugs it to his chest. I stare at all the empty beer bottles on the coffee table and my mind is screaming, *Say something, anything*, but I can't.

But then he does.

"There's a reason why we're talking about all this, you know."

"What do you mean?"

"It's because the veil is thin right now."

His eyes are shining in the twinkling lights.

"The what?"

"The veil between realms. It's almost Día de Los Muertos."

My heart speeds up.

Joel is looking at me. I'm looking back at him.

"Do you want to come with us to the festival in Algodones Park? It's held the Saturday before."

"Okay," I say instantly.

His dimple appears.

"Okay," he says back.

Then he yawns, pulls his beanie out of his pocket, and pulls it down over his ears. He crosses his arms over his chest. I think that he's going to get up and leave, but then he stays, and we just sit there together, watching our friends slow dance, shadows flickering in the night. Our shoulders don't touch, but almost.

I wish I could stay here forever. In this exact moment.

Chapter Twelve

Dad, Bernie, and I muscle through another quiet din-ner. Underneath the kitchen table, Marty the cat weaves between our legs. His fluffy orange-white tail brushes my ankles as he rubs his chin on everything.

This week at school has been another blur of dense paragraphs and unbalanced equations and trying to pry my eyes open in the mornings, but Día de Los Muertos is now this little beacon, blinking. Something in the future that doesn't crush me to think about, for once.

Bernie's already inhaled three tamales and helps himself to a fourth from the big plate in the middle of the table. The green chile tamales were frozen, and microwaved, because Dad couldn't find the tamale steamer and he doesn't know how to work it anyway, and the wild rice was from a box, but it's not bad, even though I did the rice and I messed up on the water ratio again. Because as I was rinsing the grains, as the water turned cloudy and the grains swirled in the pot, I was thinking about arroz and Joel Duran and all his words, and how his smile looked under the twinkling lights, and I forgot what I was doing.

Bernie is wearing an old cowboy shirt, black with a curling white thread detail around the breast pockets. It's prettier than anything I own.

"Where did you get that shirt?" I ask.

He tips back in his chair, straightening up to a height that, I swear, is taller than yesterday's.

"This shirt?" he asks, looking down at it, in all its carefully threaded detail, its buttons black and smooth like volcanic rock. He brushes off invisible crumbs.

"Yeah, that shirt. I haven't seen it before."

He takes down the rest of his water in one gulp.

"What, are you the only one allowed to have any stylistic flair in this family?" Dad asks, waving his fork at me.

"You've worn that same shirt twice this week," I say.

He looks down at his plaid button-down, chewing.

"So I have."

"I got it at Buffalo Exchange," Bernie says, snapping his fingers. "That's where I got it."

"Really?" I ask. "It looks like it's in really good shape for secondhand."

"Probably third- or fourth-hand at this point, Flubs," Dad says. "It looks like something *my* dad would wear."

Bernie raises his eyebrows.

"Really?" he asks.

Realizing his mistake, Dad's shoulders tense. He slipped up. He mentioned his father.

He places his forearms on the table, framing his plate, shaking his head and muttering something unintelligible.

Bernie and I glance at each other. We've never even seen so much as a picture of our grandpa, though we tried looking him up online once after I intercepted that birthday card. We couldn't find anything. There are too many people with his name, pages and pages and pictures of men who may, or may not, have kicked Dad out of the house, when he wasn't much older than I am now.

"Is he—"

I start a question that I'm not sure how to finish—*Is he like you, is he still alive, is he still someone you want to talk to every day, even though you can't?*

"So, do you need me to sign a driving log for you?" Dad asks. "For your class?"

My fork almost tumbles from my hand.

"What?"

"Don't you need a certain number of hours with a licensed driver before they give you the provisional license?"

He stares at me over the rims of his glasses with the heat of ten thousand suns.

"Right, they're covering that," I say, clearing my throat. "In class. With the teacher. I think we're starting next week."

"Well, let me know," he says.

My shoulders relax, just a millimeter, as the conversation collapses into the sound of forks scraping plates. Dad is staring at the tamales like he wants to punch them, and I wonder if he's still thinking about his dad.

What if he *is* dead and Dad doesn't even know it? What if Dad's in a fight with a dead person, like me?

Not a fair fight at all. Just swinging and swinging.

My phone lights up in my lap. *Joel Duran.*

He said he would send me the info about Día de Los Muertos, and he has. His mom and Tara are teaching a workshop there about altars and how to make them. The digital flyer is bordered with orange flowers. *Participants are invited to bring artifacts to honor loved ones who have transitioned from the physical realm.*

A photo, maybe. That necklace she wore? What am I supposed to bring, exactly? Mom told me about something similar she did growing up, something about celebrating ancestors. What did she bring to that?

"Hey, Dad," I say. "They have something like Día de Los Muertos in the Philippines too, right?"

Dad holds his fork, full of rice, near his face—my question stopping him, mid-motion.

"Maybe," he says. "That sounds right."

It's like my question is about a snake that's about to bite him or something. Maybe if he doesn't make any sudden movements, it will leave him alone.

But I don't leave it alone. Because I would just look this up, figure it out on my own, but I don't know what it's called.

Why didn't I ever ask what it was called?

"Mom told me something, maybe, about bringing food and drinks to the cemetery for Lolo and Lola. I think it's also around this time of year."

Dad shrugs and chews his food.

It's not something I know, I guess because it's not something we would have done here, because no one is buried here, on this side of the ocean, on this side of the earth.

But she is.

A chill runs through my body.

The veil is thin between realms.

This is what Joel was saying. That cemetery where she's buried is here. On this side of the ocean. So nobody will be there to bring her anything when the day comes.

What if she's already there? By herself?

"What *do* you remember?" I ask. "Did you ever go with her? I think she said it was like a party?"

I need to know what I'm supposed to be doing right now. I just need someone to tell me what I'm supposed to do, and he's not doing that, he's just sitting there, chewing and chewing.

And she's out there, alone. Waiting.

"Dad?"

I lean forward. Bernie has stopped moving.

Dad chews, swallows.

"Dead people can't party, Short Stack."

Bernie's fork scrapes across his empty plate. He's hunched over again, shut down, and it's right then, at that moment, when I realize that I hate my dad.

"You are such an *asshole*."

Bernie freezes.

"*What?*" Dad asks.

"You're an asshole and I hate you."

I spin out of my chair, wanting to put as much distance between us as quickly as possible. Marty is startled and bolts for the back door.

"Go to your room!" Dad yells.

"I'm already going!"

Marty is meowing to be let outside, so I wrench open the screen door and he flies into the backyard, bounding off into the pink twilight, disappearing behind Mom's lone rosebush, the only one to successfully take root in the earth because they weren't meant to be here, they aren't supposed to grow here, they take too much water and can't be forced to bloom.

And she's there. Right there. I can see her. Crouching, in the soft evening light, with a cigarette in one hand and the garden hose in the other. Marty is brushing his orange tail against her ankle. She is gone. She isn't gone. In so many ways it feels like she's just on the other side of a door.

Why don't you understand anything?

Her shining eyes, blinking, filled with hurt.

Why can't you just leave me alone?

I fly down the hallway toward my room.

There aren't enough doors in the world to slam.

A little while later, the cold creeps in from my bedroom window. Marty's come back inside, and he's purring loudly and rubbing his face against me as I sit cross-legged on my bed.

I think he knows when I'm sad.

I give his ears a little scratch and look out the window. From here, I can see the moon nestled in a strange yellow halo. Somewhere, Joel Duran can see it. I imagine, somewhere else, another me looking up at it. Living a different life, knowing what to do, knowing how to welcome the dead.

On my phone, I scroll through my contacts until I reach Tita Violeta.

She'd know.

But what would she do if she saw my name there? What if she saw, and declined my call? After Yvonne and I fought at school, they shoved us down into chairs on opposite sides of the main office. Her lip swollen, my head pounding, and Tita Violeta came in, she was practically running, in heels and her work blazer, and she pushed Yvonne's long hair away from her face, and looked at her lip, and whispered to her. And I couldn't hear what she said.

And neither one of them looked at me.

Not even for a second. And then they left.

I hold my phone to my heart, feeling the weight of it there.

The ache is back. The tender place at the base of my throat burns and burns. I press my palm there, flat against bone. *Stop it*, I tell the sticky ball that isn't real, *stop*. My eyes ache too, so I press the heels of my hands into them until they stop, too.

There's a soft knocking at the door, but I do not want to talk to Dad.

"It's me."

Bernie.

I set my phone on my nightstand.

"Come in," I say.

He pushes open the door, slowly. I turn on the lamp and sit up in bed. The warm light of the lamp blots out the cool light from the moon. Bernie leans against the doorframe, his hands in his pockets.

"It's called Undras," he says quietly.

"Really?" I ask. "Why didn't you say so earlier?"

He shrugs, staring at the floor of my bedroom, which is covered with dirty laundry.

"I found an article about it, though."

"Send it to me?"

He pulls out his phone and texts me.

My phone lights up on my nightstand and I grab for it, clicking through to the browser to read it. My eyes jump all around, trying to drink in the words faster than I can make sense of the sentences, words like *All Saints'*, and *All Souls'*, and *Araw ng mga Patay*, and *Commemoration of All the Faithful Departed*.

I'm still scrolling and clicking through to different pages when I realize Bernie has closed the door and is gone.

Undras, or sometimes it's called Undas, comes from a Spanish word, or maybe it doesn't; it's the same thing as All Saints' Day, or maybe it's not; it comes from Spanish colonizers, from the Mexica festival honoring the goddess Mictecacihuatl, from Catholic priests, it comes from when Mexico and the Philippines were *both* called the Viceroyalty of New Spain, and anyway, it's a word for the day when the veil between the realms is thin and the hungry ghosts return.

When Dad told Mom about the place where he grew up, what did he tell her? He wouldn't have said, *My dad used to take me fishing at El Vado, or Rio Chama.* He hated his father, but he loves this place. He must. They could have gone anywhere, but he brought her here. Would he have told her about how piñon smells burning in a fireplace on a cold night, or how at dawn you'll find your car windows so coated with ice crystals, spread wide like spiderwebs, you can hardly see the mountains in the east, capped with white? Did he tell her how in summer storms, we'd huddle together, watching tables topple as lightning cracks across the purple sky? How bone-dry dirt comes up bursting green after a shock of rain, and when the clouds clear out, the storm wiped away, the sky is blue, so blue? How the flowers punch up at the hot sun and go to seed before moonrise?

She almost never talked about the place called Manila, where she was born. Not directly. It seemed to hurt too much. But she'd curse the dirt in our garden. Dry and cracked open under the July sun. *Nothing grows here.* But it's not true, things do grow here, lots of things, strong and quiet things; their roots go deep, and sometimes they appear to be dead, but they're only asleep. Dad did say that when they moved here, many of these roads were dirt and these strip malls weren't built yet. Sometimes they'd go out into the desert and drive fast. They would drive and drive. What is it that they were trying to leave in the dust?

I hold my phone to my heart after reading all the articles and blog posts I could find about Undras. I have to tell Joel Duran what I found out.

My phone vibrates. It's Elizabeth Parker.

What are you up to tonight?

It's a school night, a Thursday, but who cares. The walls of the house press in. The moon is calling me.

I dial Elizabeth's number.

"Hey," I whisper when she picks up the phone.

There's a house show tonight, she says. One of Tara's college friends is hosting a tour of out-of-town bands in his basement, and one local band will be opening for them: Los Tumbleweeds.

"I can come get you, if you want to go," Elizabeth says.

"I just have to wait until my dad's asleep," I say.

It should be soon, it's almost ten.

"Just text me. I'll go pick up Tara first," she says, then hums along to the music playing in the background on her end. "Joel is meeting us there."

I throw my comforter off.

This time, I won't be caught off guard in a dumb shirt.

Chapter Thirteen

THEN

"You ready, Short Stack?"

Dad's standing in the doorway to my bedroom, wearing a tie, which just looks ridiculous. There's nobody who looks more unnatural wearing a tie than him. It doesn't match his shirt and it isn't even straight, but he is wearing it. For her.

I glare at his reflection in my mirror, where I'm swiping at my eyes with a cotton ball doused in makeup remover, because my mascara and eyeliner are all smeared and running down my cheeks because I have just been crying, and screaming, while my mom cried and screamed right back at me.

She was screaming at me *because* I had too much mascara on, and too much eyeliner, so it's ironic that both are now so commingled with tears that they are the consistency of sludge and I have to take it all off, anyway.

We're late.

Mom is getting an award tonight, from the Filipino-American Association, for her community service.

Yvonne is also getting an award. The Outstanding Youth Award. Now that we're freshmen, I would feel kind of dorky to be called a youth, and what she is being awarded for, exactly, I do not know.

Probably for her outstanding ability to put on enough eyeliner to look *pretty* but not quite enough to look *like a dead person*, which is how much eyeliner I had put on for the awards ceremony, according to my mom.

"Maybe we can just enjoy the night," he says.

I look at him, in his tie, which I know he hates wearing, and nod.

But then Mom appears beside him in the doorway. She barely comes up to his shoulder. She's wearing a dress that I've never seen before. The bags under her eyes are caked with makeup two shades too light for her.

She has that face on, her determined face, determined not to let this die, not yet.

"And why," she asks, "can't you wear that dress we got you for confirmation?"

My blood turns to acid. It feels like we're always picking up in the middle of an argument. In the middle of a sentence. In the middle of a long debate that will never end and I can never win.

She pushes past Dad, into my room, which I hate. Dad knows better than to enter. He stays behind the invisible line at the doorframe.

"Mom, *get out* of my *room*!"

"You never wear that dress, and it was expensive."

Ignoring me, like I don't even exist, she pries open my closet doors, and a pile of neglected dirty laundry spills out.

"Mom, *stop!*"

"Oh my God," she says, bending at the waist and scooping up all the dirty shirts, and, horrifyingly, underwear, that have fallen out of the hamper.

"Asawa, we need to get going," Dad says.

"Let me just put a load of laundry in, because our daughter can't even take care of herself."

"I can do it later, Mom. Let's just go!"

"Are you going to change?" she asks.

I smooth down the front of my shirt, which is actually Dad's. Something that he never wears and he was going to give away, but he said I could have it. I cuffed the sleeves and paired it with a vest and a long black skirt that Yvonne had rejected as a hand-me-down from her mom, but I loved the lace detail on the bottom and the crushed velvet. And I like how I look. And I hate the confirmation dress, I hate how it fits me and hugs my rib cage and how the collar choked me as the bishop anointed me with oil, how it made me sweat under the heat of everyone watching me like they were waiting for me to mess up, to say the wrong thing, like they could tell the dress was a costume.

"I don't care how much that dress cost," I say. "I hate it."

Bernie calls out from down the hall. "Are we going, or no?"

Dad clears his throat.

Mom pinches the place between her eyes.

"At least you don't look like a dead person anymore," she says.

"If only I was," I snap.

All the dirty clothes spill from her arms and land in a pile at her feet.

Her eyes are filling up with tears, again, but her makeup is staying perfectly in place anyway, her pretty red lip and her soft brown eyeliner immovable through the whole fight even now.

"Don't you ever say that again," she says.

Chapter Fourteen

NOW

A pile of rejected outfits is growing on the bed. I'm listening to Los Tumbleweeds, with my headphones, so that I can sing along at the house show, and trying on outfit after outfit.

There's a YouTube tutorial playing on my laptop, "How to Create the Perfect Braid Crown." I keep my fingers steady, carefully tugging and pulling my hair into place in the glowing light of my laptop.

I sit cross-legged in front of my full-length mirror and remove the cap from a lipstick tube that was my mom's.

It's red. Really red. She didn't usually wear it, but when she did, it looked like it was made for her.

I remember how, sometimes, I'd touch all the hems of the long dresses in her closet. How I'd watch her getting ready in the clothes that weren't the blue scrubs that made her invisible and disposable to everyone. The florals and the gingham. The boots with heels. The lipstick.

I sweep it on, the creamy red. I tilt my chin and look.

She's there. I can see her. From certain angles.

❋ ☀ ❋

"I can't get over this red lip on you," Elizabeth says from the driver's seat. "I'm obsessed."

Tara rides shotgun, her feet propped up on the dashboard of Elizabeth's car.

"Oh my God, just park on the street," Tara says.

The small house's driveway is already packed with cars, their bumpers practically touching, and the last one is technically *in* the street. A long row of bikes are U-locked to the front porch. One of them is Joel Duran's.

"You okay, M?" Tara asks me.

I pull my jacket tighter around myself and stare at Joel's yellow bike, letting my lungs fill with anticipation.

"Yeah." I smile and shrug. "Whose house is this?"

"My friend Paul's," Tara says. "He hosts a lot of these things."

The three of us walk up to the house party, inhaling the crisp smell of nighttime mixed with the scent of smoke and something cooking. In the backyard, a group of college kids gather around a small fire pit. They seem so much older than me. I search the laughing faces in the yard. No sign of Joel, but I'm ready, in my most mature-looking outfit. I even put eyeliner on, but then I poked myself in the eye with the eyeliner pencil, and cried the eyeliner off, and it was ruined, and my eye is still a little red. At least it's dark.

The front door opens.

"Paul!"

Tara jumps into the arms of a tall, skinny white guy in all black, from his black shirt to his black shoes. He's maybe in his early twenties, and he looks familiar, but I can't place him. His house is crammed full of people, and a mess. The coffee table is covered in crumpled beer cans and ashtrays overflowing with cigarette butts.

He kisses Tara on the top of her head.

"What's up, Tiny Tara?" he asks, then turns to give Elizabeth a high five. "What's up, E.P.P.?"

He pronounces each letter individually.

She snorts. "And what is E.P.P., exactly?"

"It's my new nickname for you, since you hate nicknames." He gives her a wink. "Elizabeth Pilar Parker."

"I do, usually. Hate nicknames, that is. But I don't hate E.P.P., for some reason. Has a nice ring," she says, winking back at him.

"Man. If you like it, that just takes all the fun out of it, *Liz*."

"Nope," she says, pointing a warning finger at him. "None of that."

He grins. There is a black bandanna hanging out of his back pocket. He gives me the *what's up* nod.

"Paul is the store manager at Charlie's," Elizabeth explains to me. "Paul, this is Marisol. She goes to school with me."

"I thought you looked familiar," I say. "Big fan of the place."

"Well, we're actually a little shorthanded at the moment," he says. "So if you're looking for a gig, let me know. I already told Elizabeth she should apply. If she promises to stop insulting the customers who wander in from the new Starbucks across the street."

"Listen," she says. "Unless they want to go through life imagining that coffee is *supposed* to taste shitty and burned—"

Tara holds up a grocery-store tote bag. "Beer."

"Fridge," he says, and points.

Just then, Joel's at the front door, with his own canvas tote bag, the slender neck of a wine bottle sticking out of the top. When he sees us, he waves, then smooths down the front of his T-shirt, neatly tucked into his jeans.

"Gasp!" Elizabeth says, snatching the wine from his bag. "Que sofisticado!"

"Hello to you as well," he says. "I'm sorry, I brought that as a special request, actually."

"For who?" Elizabeth asks, handing the bottle back over.

But Joel doesn't say for who, because he and Paul are clasping hands, doing their man-hug thing, patting each other on the back.

"Nothing special for your one and only sister?" Tara says, miming a dramatic faint.

"You said red wine tastes like dirt," Joel says.

Tara wrinkles up her nose and crosses her arms. "Well, it does."

"We're working on developing her palate," Elizabeth says, intertwining her fingers with Tara, who is rolling her eyes good-naturedly.

"Anyway, hi," Joel says, hugging each of them in turn. "What are we talking about?"

"Paul's trying to get us to come work at Charlie's again," Elizabeth says.

"Well, that's perfect for you, Elizabeth." Joel grins, putting his arm around his sister. "Since Charlie's is right next to Fix, you'll get even more face time with your favorite person . . . me."

Tara shoves him away.

I cross my arms, but then he turns to me.

"Hey, how are you?" he says.

Smiling like he's actually asking, like he actually wants to know.

He leans in, and I feel that magnetic tug at my heart.

I open my arms to him, and he smells so good as he pulls me into his chest.

"What did you think of that cow eyeball?" he asks into my ear.

A shiver runs through me—and he holds me a little longer than a friend would, doesn't he?

"The eyeball?" I laugh through the nerves and break the hug. "It was like cutting through a rotten pudding while it stares at you."

"Accurate." He grins. "So gross, right?"

When he's smiling at me like this, it's pretty hard to form thoughts, but I manage this one: If Elizabeth and I were to work at Charlie's, and he and Tara work at Fix, then surely they'd be coming into Charlie's to take a break from fixing bikes. The four of us could hang out all afternoon, listening to the new albums that came in, the golden sun warming everything.

"Paul, I'm interested in helping out at Charlie's," I say.

"That's awesome," he says. "Here, put your number in my phone so I can text you the details."

"Hey, the show's about to start," Tara says.

After I finish tapping my number into Paul's phone, I readjust a couple strands of hair in my braid. I came ready to impress Joel with my extensive knowledge of the Albuquerque music scene, and now is the time. I sidle up close to him as we make our way downstairs.

"I love Los Tumbleweeds," I say.

"Yeah?"

"Yeah, my favorite song is probably 'Laundromat Daydream,'"
I say.

I'm feeling the power of my red lipstick as Joel listens. Looks.
I keep talking.

"I love how their stuff is so playful it makes you feel like
dancing the two-step or something, but in a punk rock way?"

"For sure!" he says, and laughs.

Our shoulders brush and my fingers are aching to reach for
his.

At the bottom of the creaky stairs, the basement is unfinished, with dirt walls and a single light bulb that swings just
above our heads. Basically, it's the sort of basement that would
be super creepy were it not filled with a bunch of kids with
beer bottles and red plastic cups.

"Oh, that's them, right?" I ask, pointing to the far corner,
where a scruffy dude with a violin and a girl with long, sandy
hair stand amid a cluster of amplifiers and guitar cases.

"Yeah, that's them!" Joel says, smiling. "I'll be back."

"Okay—" I say.

And then I watch him walk right over to Los Tumbleweeds.
Actually, he's walking over to the girl with the long hair. And
presenting the bottle of wine to her.

Her.

"That's—" I grab Tara's arm, my brain glitching. "That's the
Tumbleweed girl, right?"

The singer, whose gorgeous, raspy voice I was listening to as
I got ready to see Joel Duran, and this girl who is now talking
to him and touching his arm. They're the same person.

Tara stands up on her tiptoes so that she can see over all
the others.

"Yeah!" she says. "That's her. Lila."

Lila is laughing at something Joel Duran is saying, with a mouth full of bright white teeth. The Tumbleweed guy stops tuning his violin to join their conversation.

Joel is gesticulating, like he's telling them something pretty funny, and he must be, because all this girl can do is laugh her freaking head off. *Look at her, with those teeth*. What, like her dad's a dentist or something?

"Actually, Lila's *amazing*," Tara continues. "I mean, she's a really talented musician, but she's also really smart."

"Great," I say. I'm staring.

Tara tucks a tuft of black hair behind one ear and tilts her head to the side. She raises a dark eyebrow at me.

My eyes are starting to water.

"You sure you're okay?"

"I'm fine," I say. "It's just smoky here."

Los Tumbleweeds position themselves at the mic stand, among the amps, Lila with a guitar that she grips like a weapon.

"Hey, what's up, Burqueños?" Lila shouts. "One, two . . . one, two, three, four!"

The beat is fast, and Lila's voice is soaring, and I don't love this song as much as I did before, because how could I?

Elizabeth spins me around with one hand and Tara with the other.

I force myself not to look at Joel, because I can't take it.

I can't take him looking at her, because how does she do that? How does she make her face all open, all beautiful? When she looks out into the room, she commands us to look back. Her feelings are all right there on the surface, and we see her, and he must see her, too, and it doesn't kill her to do it.

I shove away all the embarrassing thoughts I had about dancing with Joel tonight. About him singing along, and me singing along, and him, maybe, pulling me close, his lips grazing my ear.

Then I do look.

And he is looking at her, of course.

One single song feels like it lasts a thousand years. Five songs feel like ten thousand. My feet hurt. My eyes are stinging from the smoky basement, and I just want to go home. I'm mad that I'm wearing this stupid outfit and that Joel is clapping and bobbing his head up and down while Lila sings.

"I'm kinda tired," I say in Elizabeth's ear.

"You'll love this singer who's on after them," she yells over the music, putting her arm around me. "I promise, she's amazing."

I tug at the edge of my sweater as the song swells, tired of these amazing girls and their amazingness, and now everyone's clapping and I have to get out.

"I'll be right back," I shout.

Elizabeth waves over her shoulder as she and Tara begin to cup their hands around their mouths to sing along with the next song. Lila pumps her fist in the air and I turn my back on the show, pushing my way through the crowd and up the creaky wooden steps.

The screen door slams behind me as I step into the cold night.

Moths scatter from the porch light hanging over the door.

I breathe the harsh air slowly, deeply.

It's so cold it hurts, but no more than seeing Joel and Lila together did.

So what if Joel Duran invited me to Día de Los Muertos? I said my mom was dead, out of nowhere, like a fucking weirdo, and he probably felt sorry for me. He was just trying to be nice, because he's a good person, a really good person, that's what I've always liked about him and why I knew he'd never feel the same, because I'm nowhere near good enough. Not even close.

"Marisol?"

I blink into the glare of the porch light. As my eyes adjust, a group of kids with beanies pulled down over their ears, leaning against a nearby tree, come into focus.

It's Bernie.

Bernie and his friends.

Bernie with a beer in his hand.

"Shit," Bernie's friend Scotty says as they all scatter in different directions.

I'm so surprised to see Bernie here that I can't even process it. It's like you can't even recognize people when you see them where you don't expect them. Where they don't fit. Bernie isn't supposed to be *here*. He's supposed to be at home.

I walk up to him and snatch the bottle from his hand.

"Mari, it's just a *beer*, chill!"

But he looks too comfortable with it. Like it's not his first one or anything.

The bottle is heavy in my hand.

"What are you doing here?" I ask him.

"What am *I* doing here? You're the one who wore a braid crown to a punk show," he says, laughing.

"Bernie."

He shrugs. "Whatever, we came to hear the band."

"*You* know about Los Tumbleweeds?" I ask, my voice rising.

How? How does he know this shit? He's in the ninth grade. This is a house show. Paul must be twenty-one, at least. And yet, here's Bernie, who's just a kid, standing here all casual, drinking a beer like it's nothing.

When did this start? How did I let this happen?

I wasn't paying attention like I should have been. Like I was supposed to. I'm the oldest, and so it's my responsibility and I fucked it up.

And then I'm in the emergency room again. Just like in the nightmare. Bernie is standing outside the room, just on the other side of the glass. He's afraid to come in. I know he is. I should move. I should put my arms around him. I should tell him what the nurse told me. *Talk to her, babe, she can hear you.* But her eyes are so swollen. She doesn't look like herself. This doesn't feel real at all. It's the middle of the morning on a regular school day, and this isn't real. Bernie is okay and I am okay and Mom is okay, too. Or she would have been, if only, if only, if only *something*. If only I could figure it out. I feel like it's just out of frame. Like it's on the next page.

"Mari?" Bernie asks.

I rub my palm over my heart in circular motions until I'm back in the yard, in the cold, and I just need to fix this somehow.

"When Dad finds out about this, you'll be grounded for your whole freshman year."

"You're going to rat on me?" he asks.

He blinks as the patches of anger rise in his cheeks. I can see them, even in the dim light. When he's really angry, even the skin all around his eyebrows gets red.

"You can't tell him you saw me here," he says. "Because then you have to tell him that *you* were here."

"Well, what if I told him that *you're* skipping school?" I ask.

His mouth falls open. "Who told you that?"

"It doesn't matter."

"Fine," Bernie says. "Then I'll just tell him that you haven't been going to driver's ed."

I suck my teeth, look down at my shoes in the dirt.

How does he know? Maybe he's bluffing.

"What are you talking about?" I ask.

"I'm talking about the fact that you're not learning to make left turns, or to merge, or to parallel park," he says, crossing his arms over his chest. "You're full of shit."

I glare at him, wishing I knew what I was supposed to do. If Dad finds out I'm not going to driver's ed, he'll pull me out of school. No more shiny new friend group, no Elizabeth Parker, no Charlie's, and no Joel Duran.

Bernie knows he's won. He sees that I'm folding.

"You want me to leave?" he says. "I'll leave."

"How did you even fucking get here?"

"Scotty's brother drove us. He's straight-edge, okay? So you can calm down."

A car passes quietly on the road, its headlights falling over Bernie's face. I have to look up at him, and more and more when I look at him, I see Dad.

A chill runs through me, and all of a sudden I'm not mad anymore, just sadder than I've ever been, which I didn't think was possible, and I turn away from him and walk toward the house.

"So, you're not going to tell Dad?" Bernie asks my back as I'm pulling open the screen door. "That I was here?"

I turn around and stare at him.

Alone in the yard, in the circle of the porch light, he looks small again.

"I won't."

I pour out Bernie's beer into the kitchen sink and set it into a cardboard box full of other empties. It's gotten quiet inside, and as I make my way back downstairs, I have a weird feeling like everyone left without me noticing somehow. Like they just disappeared.

But I can feel the heat of the bodies.

Then I hear a voice.

"Y'all can sit down, if you want."

There's a rustling as everybody in the room settles in. A scraping of stools and boxes dragged across the cement floor, and as they all sit, I see her, the singer.

She's a brown girl with a completely shaved head, and maybe it's because of that that her face strikes me so much, but it's not just that, it's because I wasn't expecting it—she's Filipina. Or at least, I'm 99 percent sure. A Filipina who says y'all with an electric guitar and a full-sleeve tattoo in a basement in Albuquerque, New Mexico.

I grip the banister and sink down onto a creaky step as she positions herself on a milk crate with her guitar in her lap, plugging it into a cable that winds along the ground at her feet. Glittering jewelry all up and down her ears catches the light, and her arm is wrapped in ink, green and blue and pink. I think of Yvonne's secret tattoo, small and hidden at her hip, something she'd never let Tita Violeta see, because if she saw it, she'd cry, *Why? Why did you ruin yourself? My perfect baby.*

The musician cradles her instrument like it's a present that she's pausing for just a moment to open. I'm drawn to her, like maybe, somehow, this singer has the answers.

Elizabeth and Tara lean against the far wall, fingers knitted together.

Then the girl begins to sing.

She has this sad, ghostly voice, and I feel like she's singing right to me. And it breaks my heart. Her voice sounds like the smell of an orange on your fingertips, or like the first step into a patch of perfect snow, too perfect, and then it's gone. Here in the basement, there is heat, and the smell of people pressed close together, and a feeling of being part of something bigger than my body. I feel adrift and at the same time fixed in this spot. Lonely and surrounded by strangers, all pointed in the same direction, like we're looking at the same moon from all different parts of the city, and we can't ever really know each other even though we're right next to each other, and it hurts. All because of guitar chords and words and a human voice. And I desperately want to talk to her after the show, the singer. To ask how she did it, how she got all that down into words, into chords, but I already know that I won't, of course I won't, because she'll probably be talking to *her.*

The Tumbleweed girl has her long legs stretched out in front of her, ankles crossed, on the stairs just a few steps below me, and she's smoking a cigarette. Joel is sitting on the step below hers, his left hand on her knee. Her cigarette smoke swirls above her, a halo, and I stare at her pink shoes.

❁ ✳ ❁

My window screen pops out easily into my hands as Elizabeth's car pulls away into the darkness, around 1:00 a.m. Sitting perched in the window frame, I knock my shoes together, as quietly as possible, to shake off the dust from their soles.

Marty appears from underneath a shadow, meowing, and jumps cleanly into my room.

I follow.

I have a text from Paul. It's a link to a job application for Charlie's.

Even though I'm flooded with embarrassment at my stupid fantasy of our after-school job double dates, it's not like I'm doing anything else after school except pretending to be in driver's ed.

But I'll have to double down and commit if I want to keep that lie going.

It's not hard to find an example of what I need online: *permission slip for student driving hours with instructor*. After making some edits, I hit print.

The white paper looks too fresh, so I fold it a couple of times to make it look like it spent some time in my back pocket, or the bottom of my backpack.

Parent/guardian signature.

In the morning, as I'm brewing coffee before school, Dad signs it.

Bernie follows Dad out to the car, his violin case slung over his shoulder.

They don't say anything to me and I don't say anything to them.

And that's fine.

Chapter Fifteen

NOW

It's a clear, cold day, not one damn cloud in the big blue sky. I leave the house early in the afternoon with a backpack full of cookies and a small photo of my mom in my pocket. I peeled it out of my baby album. There's a worn crease in the middle, as if it had once been folded up into a wallet.

I didn't even tell Dad I was leaving, just walked clean out the front door.

I thought it would feel good, but it didn't.

This picture of my mom is my favorite because it's not posed. It's just a random moment. The kind of moment you wish you could get back, that you could live in again, that you just *know* you would appreciate, this time, if only you knew there weren't going to be any more. Her long, dark hair reaches down to her hip. She's adjusting her sunglasses. On the back it says, *Anita at the beach* in my dad's neat teacher handwriting.

I made the cookies last night. Bernie saw me doing it, but he didn't ask me what they were for.

He probably knew anyway, since he knows everything.

Biscochitos, they were her favorite kind. These are the kinds of things you put on the ofrenda. I read through the links on the website Joel sent me to prepare for the altar-making class with his mom and Tara. I'm nervous to meet her. I changed my outfit a bunch of times.

When Elizabeth picks me up, Tara's in the front seat, so I slide into the back next to a bunch of tote bags full of orange tissue paper and shoeboxes and mason jars filled with scissors and paintbrushes.

"You look nice," Elizabeth says as she backs out from the driveway.

I can't stop touching my hair, because it isn't cooperating. I sit on my hands and watch as Tara adjusts her bolo tie in the mirror.

"Tara, you do this workshop every year?" I ask. "You and your mom?"

My leg is jumping up and down. I place my palm on my knee to stop it.

"She's been doing it forever," Tara says. "Me, just a few years. You got the info that Joel sent?"

"I did," I say, hugging my backpack full of cookies to my chest.

One of the Los Tumbleweeds songs comes on. Elizabeth starts belting the lyrics as the car picks up speed. Tara is doing an interpretive dance in the passenger seat next to her and Elizabeth is laughing at her expressive movements.

"Stop distracting the driver," she says.

The violin is going faster and faster, and all I see is Joel's hand on Lila's knee.

"Can we change the song, please?" I shout over the sound of Lila's voice.

Tara twists around to look at me as Elizabeth reaches for the skip button.

"So, correct me if I'm wrong, but based on your subtle cues . . . ," Elizabeth says, glancing at me in the rearview mirror, "I'm guessing that you're not a fan."

"Fans of Los Tumbleweeds are called Tumblers," Tara says playfully. "You're saying you're not a Tumbler?"

I think she must be joking, but *still*.

Another song begins, by some other band, yet another band I've never heard of. I don't know how Elizabeth can catalog so many of them in her brain. Sometimes I think there's a secret guide to being cool and knowing about stuff that only some people have access to, and I'm not one of those people.

Elizabeth and Tara definitely are. And so is Bernie.

And so is Tumbleweed Girl. And all her little Tumblers.

"They're fine, it's just—" I say, but I haven't got my story straight, so I stare out the window at the trees in the bosque, their yellow leaves against the blue sky, until something comes to me. "Yeah, they're not my favorite."

"Copy that," Elizabeth says.

I feel Tara looking at me still, so I concentrate on the trees flying by.

Elizabeth pulls up to the curb next to the park, beneath a big cottonwood tree. The park is filled with a sea of white tents, like clouds that fell to earth out of the blue sky onto brown grass. Paper flowers are piled on every table—orange, turquoise, and pink. We step out of the car, and ranchera music and smoke billow over us, the scent of green chiles tumbling in roasters, and the pine needles underfoot, and the crisp fall air.

We're early so that Tara can help her mom set up for the altar-making workshop, but there's already a huge crowd, families and groups of friends spilling from cars and walking over from the side streets of the neighborhood.

I step out of the car and search the sea of faces, until it parts, and there he is, Joel Duran.

He sees me.

It's a day so beautiful it hurts, because you know it can't last. The sky is bluer than blue, heavy with the smell of fall.

The leaves on the trees lining the streets have turned a brilliant yellow.

Joel Duran is walking toward us. He has a picture frame tucked under his arm.

In my pocket, my fingertips graze the crease in the photo of Mom.

The sun is so bright, and sharp, like it gets on really cold days.

He's walking right up to me.

I grip the car door.

Right in front of me. So close that I can see the two freckles under his left eye.

"Let me help you with that," he says, reaching past me to grab one of the tote bags full of orange tissue paper from the back seat.

I move aside, swallowing my heart.

We're gathered under a long, open tent at tables lined up in rows.

Mrs. Duran has long black hair with gray at her temples and glasses that rest on her round cheeks. And while she is talking, welcoming us to the workshop, she places her hand on Joel Duran's shoulder, and he places his hand on her opposite shoulder, easily, like they're always connected, even when they aren't standing like this, facing this world together with their hands on each other's shoulders.

Mrs. Duran talks into the microphone, the silver rings on her fingers catching the light. Her voice, steady and warm, tells us what to do and what it all means, the levels, earthly, heavenly, and purgatory, who we honor, and how. When she passes the microphone to Tara, she watches her the whole time she's talking, nodding sometimes at what Tara has to say about the ofrendas, like maybe Tara is saying the same thing she used to say for this part, echoing her mother's words and repeating them now like a prayer, familiar and worn and close to the heart, keeping the words alive. Mrs. Duran is looking at her like she's been looking forward to this day. Like as she's watching Tara speak about her antepasados, she sees her daughter as she was when she was a little girl, and at the same time, she's looking into the future, and she can see all the things that Tara will do and be one day.

The way she is looking at Tara makes me wish, and wish again, for the thing that I can't have. It aches the way it did to see Tita Violeta make up a plate for Yvonne. To see her tenderly touch her swollen lip, the bruise blooming at her cheek. It aches the way that wanting impossible things does.

I thumb the creased photo of my mother in my pocket.

In front of us are piles and piles of orange tissue paper to make flowers for calling the dead home.

Elizabeth bumps her shoulder into mine as Mrs. Duran and Tara start weaving through the tables to answer questions.

"Isn't she great?" Elizabeth asks.

Tara and her mom are laughing together with a neighbor who has just handed each of them a cup of hot chocolate.

"She's so great," I say.

But Elizabeth is looking at them now in a way that looks more complicated than simply pride.

"What's wrong?" I ask.

She shakes her head like she's trying to clear it out, then stabs a piece of cardboard with her craft scissors.

"My legal guardians are being quite annoying at the moment. That's all."

"But they seem so laid-back and easygoing," I say.

She cracks a smile, reaching for a glue stick.

"It's about Tara. I wanted them to come and see her give the workshop. And meet the Durans. But they said no."

Her eyes are filling up and I see it again, the heavy weight she carries with her, this pressure from her parents.

"It's like," she says, "they think it's cute that I like her, but they keep asking me all these annoying questions like, 'But why date in high school? What's the point?' Maybe it's because she's in college. My mom said she hopes I'm not thinking about staying here to go to UNM, you know, just because Tara is there."

I tilt my head to the side.

"Are you?" I ask.

"That's the annoying thing," she says, rolling her eyes. "Sure, I'm thinking about it. As just one good option among many."

She shakes her head again, side to side.

"But why does everything have to have a *point* anyway?" she asks, an edge to her voice that's not usually there. "Can't I just be in love? Isn't that point enough?"

I put my scissors down.

"So you're, like, *in love*?"

She swats a tear from her cheek and looks at me sideways.

"Well, I mean, I haven't told her that. Yet. Exactly."

"Oh my gahhhh," I say.

A few yards away, Tara is throwing her head back in laughter, talking to someone new.

"Well, don't *look* at her!" Elizabeth whispers.

A gust of autumn wind kicks up some of the orange tissue paper and Elizabeth catches it, blushing. Her guard is down. It's amazing.

"Have you ever said it?" she asks.

My guard comes up. "What, 'I love you'?"

I glance all around, nervous, but it's not like anybody is listening to us. Joel Duran is kneeling down, showing a little kid how to twist two pipe cleaners together to make a flower crown, and I might actually die, but Elizabeth is looking at me, so I pretend to be studying the crew setting up a stage for a live band behind where Joel is standing.

"Like . . . were you and that guy Nick . . . ?" she asks.

I twist the bottom of my sweatshirt up into my hands.

"No," I say. "No, it wasn't like that."

I don't know what it was, but I know it wasn't like that.

"Is there somebody else?" she asks.

I shake my head and blink back tears. Stupid. What am I thinking? I can't admit that I like *Joel Duran*. Especially not that I like him as much as I do, especially not to Elizabeth Parker. Because they're friends. And what if she tells him? Then what? He's with Tumbleweed Girl anyway. I can't believe I was going on and on at the house show about "Laundromat Daydream" in my stupid red lipstick when he came there to see her.

"No, there's nobody else. *Nobody* at LMHS is cool," I say, deflecting. "You know that."

She snorts. "So true."

If you don't want anything, you can't be disappointed when you don't get it. I can't keep wanting things that I'll never get; it hurts too much. I really don't think I can survive all this wanting.

So I'll just stop.

A speaker on the stage screeches to life, and everyone covers their ears and laughs.

Joel appears, smiling, but I don't smile back.

He puts his hand on my shoulder.

"Do you want to come meet my mom?"

Elizabeth looks at me, her eyes lit up for some reason.

My heart races as I smooth down the hairs at my temples, the hairstyle that I did because I wanted to meet her, and I'm wearing the clothes that I picked out because I wanted to meet her, because I wanted him to be touching my arm just like this, on this beautiful day. I wanted to talk to him about all the things that I read about Undras, and I wanted it to be like when we were talking on the couch at the party, but now that it's here, I can't. I can't do it.

"Maybe later," I say.

"Okay," he says, shrugging good-naturedly.

Elizabeth shows him what she's been working on.

And the moment goes by. And it's better this way.

When the parade starts, the four of us join the cheering crowd spilling over the sidewalk to watch the dancers in long, wide skirts, twirling in unison, frills, frills, frills. Our school's marching band rounds the corner, waving LMHS banners. I clap as the sky-blue lowrider rolls slowly by, hands waving out the windows, its hood adorned with marigolds. Esqueletos on bicycles, and in pickup trucks, a bride and groom holding hands, a mariachi band, a troop of Girl Scouts, bikers in leather jackets. Grandmothers, babies. Everyone.

We walk along the parade route until we end up where we began, in the park lined with towering cottonwood trees, their yellow leaves bright in the sunshine. Tara buys tamales from the truck with the longest line and hands a white paper plate to each of us. My mouth waters as we sit atop a picnic table near the stage, where another mariachi band is tuning their instruments. I peel away the corn husk and hold the warm tamale up to my nose to take in the sweet, salty smell, savoring it before I sink my teeth in.

The band begins to play, and the familiar sounds of horns, fiddles, and trills fill the park. A young woman with slicked-back hair and bright red lips adjusts the microphone, then raises her arms to meet the crowd's applause, the sun glinting off the silver buttons that run all along her black sleeves.

"Bienvenidos," she says. "And thank you to the organizers of this event."

She begins to sing, and Tara and Elizabeth stand to dance and sway to the music.

I'm clapping along until I notice a familiar figure in the crowd. The flash of a checkered shirt, faded jeans, a familiar gait. Hands in pockets.

Dad.

But then he's gone.

"I'll be right back," I say, sliding from the table.

Joel nods and watches me go.

I search for him, pushing through the crowd.

What's he doing here? Is he looking for me?

A little kid in Wonder Woman boots darts out in front of me, before the parent scoops her up and shoots me an apologetic glance.

Maybe Bernie sent him the article about Undras, too. Maybe he read it and remembered what Mom told him, and he knows what to do now. Maybe he's here with another picture of Mom, creased from his wallet, to tell me that he really *was* listening to her. That he gives a shit after all. That he's—

The crowd parts.

And it isn't him.

Just another dark-haired man in jeans and plaid. He waves at someone I can't see and disappears.

I'm alone in the crowd as it swirls around me.

He doesn't care what I think. He never did. He didn't care that I wanted to wear his button-down shirts instead of the lacy collared dresses Mom wanted, not because he thought it was cool, but just because he flat-out didn't care. All those times when I wanted to sit next to him to watch him organize his tackle box, he let me, as long as I was quiet. He tolerated me. But he didn't want me there.

As the crowd thins out a bit, it's getting on dusk now, the community altars are revealed, set out by participants from the neighborhood on long rows of tables, big and small, under white tents. Flowers, soda cans, and framed photos. In her presentation, Tara said that we offer our loved ones the things that they enjoyed in life. I run my finger along the edge of the photograph in my pocket.

In the photos, some people are young, like this sepia-toned photo of a man in a military uniform. Some people are remembered as gray-haired and wrinkled, like this grandfather opening up Christmas presents, a red bow stuck to his balding head. I wait until I get to the very end, to the edge of the park, to a table underneath a big arch of paper skulls and pink streamers blowing in the breeze.

Some little kids run by, laughing.

I take the photo out of my back pocket and tuck it behind a tea light. From my backpack, I pull out the cookies that I made last night and place them next to the photo.

They don't look very pretty, sitting there in the gallon-sized freezer bag I brought them here in. I've seen a lot of food laid out on real plates. I hope she wouldn't care, but I know that she would. She liked things to be done right. I add two of the orange-tissue-paper-and-pipe-cleaner flowers I made in the workshop on either side and take a step back.

Anita at the beach.

The sun is starting to go down now, and all around me people are carrying little tea lights.

"Hey," I hear a voice say.

It's Joel.

With a picture of his grandmother in a wooden frame tucked under his arm.

"That's your mom?" he asks.

The picture frame he's brought is so beautiful, and suddenly

I can't stand the stupid ugly plastic bag and the crease in the old photo.

I should have brought a frame to protect it, like Joel did.

"I didn't do it right," I say.

My sinuses ache, and my eyes ache, and the sticky ball that isn't real pulses with heat, and I look down at my shoes, my face flushing.

I'm so ashamed.

Then Joel Duran is putting his arms around me, wrapping me close. I see the fibers of his coat growing blurry through my hot tears.

"You did great," he says.

"No, no, that's the problem," I say.

I choke out the words that have been right here, beneath the surface, this whole time.

"Everything I did was bad."

I was bad.

I was a bad daughter, and if I hadn't been bad, this wouldn't have happened.

If I hadn't been so horrible to her, she wouldn't be dead. It's that simple. It was my fault. It was.

"I know that's not true," he says.

He says this like he believes it, but he doesn't *know*, he wasn't *there*, he doesn't know how it was.

"I was horrible. I was mean."

My breath is catching and shuddering as I shake my head, all the horrible things I said cycling through my mind again and again, and no matter how many times I've written them down in my notebook, they're still there, horrible, horrible, horrible.

He holds me tighter.

"Everyone is horrible and mean sometimes," he says. "What about the other times?"

What other times? I think bitterly, but then I remember.

Chapter Sixteen

THEN

When Mom and I get to the community fridge and pantry, Mrs. Trujillo is there. Mom asks her if she can give Bernie a ride home from his orchestra practice for the end-of-semester concert next week, which she can, and Mrs. Trujillo walks away with a gallon of milk and three cans of beans in her tote bag.

It's early morning, so quiet that our footsteps on the crumbling asphalt echo in the dawn. The train's whistle sounds from across town. A gentle swishing of cars on the highway, behind the sound barrier erected to shield the little rows of brown houses that line the frontage road, like the one we lived in before Bernie was born.

Mom and I haven't said a word to each other since last night, through the entire Fil-Am dinner, even when Yvonne asked me to take a picture of them together, with their awards, in the hotel lobby. I didn't give them a countdown, like Yvonne has trained me to do, but I did take at least ten pictures so that one would be good enough and I wouldn't have to do it over, and the whole time I was wondering if the people coming in from outside thought that *they* were mother and daughter and I was just somebody taking a picture.

Mom and I navigate around one another wordlessly. The

path from the car's open trunk to the pantry shelves is criss-crossed with chilly silence.

When we finish unloading the car, Mom hesitates with a loaf of soft white bread. She inspects it, her brow coming together, and then holds it up close to her face.

I chew the inside of my cheek. I don't *want* to be the one who breaks the silence. Even though I want the silence to be broken. I want the silence to be shattered across the pavement like a sheet of ice. I just don't want to be the one to do it, for once. I'm clumsy with breaking silences. When I break them, even more gets broken, and I just keep on breaking and breaking and wrecking until it's silent again.

A blue-tailed lizard skitters across my shoelaces and disappears into the brittlebush and mesquite.

I sigh.

"What's wrong?" I ask. "Is it moldy?"

"Don't you think," she asks slowly, "that bread is cute?"

I bark out a laugh, almost choking it out, as if it had been lodged in my throat all this time, waiting for her to say something as strange and unexpected as *bread is cute*.

"I'm sorry, what?" I ask, snorting. "Has it finally happened? Has the perpetual sleep deprivation finally addled your brain?"

Her eyes dance and she cackles explosively, her laughter ricocheting across the empty parking lot and the quiet morning.

"My brain is fine," she says. "I took my ginkgo biloba. But bread is cute, and squishy. Admit it!"

"I will not. Because bread is food, and food is not cute."

She pouts and gently presses the loaf to her cheek, its thin plastic bag crinkling.

"You're cute when you're grouchy," she says. "Cute like bread."

"*Mom!*"

And then I'm laughing, because she's being *so* weird, and I can't help it.

I try to snatch the bread away from her and she shrieks, spinning away from me. I grab her around the waist.

"Stop playing with your food!" I say, doing my best impression of her.

She roars with laughter as she twists away from my grip.

And then we can't talk anymore, because we are laughing too hard, and being too loud, and being some way that maybe we both wish we could be all the time, if only we weren't ourselves.

Chapter Seventeen

NOW

The sky gives way to a pink dusk. Little kids laugh and run in the dry grass as the live band turns it over to a DJ with green hair, bass pumping and hips swaying in front of the stage next to the ofrendas.

Joel is still holding me.

My breathing slows, steadies, as he tucks his chin over the crown of my head.

"Better?" Joel asks.

I nod into his chest, and I let my head rest against him for a little while.

As we make our way back to our friends through the crowd, suddenly, I'm feeling shy. I can't believe I told him all that. And now, on top of everything, the sight of him during magic hour is a little too much for me to take.

His hand brushes against mine.

Tara's voice calls out to us.

"Hey, over here!"

I spot her in the crowd. She's dancing with Elizabeth and—

The Tumbleweed Girl.

Lila. Her laughter cuts through the music spilling from the speakers on the stage above. She waves to us with her free arm, and the other circles Elizabeth's waist, as they weave their hips in time to the music.

"Hey!" Joel says, brightening.

He jogs to reach them more quickly, and my hand involuntarily lifts, just for a second, as if I could stop him. As if I could stop time from its brutal march forward into the next moment and the next.

As Joel reaches her, the Tumbleweed Girl, she spreads her arms wide and he lifts her into a spinning hug.

She immediately starts telling him a story.

"I forgot to tell you about—"

But then the beat drops, and everyone laughs and lifts their arms to meet it. The breeze is swaying the branches in the cottonweed trees gently, very gently.

Elizabeth spins, sees me, and her smile fades.

Because she knows.

She knows even though I don't want her to know, even though I don't want her to see how much it hurts.

So I shake my head and smile and I close the gap between her and me, between the past and now, between the horrible things and the good, and move my body with the music until there's nothing to see anymore.

By the time I get home, the evening has turned my nose cold in the short span between Elizabeth's car and my front door. My hands cupped over it barely make any difference.

I turn the key in my front door.

It smells like Dad is starting to get dinner together in the kitchen. I should help him. It usually takes our combined remedial culinary skills to produce even one marginally edible meal. But I don't want to fight again. And I don't know how to make him understand, to make him care. I used to think Mom and I were the ones who couldn't talk to each other, didn't understand each other.

I was wrong.

He calls out to me when he hears the screen door slamming behind me.

"Short Stack?"

So, now we're back to nicknames. We're just not going to talk about how I said I hate him. We're just not going to talk about anything, like always.

"Yeah," I say.

Bernie walks in the front door right after I do. The screen door slams behind him, too.

"Flubs?"

He slips his violin case off his shoulder.

"Yeah," he calls out to Dad.

Bernie eyes me warily as we kick our shoes off in silence.

"What's your problem?" I mutter.

"How's driving class?"

I glare at him.

Dad enters the foyer, wiping his hands on a dish towel, and clears his throat. He's wearing his work boots, like he's been in the yard.

I thought I was too sad, too tired, to be mad anymore. But seeing those boots, sinking into the hallway rug, dusty, with a cluster of spiky goat's-head seeds stuck to the laces, makes me realize I'm not.

"You know," I say, heat rising in my bloodstream, "leaving shoes at the door is not some weird *superstition*, it's because shoes are *disgusting* and you shouldn't wear them in the house!"

My dad's mouth opens and closes several times as I push past him.

In my room, I flip to the last drawing I did, of that day in the mountains.

The plumes of dust under Dad's sneakers.

The flowers on Mom's dress.

What was it about that day? If I'd caught the ball instead, what would have happened? If I had opened up to Yvonne and Tes, what would have happened? If I hadn't said the wrong thing to Mom, all the time, every single time, what would have happened?

I turn to a blank page and stare and stare and stare.

It doesn't matter if I sleep with the lights on or off. It doesn't matter if I leave the blinds open or close them. It doesn't matter if I fold all my sweaters and stack the books on my desk neatly, or if I leave everything a mess, in heaps and piles.

The nightmare still comes.

It's like she's still here and I'm there. There's all that beeping and machine lights blinking.

The nurse is there, saying, *Talk to her, babe, she can hear you.*

And the nurse can tell what a bad daughter I am by the way I freeze. By the way I let the tubes and swelling and the stale hospital air keep me away from the side of her bed. How I let the sight of my own mother repel me.

Talk to her, babe.

I feel someone's hand around my throat and I can't speak.

It's my hand.

Chemistry is probably rough enough when you've had a proper night's sleep, and I haven't had one in a really long time, since before I failed this class last year.

In an effort to keep my eyelids open, I focus on Mr. Tafoya's weird arm tattoo. It looks like he did it himself. When he was a sailor. In the 1800s. In the dark.

I'm trying to do the thing where you pretend you're looking down at your notebook to write something down, rest your eyes, then look back up, pretend to read the board, repeat.

But then I'm too tired for even that. When the bell rings, I jerk suddenly and find that my "notes" are just a series of loops across the page, plus the doodle of Marty the cat flying an airplane that I did at the beginning of class.

Elizabeth is already at her locker when I get there, spinning her purple combination lock with her manicured fingertips. I ball my chewed-up nails into a fist involuntarily when I see them and lean on the locker next to hers, downing a soda from the vending machine.

"Hey," she says, opening her locker. "You okay?"

"Perfectly okay," I say.

I don't want to talk. My eyes are closing on their own now, just from the weight of this day, and it's still morning.

Elizabeth shrugs, dumping her precalc book into her locker.

"Are you sure? Because you're drinking a Coke at ten a.m."

"Wait, is this a Pepsi school? My bad."

She raises her eyebrows, fluffs her hair in her locker door

mirror. She wipes away a smudge of eyeliner that has crept down into the corner of her eye.

Then she turns to face me.

"Are you upset because Joel was talking to Lila on Saturday?"

Shit. I crush my soda can with my hands. I knew this would happen. That if she knew about Joel she'd want to talk about it, and if we talk about it then it's not just in my head anymore, and if it's not just in my head anymore, then it's terrifying and I hate it.

"Why would that upset me?" I ask.

"Oh, I don't know," she says, sighing. "Maybe because you *like* him?"

"No, I don't," I say too loudly.

I catch myself practically shouting, and then look around the crowded hallway.

"Hey," she says, looking at me. "You can tell me. You don't need to be all secretive."

I purse my lips. There's nothing to tell. I've already decided. And he likes the Tumbleweed Girl anyway. So, what's the point?

But Elizabeth Parker is still shaking her head like she can read my thoughts, and she's being really freaking Elizabeth Parkery about this. I hate that she's seen through me this way, that my secrets maybe aren't so secret after all, like there's nothing I can keep protected and hidden inside, not really, that there's no piece of me I can keep for myself, to protect it.

"Because they're just friends," she's saying. "And if Joel only knew what—"

The bell rings.

"There's nothing to know," I say.

Elizabeth sighs again and glances down the hallway, probably worried about getting her first tardy ever.

"Okay," she says, her earrings catching the light. "Whatever."

When I feel her giving up, I flinch. Yvonne got tired of trying to pry stuff out of me eventually. Elizabeth is turning away now, but maybe there's something else I can let her do.

"Hey, so," I say, reaching out for her arm. "I do need your help with something."

We wait until the seniors who have off-campus lunch make it to their cars and pull out of the parking lot to give us more space.

Elizabeth is practically vibrating with excitement in the passenger seat of her car. She lives for this kind of thing, I can tell.

"I'm a really good teacher," she says. "I'm teaching Janelle and Karina."

My palms are already sweaty.

"It's not that I don't know how," I try to explain. "I'm just out of practice or something. I just need to get back into it, and the class already started and . . ."

"So, you've really been lying to your dad this whole time?" she asks. "How come?"

"I don't know," I say. "After I missed the first day, and then the next one, it was just easier not to go or something."

When I put my hands on the steering wheel, it doesn't turn.

"You have to start the car before the wheel can turn," she says.

Right. I suck on my teeth.

This all seemed like such a great idea before.

"Feel free to adjust the mirrors if you can't see out of them."

She seems totally calm, leaning back in her seat. My heart starts beating faster. Why is she so relaxed? How could she trust me behind the wheel of her car? She doesn't even hardly know me at all. If she really knew me, she would never.

"And the seat, too."

Oh. My feet don't reach the pedals. Elizabeth is taller than me, so she has it set much farther back. I scoot the seat up in order to close the gap.

I put the key in the ignition and turn it, and it makes a horrible sound.

She laughs and I wince. I feel like an idiot. I should be able to do this. There's no reason why I shouldn't be able to do this. No logical reason.

"Finesse," she encourages.

The engine is humming now, though, and the dashboard seems to have come to life. I buckle my seat belt.

My hands find the wheel again.

"Okay, keep holding down the brake pedal, and try backing up."

I close my eyes before I can change my mind—I shift into reverse.

"Release the brake," she says.

I do, but then we go shooting back superfast, and super far, so I slam my foot back down onto the brake again. Our seat belts throw us back against our seats as the car comes to a stop, sticking out diagonally from the parking spot. My seat belt is still locked. I can't breathe.

"Okay," she says, laughing. "Good! Now, more slowly this time?"

All of a sudden I can't stand her looking at me. I know that I look ridiculous. Can't even back up.

"Could you stop fucking laughing?" I ask.

"Whoa," she says. "Sorry, I'm not laughing *at* you."

"Well, it feels like it. I know I look stupid, okay?"

I throw the car into park and grab my backpack from the back seat.

"Forget it. I don't need your help," I say.

"Wait!" she says, but I'm already slamming the door.

I wrench open the heavy metal door to B Hall, slamming it against the doorstop as hard as I can. I want to punch something. I try to pass by the cafeteria without even looking, because I don't want to look, but I know they're in there, so I do. Sitting by the window, bathed in the warm light of the sun, Nick's arm around Yvonne's shoulders. Tes is writing something carefully in her planner, probably with her favorite pink felt-tipped pen.

Nick's looking at Yvonne. Only her. The same way he's always looked at her. Like there's nothing else in the entire world. He buries his face in her hair and she laughs. Yvonne's backpack occupies the space where I used to sit. Where Nick nudged me with his elbow and tapped his index finger on the doodles at the corners of my biology notes.

Those are good, M, he said.

He's the one who kissed *me*. If I hadn't kissed him back, I'd be sitting where Yvonne's backpack is sitting, because we never would have fought and I never would have got sent to juvie and I never would have heard about the sticky ball, and Elizabeth Parker would never have invited me to a party where Joel Duran would sit under the twinkle lights and *actually* talk to me and give me the stupid hope that he'd want to *keep* talking to me.

If Nick hadn't given me the stupid sketchbook in the first place, I wouldn't have kissed him back at all. It was all because of that stupid sketchbook.

Before I know what I'm doing, I'm at the edge of their table, heart pounding. Nick stops talking mid-sentence, shifting uncomfortably. He looks terrified, actually, like I've come to ruin his life. Tes smiles at me, sadly, but stops before Yvonne sees.

Yvonne looks like she feels bad for me. Her capacity for pity is so deep, so Christlike, and I can't stand it.

Such a good girl.

"Why—" I say, gripping my backpack straps.

I take a deep breath.

Stare at Nick, his dark eyes darting all around the room. But I'm not going to tell Yvonne about that night after prom, because it wouldn't matter. She's made that clear. There's something else I need to know.

"Why did you give me that sketchbook?"

He sits up straighter, his eyebrows coming together in confusion.

Yvonne looks at him. "What sketchbook?"

Nick looks at her, then me, putting his hands up like he has no idea what is transpiring right now, but he definitely has nothing to do with it.

"I don't know," he says. "I don't know what she's talking about."

"You left it for me. At my mom's funeral."

The only solid thing left on earth.

He shakes his head and shrugs, like he really doesn't know.

Wait.

But it was a *sketchbook*. It just made so much sense because of all the lunch periods spent right here, at this table, me watching him draw. Copying him. Me doodling little cartoon people having little conversations because drawing, moving the pen, writing the words, it helps me think things out. I thought that Nick had been watching me, like I had been watching Joel, understanding something from a distance.

But no. And now Tes, Yvonne, and Nick are sitting in a row, looking like some perverse panel of judges, and now I know what they probably have known this whole time.

I was lying to myself before.

I was lying to Yvonne before.

The rain was coming down in waves and I kissed him back. I kissed him back for real. Because I wanted it to be true.

That somebody understood me.

Yvonne and Tes cast their eyes down to the floor, like they're both dying of secondhand embarrassment on my behalf.

The cafeteria feels sideways, backward. The sounds, the smells, drain away.

Nick, seeing my face, looks away, too.

My cheeks burn as I push through the crowded cafeteria, my heart clenching.

❄ ✳ ❄

Dad and Bernie are watching another old kung fu movie.

I've been wearing these sweatpants since I changed into them yesterday after school and I have no plans to change out of them, ever. Elizabeth has texted me a couple of times, but I don't respond, I ignored her all week at school.

I'm still too mortified.

Bernie's wearing another button-down shirt that looks like it's been ironed, even though it's Saturday, and I have no idea where the iron even is.

"What?" Bernie asks, raising an eyebrow at me.

"What do you mean, 'what'?" I ask.

"You're staring at me."

"No, I'm not."

Bernie narrows his eyes.

I do the same.

"Cut it out," my dad says. "The assassin just scaled the walls of the Forbidden City."

Bernie and I both roll our eyes.

My dad collects these weird old movies at garage sales. His favorites are martial arts movies and B-level horror movies circa 1965. We still have a DVD player, and because just about everyone else has moved on, DVDs are pretty easy to come by. People are just selling them by the box now. Just big brown boxes, usually labeled $5.00.

Marty is resting on the carpet in the middle of a sunbeam, which is a cat's ideal situation, as far as I can tell.

I poke him with my toe and he begins to purr, closing his eyes and rolling onto his back.

It's so sweet, so simple, and my eyes begin to water for no reason, and I clench my jaw. I haven't been able to open my sketchbook since I learned that it wasn't Nick who gave it to me.

It sits on my desk, silent as a stranger. I feel so stupid. So embarrassed.

"I need taquitos," I say, clearing my throat.

"Check the freezer in the garage," Dad says, without looking away from the screen.

"I can get them," Bernie says suddenly, sitting up.

"Um, what's up with the chivalry all of a sudden?"

"Jeez," he says, sinking back into the couch and crossing his arms. "Just trying to be nice."

I eye him, but when he says nothing more, I give up and head for the door off of the living room.

My eyes need a moment to adjust to the dimness in the garage. The swinging light bulb is burned out, and replacing it has become one of those chores that gets mentioned in passing but is never completed.

Something unexpected catches my eye in the darkness— movement. I hope some animal wasn't inadvertently trapped inside when Dad came home last night.

I walk around the car to check it out, and for a second my brain can't even process it.

The light splashes onto the wall from the crack in the

garage door. The words float up from somewhere in my subconscious—camera obscura. Projected onto the blank wall of the garage is the image of the house across the street, distorted and stretched, but it's all there—the green tangle of cactus in the neighbor's front yard, the row of juniper trees, the car in the driveway, everything specked with the dust suspended in the airy light, like a memory.

I don't know how long I stand there, but long enough that the light changes and the image fades away, like it was never there.

Leaning against the wall where the image was, among a pile of other garage crap, is the telescope that I knocked loose with the car.

Untouched since Christmas, when, without her, everything felt raw and strange.

Everything is still raw and strange. Time has passed, but it doesn't matter. It may as well still be that cold winter night on the sidewalk, when Dad tried to piece us all back together.

Bernie bursts into the garage.

"What's taking you so long?" he says.

His eyes bounce all around the garage, until they finally settle on me, tucking the telescope under my arm. I cock my head to one side.

"I'm . . . bringing this inside. Is that okay with you?" I say.

"Oh—okay," he says, his eyes lingering on the jumble of cardboard boxes at my feet. Probably more DVDs that nobody wants.

He stands there in the doorway as I squeeze past him, stuffing his hands in his pockets.

"You didn't even get the taquitos," he says.

"You get the taquitos if you want them so bad," I call over my shoulder.

Dad glances at me, and I'm hugging the skinny telescope box to my chest.

He adjusts his glasses, and I feel like I've broken some kind of pact that I didn't even know I made.

He blinks first, and I carry the telescope across the threshold.

Chapter Eighteen

NOW

Early on Tuesday morning, I wake up to the beep of a car horn outside. Just a brief tap. Marty, who's been asleep at the top of my pillow, darts away as I sit up. Everything is so quiet and still, I think maybe I've just dreamed it, until I hear it again, *beep*.

I get up to part the blinds.

Elizabeth's car idles at the curb.

My phone lights up with a text from her.

Coffee?

It's still dark out.

I text her back.

five minutes

I hop down from my window with my backpack, quietly. Marty jumps out after me and then bounds away.

Elizabeth rolls down her window as I approach the car. She's wearing sunglasses despite the predawn dark. She hands me a warm to-go cup. I can see her breath on the air.

"Sorry," she says.

"What are *you* sorry for?" I say.

"Come on, we're going to miss it."

"Miss what?"

❊ ✳ ❊

Elizabeth drives north, weaving through back roads into the foothills. It's super creepy, because the headlights are really the only lights up here.

"Every time you turn a corner, I keep expecting a ghost, or a deer, or a ghost deer to jump out in front of us."

"No, not a ghost deer!" Elizabeth says. "Such gentle, tender haunting they do!"

We climb higher, cracking dumb jokes, winding into a neighborhood where huge houses sit right up against mountain rock, their long driveways lined with cacti and twisting trees clinging to the earth.

She swings the car into the empty parking lot at the base of the tram that carries passengers to the peak and pulls into a spot overlooking a ridge, among the junipers and the ponderosa pines.

The foothills and the city lights lie below us as we get out of the car and sit on the hood, the metal warm against my butt. The night is thinning out, slowly, as the sun threatens to come up over the mountains.

"I wasn't thinking," Elizabeth says, looking out over everything, "about how maybe driving would be weird for you, because of your mom."

I wince and sip the coffee she brought for me, bitter and hot.

It's not that it's *weird*. Maybe it's not even about driving itself. I don't know what it is.

"I'm sure it'll just take some time, or something," I say.

I say these words even though I don't mean them at all. What could time possibly change? Elizabeth tugs on the cursive *E* at the end of the silver chain around her neck.

A thin yellow glow clings to the earth before giving way to the deep purple night sky suspended above it. A red light winks against it, an airplane preparing its descent into the airport in the south. It's too dark to see them, but I can picture the bison herd moving in the north, the pueblo ranchers up already, earlier than this, every day.

A shiver passes through me. I was born here, within this grid, and I've barely strayed beyond its perimeter. I am looking down on every person I have ever known, and every place I have ever been, since the day I was born. I'm looking down at a map of my own life, a bowl of marbles in the dark: there's our school, there's my house, there's the house we lived in before Bernie was born, there's the library where the community fridge is, then, right there, there she is.

The cemetery where we buried my mom, a darkened parallelogram nestled in the blinking lights, which are fading now, blurring against the gathering dawn.

Did she know when she came here that she would never leave?

There's a lump rising in my throat and I swallow it hard, concentrating on the slow blinking lights of planes taking off at the airport across town. What if I were on one of them? How quickly would that parallelogram disappear? I'd blink and my whole life would be gone.

My eyes are stinging.

Elizabeth doesn't say anything more. Just leans her shoulder into mine, and we look down at the map of our lives, a glowing city grid, winding paths that switch back and lead to where they started.

The sun comes up. We didn't miss it.

"I do like Joel Duran," I say.

It's the most obvious thing in the world at this point, but there it is.

"So why not say something?" she asks.

The sun touches the volcanoes in the west, sitting dormant and quiet on the edge of my life.

❁ ✳ ❁

I get a call from Paul at Charlie's on Sunday saying my application was approved and asking if I'm ready to start.

"Can you come in tomorrow? How are weekdays after school for you?"

"They're great. I'll be there," I tell him.

"You'll be where?" Dad asks, passing by my bedroom just as I hang up with Paul.

Shit.

"Oh, just the library at lunch tomorrow. For a group project thing."

He leans in my doorframe, hands in his pockets, lingering.

But I wish he'd just go away.

"Can you sign my driving log?" I ask.

My fake driving log. I pull it out from underneath my

sketchbook. He joins me at my desk, producing a pen from his shirt pocket.

"How is the class going?" he asks, scratching out his signature.

"Watch out for bikers, etc.," I say, and hope that I haven't already given this same fake answer to a previous driver's ed–related inquiry.

As long as I can remember to turn my phone off every day after school when the bell rings, he won't be able to see that I'm not there anymore on that stupid tracking app of his.

"See—and that driving school wants to charge me five hundred bucks? Extortion!"

"Ha, yeah," I say.

He clicks his pen and slips it back into his pocket, his eyes lingering on my desk. My sketchbook. It's clear that the first half of the pages have been filled by the way they don't lie flat, and from the gray lead smudges that are seeping out onto the edges.

"Have you been drawing?" he asks, his body leaning forward, like he might reach for it. My heart jumps as I grab it and fold it into my arms protectively.

"Yeah, sort of," I say.

He looks at me with an expression that I can't read.

"Okay, well." He clears his throat. "I was thinking we could do those chicken thighs tonight."

"Oh, good," I say, shifting my weight from one foot to the other. "We need to use them before Tuesday, probably."

"Good," he says as he walks away, but it doesn't sound like it's good.

Not at all.

I hug my sketchbook to my chest. It's like there's this vast, deep gorge, with jagged rocks reaching up from the bottom. Dad on one side, me on the other.

※ ✳ ※

On Monday, I shut my locker to find Elizabeth standing there, in a lavender sweater.

"Did you hear from Paul? About Charlie's?" I ask.

"Yes! Are you in?"

"Of course I'm in," I say. "Are you in?"

"Heck yeah, I'm in!" she says as the bell rings. "We should have plenty of time to get there after our last class. Let's talk more in fourth period?"

I nod and wave at her as she disappears into the crowd.

But when fourth period starts, Elizabeth hasn't shown up. I stare at the door of the English classroom, plastered with Shakespeare quotes.

Where is she?

I make an attempt to subtly reach into my bag for my cell phone.

"Ms. Martin?"

Snapping to attention, I find Ms. Moustafa raising her perfectly sculpted eyebrows at me from in front of her smartboard.

There's an image of a dense green forest displayed behind her.

"What can you tell us about the symbolism behind the forest? In the play?"

I look down at my book, clear my throat. The forest. The places beyond the grid of the city lights. The places where the characters have yet to go.

"The unknown?" I ask.

She nods. "Good. The unknown, the wild, the mysterious."

As Ms. Moustafa paces the front of the classroom, I watch the door for Elizabeth.

But she never shows.

After school, I call her from the hallway, but she doesn't pick up. What am I supposed to do?

I could just flake out. Except Paul was so cool at that house show. And Charlie's was this great place, full of weird people being alone together, sitting with their books and laptops and shuffling through boxes of old crap. And he said he needed help.

And I said I'd be there.

When I punch the address of Charlie's into my phone, it looks like I'll have to take two different buses to get down there, and I might be late, but I can do it.

As I board the bus about half a mile from school, I wonder where Elizabeth could have gone. All along the way, there are nothing but flat, gray-bottomed clouds crowding the sky. The evidence from last night's freeze has mostly disappeared; a few stray ice crystals cling to the clumps of grass that grow in empty lots and under brittle brown bushes.

After jumping off the bus, I stuff my hands into my pockets and rush past Fix, hoping that neither Joel nor Tara are in there to notice me.

I can't face Joel anymore. And what if the Tumbleweed Girl is in there?

Outside Charlie's, I pause to check my reflection in the window, just in case I do run into him. I had put my hair up in a messy bun at the top of my head like I've seen Elizabeth do sometimes. On me it looks stupid, so I yank out my hair tie and march down the cracked sidewalk toward the front door with my head down.

Charlie's is situated on Central Avenue, which used to be part of Route 66 a long time ago. It sits among rows of shops and motels with funky neon signs. Square adobe buildings that house the tattoo shop, comic book store, and hair salon are all lined with luminarias, a sign that we're already sliding into the holiday season, somehow.

A little bell rings when I push through the door. I scan the store, from the rows and rows of vinyl and CDs, to the bins full of cassette tapes, to the mismatched café tables, filled with customers, college students probably, from UNM and CNM, computer cords tangled up beneath their feet, an older couple, folding and unfolding a newspaper, a big fluffy dog at their feet. The dog yawns.

Paul looks up from counting a stack of tapes and waves to me from behind the counter.

"Hey," I say, relieved not to be late. "Is Elizabeth here?"

"Not yet," he says. "How's it going?"

Paul's wearing the same all-black look he had on at the house show. I'm glad to see there's no dress code, because I hadn't even thought of that. If Paul stepped out from behind the counter, he'd look the same as every other kid in here, beanies and jeans and lip rings and T-shirts.

"Can't complain," I say.

"Come around back and we'll get you started on these. We have boxes and boxes of backlog since NPR did that story on 'Cassette Tapes: Young People's Latest Nostalgic Obsession.'"

I tuck my backpack underneath the register.

"I was just about to put Miriam's album on," Paul says. "From the house show? She left us some copies."

On the counter next to the register, a stack of flyers from the house show still rests, featuring a photo of the Filipina singer and her guitar, her name and the names of the other bands scrawled along the border. *Miriam Almajose.*

Paul sees me studying the flyer as he moves over to the stereo to change the music.

"Unless you're in more of a Tumbleweeds mood?"

I scowl without thinking about it, and Paul starts laughing at me.

"Message received," he says. "Negative on Los Tumbles."

"No, no, they're really good," I say quickly.

I shove my hands in my pockets and look at the floor.

"They're just not really my thing, if that makes sense."

"To each their own," he says, fiddling with the sound system until Miriam's voice fills the store. "There we go."

This song, *God*, this song. It's like it's stabbing me in the heart, but I know that I'll play it again and again and again.

"You can toss those flyers into the recycling bin," he says.

I take the stack into my hands but hesitate to discard them. They're now a historical artifact, the date of the show scrawled in cool lettering across the corner. Albuquerque was just one stop on Miriam's tour. Where did she come from?

Where is she going now? How long has she been writing her songs? Will the Tumbleweed Girl go on tour one day?

As they drive away and out into the desert, how long until the city lights, and all of us, disappear?

"Can I keep one?"

Paul shrugs. "Of course."

I take one and tuck it into a folder in my backpack, careful not to crease it. Maybe Paul thinks I'm a dork, but I don't care. I put the rest of them into the recycling bin.

"So, about these cassette tapes," Paul says. "You know what tapes are, right?"

He fishes out one and shows it to me, like Exhibit A, and I snort.

"Of course I do," I say.

"Well, per the sign out front, you can buy, trade, and sell 'em here. How much do you know about post-hard-core math rock?"

This is it. The moment I get exposed as the total fraud that I am.

"I'm just kidding," he says.

"Okay good, because, to be honest," I say, putting my hands together like a prayer, "I don't know anything. About music."

I look at him helplessly.

"Hey, no worries," he says. "This is a retail job. So as long as you're pretty confident with your people skills?"

I stare at him.

"Well—" he says, and then starts cracking up. "Okay, let's start with the basics."

We have just started to sort the used cassettes by genre and artist when Elizabeth pushes through the door in a hurry.

She has her hair up in that same messy high bun that I attempted earlier, and of course on her it looks perfect.

In her rush, her book bag slips off her shoulder, and she gives me an apologetic look when she sees me.

Dude, I'm so sorry! she mouths.

"Hey, Elizabeth Pilar Parker," Paul sings.

"Hey," she says. "I'm so sorry I'm late."

As she makes her way around the counter, I can see her puffy eyes. She seems to have applied an extra-thick coat of concealer underneath them.

"No worries," Paul says, clapping his hands. "Now that you guys are both here, let's go over to the other side. I can show you both how to work the espresso machine. It's somewhat temperamental."

I let her walk ahead of me as we follow behind Paul.

The store really is crazy busy, but in between helping customers and accepting boxes of used media, he manages to explain to us how to use the register, gives us tricks on how to get the temperamental espresso machine to work, and asks us to shadow him while he helps a few customers look for obscure records.

As we sort through all the tapes for resale, I ask her what's wrong and she says it's nothing, but it's obviously not nothing. So I start belting out Miriam's saddest song, which we've been playing on a loop all afternoon, and then Elizabeth finally, finally laughs.

"Oh my God," she says, clutching one of the cassettes from the box. "It's the soundtrack from *Romeo and Juliet*!"

"Like the play?" I ask.

"Like the classic 1996 Baz Luhrmann film!" she says,

jumping up and down. "Paul, you'll never believe it. We can't sell this. We have to put it in a display case on a velvet pillow!"

As Elizabeth starts reading off the title and artist of every song listed on the back of the tape, I imagine coming back here tomorrow, and the next day, and the next, and for once, the future doesn't feel so crushing. I'll have to keep coming up with random excuses for my dad as to why I'm coming home late, but I'm sure I'll think of something. It's worth it.

When the day is coming to a close, I'm straightening up the sitting area, collecting copies of the local paper and stacking them neatly. I'm surprised at how good it feels to see all the stacks we've organized, the balanced register, the chairs turned upside down on top of tables.

The soothing order of having done things.

Just as Paul is locking up, somebody knocks on the window. The sky is going orange and gray above them.

Paul pulls open the door for the bubbly, smiling, purple-haired person standing there with a too-heavy backpack and a notebook tucked under their arm.

"Sorry, we were just closing up," Paul says.

"Do you have just a sec?" they ask. "I'm from the Nob Hill mutual aid group. We're looking to establish a new free fridge, and we need a place to plug in."

A lightning bolt passes through me. I almost drop the broom I'm holding.

"That's cool," Paul says. "But I'll have to—"

"We should do it," I say.

"Yeah! We should!" Elizabeth says, coming up behind me. "What are we doing, exactly?"

Purple hair is grinning at me. "These kids are *ready*!"

"I mean," Paul says, "Charlie is usually all about this kind of stuff, but—"

"I can work with the group," I say. "I've done it before. Tell Charlie. I'll be the fridge czar."

Paul throws up his hands.

He and purple hair exchange some info about the group. By the time our shift is over, it's fully dark.

"Thanks, kids," Paul says after he locks up. "I'll let you know what Charlie says."

He takes off on his bike, leaving us standing alone underneath the streetlight.

"Where's your car?" I ask.

"*Where*, indeed," she says, zipping up her jacket. "So, my mom drove me here. Because she felt some 'urgency to continue our conversation,' aka the huge fight that we got into after she showed up at school to talk to the guidance counselor about my college prospects."

Elizabeth lets out an exasperated puff of air.

"She's mad I took the job," she continues. "Can you believe it? Because she wants me to focus on 'extracurriculars' that will look better on college applications. She's being *so* unreasonable."

I bite the inside of my cheek.

"What?" she asks.

"Nothing. It's just . . ." I tug at my backpack straps. "Is she wrong?"

"I mean," she says, staring across the street, where the luminarias are all lit up, all down the avenue. "Not technically, no."

So Mrs. Parker wants Elizabeth to go to a fancy college,

because that's what she did. That's what Mr. Parker did. Isn't that how they were able to get that four-car garage in the first place? And the kind of job where you can drive to your daughter's school on a long lunch to speak with the guidance counselor and nobody gets mad at you, the kind of job where you don't have to clock in and out?

A white car pulls up to the curb in front of us, and Elizabeth tilts her head toward it, sighing.

"Want a ride?" she asks.

Mrs. Parker is in the driver's seat. I try not to cringe. I'm pretty sure Mrs. Parker is doing the same thing. She raises her hand to beckon us into the car.

It's warm inside the car, and I unwind my scarf from my neck as I settle into the back seat, my shoulders tensing up in Mrs. Parker's presence.

"Hi, Mrs. Parker," I say. "Thank you for the ride."

"Juana," she says, pulling away from the curb. "And of course. You'll just have to tell me where to go."

Elizabeth turns on the radio and says nothing, freezing her mother out. I stare at Mrs. Parker's wrists, at her watch, at her rings. She's wearing an oversized blazer and gold hoop earrings. She looks beautiful and powerful. In control.

Except she isn't right now.

"So, mi cielo, you want to work," she says.

Launching straight back into their argument. Maybe this is a talent that all mothers have. But hearing Elizabeth called that is like being pierced straight through the heart. Like when Tita Violeta blew gently on Yvonne's rice. I swallow hard.

"Which is great," Mrs. Parker continues. "But what about that internship we talked about, the one at the Labs?"

"I do not want to do an internship where *Dad* works!" Elizabeth says.

"Why not?" Mrs. Parker snaps. "Secondhand records are your passion now? Who even listens to them anymore?"

I stare hard at the stores in the strip mall rolling by, their signs all lit up in the dark: CELEBRACIÓN LIQUORS 'N' MORE, FAMOUS PHO, PEREA'S FAMILY DINER.

"Fine, if not the Labs," Mrs. Parker says, "why not BBER or—"

"Economic research? Me?" Elizabeth says. "Mom, you can't just copy/paste Becca's stuff onto me. I'm a totally different person."

"Obviously I know that," she says. "I just wish you would—"

"Mom," Elizabeth says, sounding tired. "Can we not do this? In front of my friend?"

I chip away at the cracked polish on my thumbnail. *I just wish you'd listen. Why don't you listen? Why don't you wear that dress I laid out for you?* My mom had a lot of wishes for me. They felt like prayers. Desperate pleas. For me to be some other way in the world, as if the world would go easier on me if only I followed her script, as if that script had ever worked for her. Still. My wish now is to go back. To be a completely different person.

"An internship sounds . . . cool," I say.

Mrs. Parker glances at me, and it's obvious that she doesn't think I could get an internship at Sandia Labs even if my dad worked there, which he does not.

Elizabeth turns around in her seat to look at me like I'm a Judas, but she deserves it. She's being a brat. If my mom had a way to get me an internship somewhere, she would have. If my mom had time to talk to the guidance counselor, she would have. I'm not sure she even knew that she was allowed to.

"Karina told me that your brother's been out of class again," Mrs. Parker says to me. "Is he all right?"

I immediately regret drawing attention to myself.

"Mom," Elizabeth says, snapping her head to look at her.

"What?" Mrs. Parker asks. "I can't ask if he's all right?"

"He's fine," I say quickly.

Mrs. Parker's dark eyes narrow so I keep talking, saying whatever I think she'll want to hear so that she doesn't try to talk to my dad when we get to my house or something, because if she talks to my dad, she'll probably mention the fact that she picked me up from my new after-school job, and then I'll be screwed.

"He *was* ditching class. Before. And my dad already had a talk with him. He got in a lot of trouble. But he showed remorse. And he's been totally blameless up until now."

Christ, I sound like I'm defending a rich asshole against charges of tax evasion or something. Mrs. Parker isn't buying it, I can tell, and we're already approaching the turn into my neighborhood.

In the rearview mirror, she stares me down and I stare back.

"Mom, watch the road!"

Mrs. Parker breaks eye contact as she rounds the corner, and I can see that Dad's car is in the driveway of our house. I grip the door handle and grab my backpack strap so that I can jump out as soon as possible.

"Right here on the left," I say.

Startled, Mrs. Parker hits the brake abruptly.

"Mom!"

"Thanks so much, Mrs. Parker, bye," I say as I fly out of the car and slam the door behind me. I run up the walkway to my house without looking back.

Chapter Nineteen

NOW

I'm in the hospital room again. Mom is in the bed, in a hospital gown, bruised and silent. Bernie is standing outside the room. The nurse says, *She can hear you.* I don't say anything. Instead, I turn around and walk out. Bernie isn't in the hallway anymore. I don't know where he is. I keep walking. I walk past the nurses' station. No one is there. I hit the round metal button on the wall that says PUSH TO EXIT and I walk out of the ICU. I walk past the break room, where all the nurses are eating their lunches out of Tupperware and doing worksheets with their daughters. I walk through the winding hallways, passing by hospital room after hospital room and break room after break room until I walk through the sliding glass doors and then I'm outside in the ambulance bay. It's broad daylight. It's a beautiful day. The aspens at the mountain's crest have yet to turn yellow.

Then I'm in the cemetery. And she's going into the ground. And I don't know where Bernie and Dad are. I don't know where anyone is, there's just her coffin going into the ground. But then she's standing next to me, in blue medical scrubs and house slippers, even though we're outside. And then I'm turning away from her, and walking away, walking and walking through the trees until I reach the parking lot, but there, in the parking space where our car should be, is the telescope, propped up and pointing to the sky.

Then I wake up in my bed.

My shirt is completely soaked through with sweat, and I can't breathe.

I just left her there. I left her. She's still out there waiting.

I wake up and the sun is too bright.

Did my alarm not go off?

When I lunge for my phone, Marty jumps down from the edge of my bed, startled.

I've missed the bus. A heavy weight settles over me. I should just go back to sleep. What does it matter if I don't go to school, anyway? There's a quiz in history that I haven't done the reading for. Every time I look at Joel, I wish I'd never spoken to him about the cow eyeball, or chisme, or tsinelas, or the space that people leave behind. And Elizabeth's going to want to talk about her fight with her mom, and I'm going to have to muster sympathy when I just want to scream at her that I wish I could have my mom back for just one second, and that she could tell me to apply for all the stupid internships on earth, and I would do it.

But when I pull the blanket over my head and close my eyes, I remember the dream.

I throw my blanket to the floor.

"Goddamn it," I mutter to myself, while picking through the profound amount of crap that we keep in the garage, looking for my bike to ride since I missed the bus. Christmas decorations, old patio furniture, mystery boxes, a shopping cart—*what the hell?*

Maybe that's just what happens when you have a garage. You just fill the space.

I guess that's what humanity does, doesn't it, just creeps over the earth, filling in all the spaces with a profound amount of crap?

My bike appears, wedged between two dusty cardboard boxes.

But right next to one of them there's a crisp, new box. Not like the others, which have banged-up corners and multiple layers of old packing tape.

The other day, wasn't Bernie acting nervous, like he wanted me to get away from this area?

I move aside some of the old boxes, one by one, huffing, and then pull out my house keys to slice through the fresh packing tape that seals the new-looking box.

"Holy shit," I whisper.

Neatly folded men's shirts. With the tags still on. The box is completely full. I riffle through them, counting. Ten, fifteen, twenty. My fingers grasp a price tag.

$115.00.

"For a shirt?!"

When I pull the stack of shirts onto my lap, underneath there are two pairs of fancy dress shoes. Size twelve. Which are two sizes bigger than Dad's.

Bernie.

Where did he get this stuff? He doesn't have money. But they couldn't be stolen.

Could they?

I have to get to school and find this kid. My frantic palms close the box quickly, not bothering with the now unsticky tape. I wrench my old bike from a tangle of extension cords. It seems rideable, but hanging from the handlebars is my helmet, which is embarrassingly, violently pink.

Oh well. I snap it into place.

I have a brother whose ass needs kicking.

I'm wobbly in the saddle at first, but then I find that my body remembers things. To lean this way or that. When I arrive at school, the buses are depositing students into the parking lot. Elizabeth's car is sitting in her typical parking space already.

I almost crash straight into the curb when I see Joel Duran, digging in his backpack for his U-lock right next to the bike rack.

Joel looks up in surprise as I swerve and screech to a halt clumsily. I drop my eyes to the ground as I hop off my bike, but it's too late to avoid this humiliation.

"Marisol," he says.

I wince.

"Nice Barbie helmet," he says. "Vintage."

Christ.

I unbuckle it and take it off quickly, and then ruffle my hair in a way that I hope is graceful and cool, like I actually am wearing this because it's vintage and not because it's actually just my pink Barbie helmet from when I was in middle school.

"Yeah, um, thanks," I say. "I guess I should get a new one."

"Well, it looks a little too small for you," he says. "Which means it's not safe. May I?"

He takes it from me expertly and flips it around, inspecting the inside.

My mouth goes dry as he closes the gap between us, lowering the helmet back onto my head. I stare at the place where his T-shirt collar rests at the base of his neck.

His warm fingertips brush the tops of my ears as he leans from one side to the other, checking out the fit.

"Yep. Too small for this big ol' brain," he says, taking the helmet off, flipping it over, and handing it back to me. "Come down to the store and I'll help you pick out a new one?"

"Okay," I choke out.

"I'll see you in A and P," he says, snapping his bike lock shut and walking away.

Then I'm just standing there, clutching my pink Barbie helmet as hundreds of people stream past me into the school, my heart pounding as I watch Joel's retreating back.

Maybe Elizabeth was right. Maybe if I just—

The bell rings.

Shit!

I pull out my phone and tap out a quick text message to Bernie.

B. We need to talk. Meet me @ lunch

For today's discussion about *The Crucible*, Ms. Moustafa is in costume as a Massachusetts villager of the late 1600s. Seriously. She has been insisting that we call her "Goody" Moustafa, like characters in the play, for this whole entire unit. Basically, she is really into her job.

I take my seat as the class assembles and pull out my copy of the play, wondering if I know enough about the Salem witch trials and Communism to say something passable if called on during discussion.

When Elizabeth slips into her seat, Dominic Espinosa turns around at his desk and tries to talk to her, just like he does every day, even though every day his efforts are soundly deflected.

I just can't figure out if he's determined, or stupid, or what.

"You look nice today," he says, tapping his mechanical pencil on her desk, trying to get her attention.

"I know," she says as she looks over her notes. "I have a mirror in my house."

The bell rings just as Josh Aceves squeaks in on his sneakers.

"Okay, people!" Ms. Moustafa says, clapping her hands. "Today we will be discussing the first act of Arthur Miller's *The Crucible*. I'm sure you are all caught up. However, this is a *play*. Plays are meant to be performed! So we're going to do a reading."

Tyler Paulson's hand shoots up.

"Ms. . . . . I mean, *Goody* Moustafa, may I read for *Tit*-u-ba?"

A wave of snickering rolls over the classroom. This is allegedly an Honors English class. Disgrace.

Elizabeth is looking up at the ceiling in disgust in the next row. She still looks sad, maybe from the fight with her mom yesterday. I feel bad for being annoyed with her about it and scribble a short note on a piece of loose-leaf to give to her.

it's funny, because it has the word "tit" in it.

When she reads it, she covers her mouth with her hand, laughing silently.

The giggles from the class die down.

"Tyler, I hate to tell you this," Ms. Moustafa says, "but somebody makes that same 'joke,' if you can call it that, every single year."

When class is over, we meet up outside in the hallway.

"Hey," I say. "What's wrong?"

Elizabeth shrugs.

"I'm not going to be able to keep working at Charlie's. I called Paul last night and told him."

"Oh."

"I'm so sorry," she says, rubbing her temples. "My mom's just not budging on it."

The noise of the hallway feels unbearable suddenly, like I wish I could scream at everybody to shut up.

"Well, did you tell her how much Paul needed help?" I ask.

"I did, but she was unsympathetic to his plight."

"It's just that . . . there were all those tapes still that we didn't get through."

"I know," she says. "Don't have too much fun without me."

She gives me a little punch on the arm and veers off toward her next class. The crowd parts to let her through. Somebody bumps me without saying sorry.

By lunchtime, there's still no response from Bernie. I

march across the concourse to his usual spot with the rest of the orchestra kids. I swing my book bag over my shoulder and approach one with dyed pink hair and a cello on their back.

"Hey, I'm looking for my brother, Bernardo Martin," I say. "Have you seen him?"

They shake their head.

"He wasn't in zero hour, and I haven't seen him all day." They shrug and nudge past me toward the hot lunch line.

What the hell.

I hold my phone in my hand. It feels heavy. Should I call Dad?

You're going to rat on me? Bernie's voice echoes in my head.

I clutch my phone.

B WHERE THE HELL ARE YOU?

The bus churns as we start up again after a long red light. I tried not to make eye contact with the bus driver as I placed my child's bike onto the rack on the front of the bus. No word from Bernie, and now I'm heading to Charlie's, alone.

We pass by a giant "snowman" (three tumbleweeds stacked on top of each other) in somebody's yard. His arms are two sticks with workman's gloves stuck on the ends, and his head is topped with a backward baseball cap. I can't stay seated because I'm a total jumble of nerves.

When I get to Charlie's, it's packed. Paul is on the café side of the shop, taking coffee orders. I throw my hair up in a ponytail, slide my backpack under the register, and toss my coat in after it. A line starts forming at the register in front of me and I'm not sure what I should do, because I haven't done this by myself yet.

I look around and there's no one coming to my rescue. Deep breath. Of all the information that got thrown at me yesterday in training, only about 80 percent actually stuck. I force myself to smile.

"Hi, how can I help you?"

And it goes in a blur from there. It's like someone else takes over my body. I take money, count it, and make change. *Where are the LPs? Can I put up this flyer for a house show? Do you have the new posters in?* I point people where they need to go. If I don't know the answers to their questions, I say I don't know. Or just make it up.

"How much are these little pins?" a customer with blunt bangs and blue highlights asks me, pointing to a bowl right next to the register full of pins and buttons. Some of them have band names and some of them have colorful designs, but none of them have barcodes.

"Uh, those are ninety-nine cents," I guess.

I figure I'll just ask Paul later when the café clears out and if I'm wrong, Charlie will forgive me, wherever and whoever he is.

A customer in a denim jacket asks me for the bathroom key. I search around under the counter and open drawers until I find a ring with millions of keys on it.

"It's . . . one of these," I say, offering it pitifully.

Luckily, they just laugh and say, "Okay."

When the rush is over, I sigh. The little bell on the door rings as a big group of people leaves, coffees in hand, wrapping scarves around their necks, looking over their shoulders to make sure they have everyone. The door closes and their voices are muffled, but I watch them laughing through the glass as they walk down the sidewalk.

I can do this. It'll take me a while to get everything, but I can do it. Something like pride swells in my chest as I look around the shop, a place I can come and do something that's just for me.

"It goes in spurts like that sometimes," Paul says, suddenly at my side. "Nobody for hours and then everybody at once. How'd you do? Are we bankrupt?"

"Yeah, somebody asked me for all the money and I figured I shouldn't argue."

"Oh, well. You made the right decision."

"How much are these pins?" I ask.

Paul shows me a sheet under the register full of barcodes for little things like the pins. And the pins actually *are* ninety-nine cents, so, score.

"So, no Elizabeth anymore, huh?" he asks me.

I shrug.

"Well, good news," he says. "Charlie okayed hosting the fridge with the mutual aid group."

"Really?"

"Yeah. Congratulations on your promotion to fridge czar."

"Well, what do they need?" I ask, my mind turning. "Do

they already have a fridge donated or do they need one? Because you have to get one that's supposed to be outside. It's going to get really cold soon at night, and if you use an indoor one outside, then the sensor in the freezer goes haywire and everything gets ruined—"

He laughs.

"Let me give you the contact information so you can get the details," he says, reaching for the phone as it rings. "And hey, can you do me a favor and bring up the box of new stuff from the back? It's not heavy."

"Sure."

I slide around to the front of the counter and make my way through the aisles to the back room.

It would be cool to have the fridge here. Maybe, eventually, I could tell Dad about it. Not yet. But someday. And maybe he'd want to come sometime. He'd like this place, with its old movie posters and records. Maybe he'd—

When I turn the corner down the last aisle, which is where we keep all the special, vintage seven-inch LPs, I stop, mid-stride.

Bernie is standing there. By the vintage stock.

Sliding something into his jacket.

And it's like I'm seeing two moments at once. It's like I'm seeing Bernie, here, right now, at Charlie's. But I'm also seeing the time he fell.

It was this one hot summer when he was just learning to walk, and everything smelled sweet, like the lilac bushes in the backyard, which were always full of moths and little white butterflies.

The swamp cooler was rattling. Bernie was with me, but

then he crawled away somehow, and I wondered where he was hiding. I tiptoed into the weeds, not wanting to scare him, but kind of wanting to scare him. I loved to say "Boo!" to Bernie, because he was such a giggly, happy baby. I loved how his dark eyes crinkled up as his big, musical laugh burst out of him.

But I couldn't find him where I thought he would be.

When I came around to the other side of the lilac bush, I froze.

He had climbed up onto the patio table. He must have gotten up onto the chair first.

He was wiggling, happily, in his overalls, with that fat butt little kids have when they're still in diapers.

When he saw me, he laughed, and laughed, then banged the metal table with his fat little hand, and then he wobbled.

He wobbled.

I could still see my mother's outline through the screen door, just inside the house, as if she was about to return with something she'd run inside to grab—maybe a ringing phone or a bowl of grapes—and I tried to shout out to her, but Bernie was already falling.

His scream, the screen door flying open, the blood on the cement.

The moths emerging from the lilac bush in a cloud of white wings.

Later, he needed three stitches in his lip, and Mom held her head in her hands after Bernie had gone to sleep, her dark hair covering up her face, while my dad rubbed her shoulders gently, repeating, "Shh."

Bernie. Sliding something into his jacket.

And it feels exactly like that moment right before he fell off that table on the back patio.

He wobbles. He's about to fall.

When he sees me, his eyes get huge, but then he plays it off, pulling the zipper of his jacket up to his neck.

But I saw.

I saw him take something.

And I'm already charging toward him.

"Bernie," I hiss, so Paul doesn't hear. "What the hell?"

"Whoa, what are you doing here?" he asks.

I grab his arm. "I work here!"

"Since when?"

I shove him back against a Modest Mouse poster on the wall.

"What's wrong with you?" he asks, in a normal, casual tone, like I'm the one out of line, like *I'm* the one who's going to mess everything up, when for once it's not me, it's him.

"Calm down."

"Shh! Be quiet!" I hiss, grabbing at his jacket zipper. "What did you take?"

"Marisol, what the hell—"

He's wrestling away from me, out of my grip.

"Put it *back*, you're going to get me in trouble—"

I grab a handful of his jacket.

"What are you talking about?" he says. "Leave me alone!"

And just as I get a grip on his jacket zipper—

"What's going on back here?"

We both look up as Paul comes around the corner, and Bernie's jacket falls open, and a stack of LPs tumbles to the floor.

The Mamas and the Papas. The Ronettes. Queen.

Paul's eyes fall to the carpet, where the vinyl discs have come loose from their sleeves.

Bernie takes off running in a blur.

"Bernie!" I shout.

He doesn't stop.

Paul doesn't even stop him, he just lets him pass. His eyes are on the floor as he sighs, puts one hand to the back of his neck, one at his hip.

My heart clenches. He looks up at me as the little bell dings, Bernie disappearing through the front door onto Central Avenue.

That look on Paul's face. It kills me.

The disappointment.

"He's my—" I start to explain. "I was just trying to stop him—"

It's useless to find the right words.

Paul holds up his hand, shakes his head.

Tears leap to my eyes because I *know* it looks bad, but it's just so unfair.

"I want to believe you," Paul says. "But it's just, everybody always says that. And I know the guy at the pawnshop, so he can always tell me when our stuff turns up there, which it does all the time."

"Why would you automatically think it's my fault?" I ask, suddenly furious, suddenly wanting to kick his stupid precious records across the floor.

I push past him, marching toward the register to grab my backpack. I don't need this stupid job, I don't need this stupid place. My body is radiating with violence and shame at the same time, and I can't figure out why, because I didn't do anything *wrong*. I snatch my bag and I'm wiping my snot on my sleeve when the bell at the door jingles.

My dad walks in, pushing Bernie ahead of him, his hand firmly on the back of his neck.

I freeze.

Dad. Staring me down.

Dad looking incredibly, profoundly pissed.

"Well?" he says, his face red, pushing Bernie forward.

Bernie, turning in on himself like a wilted flower, trying to make himself small, which is impossible. His voice, which is a low register, hard to hear, is barely audible.

"Say again?" Dad says.

He's wearing a suit, his only one, and it's practically falling off his frame from losing so much weight since Mom died. He must have had his formal teaching evaluation today.

"I'm sorry," Bernie whispers.

Paul holds up his hands.

"Whoa, man, what's going on here?"

"He stole, right?" Dad's voice is a growl. "That's why he ran out of here?"

"Hey, man," Paul says, his brows knitting together with concern. "You can't just grab random kids on the street like that."

"He's not a random kid," Dad growls. "He's my son!"

Dad makes a fist, furious that Paul doesn't see what is so obvious.

Then he points at me.

"And that's my daughter."

He's claiming me, but not out of pride—out of obligation, a heavy burden, that's my daughter, *that's my daughter, who I'm just trying to keep out of juvie, trying to keep out of the emergency room, where I had to watch her, pale and sweat-slicked, get her stomach pumped, under those thin fluorescent lights buzzing, in that same hospital*, that same damn hospital.

"That's why I came here."

How did he find me? Did I forget to turn off my phone? Did he track me on that stupid app? I clutch my backpack to my stomach, which is twisting and twisting in knots.

"She's quitting," my dad says.

"I was fired," I say.

My dad looks at me and his mouth becomes an O, as if he was shocked that I could go any lower in his estimation but yet, here I am.

He pulls out his wallet, his hands shaking, pulls out a few twenties, and shoves them into Paul's hands.

"For what he took," he says.

He turns around and walks out of the store. The bell dings.

Bernie and I follow quietly, not able to meet each other's eyes, leaving Charlie's behind.

We trail behind Dad as he crosses the crumbling asphalt parking lot. Dried-out weeds punch up from the cracks. Daylight is swiftly fading, the sky a dusty gray-pink. The air is growing cold. When we reach the car, Bernie climbs into the back seat and I reluctantly slide into the front, next to Dad.

Dad is just sitting there. Still. Staring straight ahead.

He hasn't put on his seat belt.

I pull my backpack close to my chest and tuck my chin over the top of it.

"Have you gone to driver's ed?" Dad asks quietly. "Even one time?"

I could, at least, say I went to the first class but they showed a fucked-up movie and I ran out screaming my head off because it reminded me of Mom and I was too ashamed to tell him. If that had been the case, maybe that would make sense. But it doesn't make sense.

"No," I say.

"Great. Sure. Okay. I see."

He shakes his head slowly.

"So you've been doing God knows what for hours every day."

I set my jaw in a hard line.

"I haven't been doing anything bad."

He puts his hands on the steering wheel but makes no other motion.

"You don't believe me," I say, stating the obvious.

He doesn't say anything.

"How did you even know I was here?" I ask.

"Elizabeth's *mother* called me," he says, his voice rising again. Fucking Mrs. Parker.

"At work. To tell me that Bernie's apparently been missing school, and oh, by the way, she'd be happy to recommend some 'volunteer opportunities' that you 'might be suited for' that would look better on a college application than some 'silly after-school job' all the way downtown. To which I couldn't help but reply: 'What silly after-school job?' And Bernie—"

He can't even look at Bernie, so he fixates on the sign for the Blake's Lotaburger across the street. BISCOCHITO SHAKES ARE BACK!

"Bernie, what would *possess* you to—?" he asks, his face growing redder. "All that stuff in the garage—? You know that if you need something—just ask—and I'll—!"

I see him trying hard to make sense of it all. But I think Dad's missing the point. Bernie was grasping at something with those stolen things, grasping at getting ahold of something that cannot be held.

Bernie's not saying anything and I can't see where he's looking, but it's not at Dad. I chew the inside of my cheek in silence.

"Marisol, I'm withdrawing you from school."

A tremor passes through me.

My breath stops.

"What?"

"Homeschool. I found an opportunity to teach online classes from home so that I can work with you until you graduate," he says, with finality.

"How long have you—can we afford to do that?" I ask, incredulous.

No, no, no. How can Dad even cover the mortgage by teaching online courses?

"What about your job? Will they let you come back afterward?"

"Marisol, that's for me to worry about, not you!" Dad is yelling now. "You haven't left me any choice here. I can't trust you. That's it. So this is the only way."

It's all gone. Joel Duran putting my helmet on by the bike

racks under the cottonwood tree. Passing notes to Elizabeth as she hides a snicker behind her hand. Sorting through the boxes of tapes at Charlie's.

"You can't do this to me," I say.

But he can.

So he purses his lips into a line and sticks the key into the ignition.

And just like that, my life is behind us.

Chapter Twenty

NOW

Dad sends me to school the next day to clean out my locker and pick up some forms from the office. It seems pointless to go to class, but I also don't know what else to do, so I go.

How could so much crap have possibly accumulated in my locker since school began?

I frown into the mess of crumpled-up notebook pages and extra sweaters, and, embarrassingly, a half-eaten breakfast sandwich in grease-stained yellow paper.

How am I going to clean all this out?

"Dude, how old is that sandwich?" Elizabeth asks, wrinkling her nose.

I slam my locker.

"I'm so sorry my mom called your dad," Elizabeth says, anxiously shifting her weight from one foot to the other. "I know I said that already. I'm just . . . sorry."

"Why?" I ask, shrugging. "You didn't do anything."

The zipper on my backpack is caught, so I pull and pull and pull at it.

"It's just so typically *Juana*," she says, pacing. "Trying to control everything and everyone."

"So," I say, abandoning my half-zipped backpack and keeping my voice bright, almost manically so. "Did you read for English class? How about those Puritans? Turns out, America was basically founded by a tyrannical cult. Can't wait to see Goody Moustafa's lecture outfit one last time."

"Though the draconian antics of the Puritans amuse me," she says, "I did not read that yet, because there is no fourth period today. We have the Cultural Assembly, remember?"

Fantastic.

I will endure Yvonne Morales being an Outstanding Filipino Teen again, before slinking off into homeschooled obscurity forever.

We file into the gymnasium, crushed by the crowd. On the wall, a hand-painted banner that reads ¡CELEBREMOS NUES-TRAS CULTURAS! hangs beneath the GO PUMAS mural.

"I don't think I've been to an assembly the entire time I've been at school here," I tell Elizabeth as she plops down next to me on the bench. "You know, they'll let you go to the cafeteria and read instead, if you ask."

"Wow," she says. "They *let* you do that?"

"Yes," I say, wiggling my glasses up and down for an ultra-nerd effect.

But really, all these people, laughing and waving, so excited, and for what? To be missing fourth period, not to see whatever Yvonne and Tes have come up with to cele-brate "culture." Across the gymnasium, among the crowd, Joel Duran is finding a seat, his headphones resting on his shoulders.

"Do we have to stay?" I ask.

Just then, Principal Peña strides across the floor to half-court. She holds a cordless mic in her hand.

"Welcome, Pumas!"

"Love this jumpsuit," Elizabeth says in my ear as she joins in on the applause. "For a principal."

And suddenly, it's so, so sad. Principal Peña in her cool red jumpsuit, the assembly in the totally packed gym, and all the things I won't get to do. The corny dances, the paper stars hanging from the ceiling. Walking across the stage at graduation. All the things that Mom would have been excited about, would have embarrassed me by taking too many pictures at. I would have pretended to hate it. All of it.

"Kicking off our cultural celebration today," Principal Peña says, referring to note cards in her hand, "here to perform the national dance of the Philippines, the Tinikling, please put your hands together for your La Manzanita High Asian Club!"

As the crowd whoops and cheers, Nick stands up in the front row, clapping. I stare at his back, feeling hollow.

"So I was thinking," Elizabeth says. "Today would be a great day to tell Joel you like him."

Yvonne, Tes, Sloan, and the rest of the girls from Asian Club run out onto the shiny gymnasium floor, waving, smiling, in red checkered skirts and boxy white crop tops. Bare feet.

"What?" I ask.

"It's perfect," she says. "Romantic. Your last day at school."

The guys run on from the opposite side, swinging long bamboo poles in pairs, in loose white shirts and shorts. Joel Duran is across the room, but I don't dare look at him.

The dancers get into position and the music starts, plucky guitar.

"Come on, why not?" Elizabeth says, nudging my shoulder.

"What's the worst that could happen? Do you want me to say something?"

"I—"

"Titty-kling! Titty-kling!"

I whirl around to see who said that, but I already know. Two rows behind us, Tyler and J.J. are cracking themselves up, chanting, "Titty-kling, titty-kling."

The song swells. Rage crashes over me in waves. The bamboo poles clack against the floor and each other, *one two three, one two three*, as the dancers hop nimbly between them, spinning and leaping on bare feet.

My mom performed this dance once. It was for some community night when we were really young. Her hair was loose, long, almost down to the ground. The way she moved, fluid, her ankles narrowly escaping the jaws of the poles coming together. *Thwack. Thwack. Thwack.*

Nothing could touch her. Nothing.

Yusef takes Yvonne by the hand and spins her, her delicate curls bouncing as she raises her palm to the sky, finds her light, smiles. *Miss America.*

Everyone cheers.

"Yo, nice titty-klings!" Tyler calls, cupping his hands over his mouth, J.J. howling next to him.

One two three, one two three.

"Shut up," I say.

Too quiet. Nobody hears me. Not over the roaring crowd.

I fill my chest with more air.

"Shut the fuck up!"

Elizabeth puts her hand on my arm.

One two three, one two three.

"Who said that?" Tyler asks, scanning the rows beneath him before his eyes land on me, twisted around, staring at him.

"Mary?" J.J. laughs.

"That's not my fucking name!" I shout. Elizabeth is tugging on my wrist now.

"Don't feel left out," Tyler says. "You have nice titty-klings, too, Mary."

I launch forward, my arms pushing Josh Aceves and Dominic Espinoza apart, because they're in the way, one row behind us, but Elizabeth is holding me back from the waist.

One two three, one two three.

I'm struggling against Elizabeth's grip, but I can't hear what she's saying over the music and everyone yelling and the bamboo poles thwacking the floor.

My mom, spinning on the stage, under the lights, full of power.

"Hey, stop, stop, it's okay." Elizabeth's arms are around me, and she keeps saying, "Hey, hey, hey," until I let myself be stilled.

"I fucking hate them," I breathe, my face hot, and if only they had been closer to me, I would have— "I hate them."

Elizabeth is holding my shoulders as the crowd comes to its feet for the big finish. Tyler and J.J. disappear behind a row of bodies. The Asian Club takes a bow.

"Can we go? Can we leave?" I ask.

"Yeah, come on."

She takes my hand, and the crowd provides sufficient cover for us to slip away, running down the steps two at a time.

It's freezing today, but we roll the windows down and blast the music. Then we take off, heading north, to the edge of the city, until the concrete strip malls and parking lots give way to houses with chicken coops and corrals, and brown horses trotting in the sun.

"Fuck those guys," Elizabeth says, banging her hand on the steering wheel.

The gym, the crowd, my school, it falls away.

It's gone.

I'm never going back there.

"They're idiots," she says.

She looks so powerful there, her hand on the wheel. Like she always does. Like she knows what she's doing.

I'm chewing on my thumbnail, consumed with unfinished thoughts and shame.

I should have—Maybe I could have—Why didn't I—If only I could—-

"Hey, can I drive?" I ask.

She glances at me, at my knees bouncing up and down, and my balled-up fists.

"Of course."

Elizabeth pulls into the empty parking lot of a little brown church. It's not our church, but it looks like ours does, with its stained-glass windows and its wooden cross over the door.

We're alone here, but for a few tumbleweeds crawling across the asphalt in the chilly breeze. The Sandias rise up behind the church, and above them, the bright blue sky.

When I slide into the driver's seat, I stare at the dashboard.

The wind moves the yellow leaves on the little trees by the road, just slightly.

Taking a deep breath, I place my hands on the wheel. After I shift the car into reverse, I try to ease off the brake more slowly this time.

I turn around to look behind me, like I've seen other drivers do.

It's a good thing that the parking lot is totally empty. Otherwise I would have definitely hit every single other car near us, but I did manage to back out.

"Good," Elizabeth says.

She guides me through a series of maneuvers in the parking lot.

Beneath my fingers, the wheel. Beyond the wheel, the car. A giant piece of machinery. A two-ton beast, barely under my control. I feel its power with every jerking stop I make and every crooked turn I take too quickly.

I'm sure that the Cultural Assembly has been over for a long time when Elizabeth announces that I've taken enough laps around the parking lot.

"I think you've earned a spin on the open road!" she says.

"It's getting late," I say, and I know it sounds unconvincing.

Elizabeth sits up straighter and looks me in the eyes.

"You can do it," she says.

Damn it.

I stare back at her. There are so many half-formed thoughts that begin. So many things I'm scared to even think, to feel, thoughts I want to turn away from, because they're too big. So many things I can't say. But she knows that, somehow.

She nods.

I creep out to the edge of the parking lot, gripping the wheel so tight my palms are getting sweaty. A car comes over the hill, far away, but I still wait for it to pass before turning out into the street.

And then, I'm doing it.

Moving us along the black asphalt, commanding this huge metal machine.

I push the gas pedal too hard and we jerk forward. Elizabeth laughs, and I laugh too, this time.

But as we pick up speed, I begin to feel sweaty in my jacket, and really aware of how tight it fits me in the shoulders, constricting the movement of my arms. My eyes flit from mirror to mirror. Just as we crest a hill, a car blows past us, coming the other way, and I flinch. It would only take a small movement for it to have swerved into our path, or for me to have swerved into its path.

That's enough. We should stop. Now.

The next turn is a side street, a dirt road, and it's coming up fast.

I punch down on the brake and turn off onto it, the wheels skidding.

"Marisol—!"

And there's a dog, a big brown dog—*Cash!* I think, illogically, of Elizabeth's dog—and I jerk the wheel hard to the other side to avoid it.

The tires try to find purchase on the loose dirt road beneath us. I wrench the wheel the other way, but we fishtail, then the flash of yellow leaves—something punches me in the chest and my hair is in my face and my eyes and I think I bit my tongue, and there's the sound of metal crunching and it feels like all the air in the world is gone.

It all stops.

It's quiet.

My brain is trying to make sense of it. When I reach up to touch my face, I realize I'm not wearing my glasses anymore. Then I reach over to Elizabeth and our hands find one another and grip tightly.

Somebody is laughing. I realize it's me. Or maybe I'm crying.

"Are you okay?" Elizabeth asks. Her voice sounds really far away.

"Yeah," I say, and it sounds like someone else is saying it.

Her door opens. The sun spills in. The airbag in front of me begins to deflate. I unbuckle my seat belt with a click and follow. The gravel crunches underfoot.

"You're okay?" I manage to ask, breathing heavily.

"I'm fine," she says, and opens the door to the passenger side and reaches in to get something. "Look. My parents would flip *out* if they found out I was letting somebody else drive my car. And you don't have a driver's license, and you could get in trouble, so I think you should go."

I stand there stupidly as she presses my glasses into my hands. There's not a scratch on them. They quiver in my shaking fingers. My mouth tastes like blood. When I put them on, I see her face as it comes into focus.

Her eyeliner is running, and all the color has drained from her face.

"Go?" I ask.

She turns around and begins riffling through her bag.

"Where is my phone?" she mumbles to herself.

Almost in a trance, I open the door to the back seat and pull out my backpack. When I close the door, it finally sinks in that the front of her car is crumpled into a tree at the side of the road.

"Elizabeth," I say, taking in the sight. "Oh my God. Oh my God. I'm so sorry."

"It was an accident," she says. "That fucking dog."

"But . . ." My mouth is moving but my brain is too slow for words to come out.

"Marisol," she says, looking around. "Listen. Just *go*, okay? My parents are going to kill me for this, and if they knew it was you, they'd give me *extra* shit because—"

She looks up at the sky.

I watch for a minute as she tries to collect herself, to suck the words back into herself.

"Because why?" I press her, already knowing the answer. "Because they don't want you hanging out with me?"

"No." She pinches the bridge of her nose. "They're not like that, okay?"

"Are you sure?" I snap. "Because they seem pretty much exactly like that to me."

Elizabeth blinks. "What's that supposed to mean?"

"You know what I mean. 'Oh, *Daniel* went to *Brown*, I went to *Caltech*, he's an engineer, I'm a lawyer—'"

"She's the one who went to Brown—"

"Oh my God, I don't care where she went, the issue is that she looked at me like I was a freaking *street urchin*."

"Okay, that's a tad melodramatic, if not fully Dickensian.

She can't be proud of going to Brown? Why not? And any-body's parents are going to be pissed over a car with a tree in it!"

"This is your fault!" I scream.

Her eyes widen incredulously.

"You said I could do it!" I say, my hands gesturing wildly, because she just doesn't get it. "You're the one who *made me* want to try. You were, like, hyping me up all the time, and bugging me about Joel Duran, you made me *want* to go to *parties*, and I hate parties, and you made me want to get that job at Charlie's, and like try and shit, but maybe I don't *want* to try! I don't want to *care*. I don't *want* to go to assemblies, I don't *want* to talk to Joel, and I don't *want* to care what your parents think about me!"

My chest heaves and my face is wet.

"But you do," Elizabeth says, finishing my thought, obnox-iously always right, always right about everything.

She reaches for my arm but I pull away, wiping the stupid tears from my face.

"What did your mom say to you?" I ask. "That day when I came over after school for the first time. She said she always warns you about having friends who aren't . . . what?"

She crosses her arms and looks down at her feet.

"Tell me," I say.

"Friends who aren't . . . on my level."

"Wow," I say. "Wow."

"But she just means—you know—"

"So you're *pushing* me to get on your level?" I say.

"That's ridiculous," she says. "I was just trying to help."

"I didn't ask for your help," I say. "I'm doing perfectly fine."

"Well, I wouldn't say that."

I suck in air and glare at her, looking all smug with her quip, like she's so goddamn smart, but what does she know? I'm fine, I'm really okay, and who asked her anyway?

"I'm just saying," she says. "You're obviously having a hard time. I would be, too. If my mom died, I'd—"

"You don't know *anything*!" I say. "Just because you read a psychology book and independently studied or whatever!"

She flinches. And I feel myself coming apart, everything that was tightly held coming loose.

"I was awful to her, okay?" I say. "I was a nightmare, I was ungrateful, I was the absolute worst, and I don't mean that I chose the wrong after-school activities. I don't—I don't *deserve* to be having a hard time."

My throat is closing up, and my eyes are burning. I'm so mad that I can't see straight anymore. Elizabeth is mad too, really mad, she's keeping very still and she's sucking on her teeth, her hands posed in front of her body like she's praying.

"*I know* what it's like to want to be a good daughter. And feel like you're failing. I didn't have to read that in a book."

I see it again, how this steel in her spine comes from holding herself up, holding her mother, holding her grandmother, holding the weight of all those medals and expectations.

"I know you're really upset," she continues, keeping her voice controlled even as her folded hands shake slightly with rage. "And I get that, but please, will you just *go* and let me deal with my parents?"

Elizabeth's face is hard but her eyes are pleading. Because

she doesn't want to tell her parents it was me. Because she wants us to still be friends.

"Fine," I say.

Slinging my backpack over my shoulder, I whirl around and march away from her, down the dirt road lined with trees and yellow leaves, quivering. I walk and walk and I don't look back, not once. From up here, I can see the dormant volcanoes way out there in the west. I stomp my feet, letting my anger carry me all the way to Paseo del Norte.

The whole scene is settling over me.

And I imagine some future dinner at the Parkers', Elizabeth telling her parents some dumb story about how I wrote a really *smart* essay in homeschool, and she's encouraging me to *submit it* somewhere, and she's pretending that she wants to go to law school, and I'm pretending that I didn't crash her car into a tree, and that I didn't punch my best friend in the face, that I didn't get sent to juvie, and that I didn't kill my mom, or may as well have. As good as.

I spin around and go back, speeding up, the cold air filling my lungs as I take off running. I come over the top of the big hill just in time to see Mr. and Mrs. Parker's car pulling up next to Elizabeth's crushed one, Mrs. Parker jumping out of the passenger seat and pulling Elizabeth into a tight hug.

"It was me!" I yell from half a block away.

They all turn to look at me, their worried, tense faces passing into foggy confusion.

I'm so out of breath when I reach them that I have to stop and double over, breathing hard.

"It was me," I say again, straightening up.

With her mom's arms still circling her shoulders, Elizabeth mouths, *What are you DOING?*

"I crashed the car into the tree. It was me. She wanted to cover for me, but it was totally me," I say, veering into some kind of absurd glee at the ridiculousness of the situation. "Go ahead, call my dad and tell him."

The Parkers look between Elizabeth, at a loss, and me, out of breath and wild-looking.

Mrs. Parker opens and closes her mouth several times.

I pull out my phone. "Here, I'll do it," I say, dialing my dad's number.

He answers after one ring.

"What's wrong?" he asks.

"Elizabeth was trying to teach me, her delinquent friend, how to drive and I crashed her car," I say. "Can you come get me?"

Silence on the other end.

"Check your stalker app for my location," I say, and hang up.

Elizabeth's dad is awkwardly circling the car with his hands on his hips when Dad pulls up. Mrs. Parker has been busy shaking her head, crushing her lips together in a thin white line.

Elizabeth is staring up at the sky.

My dad jumps out of the car as soon as it's in park. After taking in the scene with quick glances, he gives Mrs. Parker an awkward nod, which she returns, and strides over to Mr. Parker with an outstretched hand, which he takes quickly.

"Daniel."

"Peter."

"Might not be as bad as it looks. Looks like maybe the axle might need realigning—"

"Oh?"

"Maybe, or—"

"And the hood here—"

Now they're both circling the car and talking about it, like that'll do anything, while their daughters stand in the dirt with their hands at their sides.

"I'm so sorry," my dad says to no one in particular, then to Mrs. Parker in particular. "I'm so sorry. Let me, ah, give you my insurance information."

Mrs. Parker nods stiffly, apparently too angry to speak, as my dad rushes to the glove compartment. He riffles through papers with shaking hands.

"I'll figure this out," he says. "I'm so sorry."

When he finally retrieves it, he looks at me for the first time.

"Get in the car," he says.

Elizabeth crosses her arms, looks at her feet.

I stomp off, slide into the passenger seat, and slam the door.

I stare at Elizabeth through the windshield while her mom whispers at her fiercely. Saying, probably, *Didn't I warn you about her?*

And she was right.

Elizabeth is sullen, looking everywhere, at everything else but me.

Chapter Twenty-One

NOW

The next morning, I pull out a frying pan and slam it down, harder than I mean to, onto the stove top. I stayed awake until the sun came up this morning. But when you don't sleep, you can't dream, and why do I need to sleep, anyway? I don't have school anymore. I don't have a job anymore. I don't have friends anymore.

Almost automatically, like my body is doing it without me, I begin making the only thing I can think of to comfort me, the only thing that I know how to make, the only thing we have ingredients for, sinangag.

My hands shake as I picture that tree, and the car, all crumpled, but they steady themselves as I begin to peel the cloves of garlic. Mom chopped garlic cloves without looking. While looking at something else. An open book. Bernie crawling across the floor. After she let me peel their papery skins off, I liked the way the tangy smell clung to my fingertips, and I'd watch her smash each clove with the heel of her hand, beneath the flat side of the knife, pulverizing them, releasing their sharp fragrance, before chopping it finely.

I cup a large egg in the palm of my hand before cracking it into the pan.

I remember watching my mom make garlic rice like this when I was younger, and describing to her, in detail, the part in that book *Hatchet* when the kid, lost in the forest after a plane crash, starving, finds the turtle eggs and eats them. After all he's been through, and how hungry he is by that point in the book, raw turtle eggs sound like the most delicious thing in the world. She nodded, and listened, and told me about how she grew up eating balut, a duck embryo served warm and still in its shell. I pretended not to be disturbed by her description of the little beak, the bluish veins, the bones, soft, all soaked in vinegar, because I could tell she was trying to shock me, and I wanted her to know that I was brave and that she could take me to the Philippines one day, and that if she did, I would chew all the little bones without flinching.

I gently slide the chopped garlic from my knife into the pan with my fingers, then add a few glugs of oil and yesterday's rice. Yesterday's rice is always best, Mom said, because it's a little bit dried out, so it absorbs the garlic and the egg and sticks to itself, easier to eat. Two eggs, which, once I got tall enough, she let me crack open on the pan.

Yesterday's rice, two eggs, two cloves of garlic, and a little bit of oil. That's it. Like magic. Her hands worked swiftly, scooping the rice from the pan onto two plates, one for her and one for me. Then she'd crack two more eggs with one hand onto the still-hot pan. Perfect, runny, golden yolk and crispy white edges. They slide easily from the pan—one onto the top of her rice, and then one onto mine. She'd carry the plates over to the table and ask me to grab the ketchup from the fridge.

If Dad was there, he'd shudder and wrinkle his nose at the ketchup.

Ignoring this, Mom would squeeze it on top of the sinangag in a generous, three-ringed swirl and sit at the table, tucking one knee up close to her chest.

Then she'd set the ketchup back on the table, in front of me.

She never did the ketchup for me. She let me do it myself. I'd add a swirl with three rings, like her. Then I'd mush it all up together with a fork. Hot, and salty, and sweet and yolky and good. Our after-school snack was her breakfast. She was usually still sleeping when we got home from school. But sometimes, when we got off the bus and walked the two blocks home, put the key in the door and turned it, I'd find that she was awake, in pajamas and a bathrobe. Gazing out the window, the light on the rice cooker blinking.

Once she was sitting outside in a winter coat, on the step, smoking, with her phone sitting next to her on the concrete. When she saw me, she looked sideways at me, then out into the cloudless, matte-blue sky, taking one last drag before stamping the cigarette out.

"Do as I say," she said, smoke curling from her lips. "Not as I do."

She coughed, cursing the dry desert air. An island person, landlocked. She used the dusty watering can under the lilac bush in the corner of the yard as an ashtray, its contents going undiscovered until after her death.

I turn the burner on, then turn to look in the fridge for ketchup. I spot it, behind a Tupperware in the back, but when I pull it out, several others come clattering to the ground.

"Damn it," I mutter.

I toss the rice up onto the counter and gather up the other leftovers, tucking them back into the fridge.

When I stand back up, the vegetable oil in the pan is smoking.

"Goddamn it!" I say.

I click off the heat and pull the pan off the burner.

A little bit of oil sloshes onto my hand, stinging. I stick my knuckle into my mouth as I run over to the window to open it before the smoke alarm goes off. I grab a towel and fan the smoke outside into the cold morning air.

Bernie appears at the edge of the kitchen.

"What are you still doing here?" I ask him.

"Dad had to go wrap up something at the district office, so I'm going to take the bus," he says, zipping up his sweatshirt.

Then he sniffs the air.

"What are you burning?"

I flap the towel harder, driving the last of the gray smoke toward the kitchen window. Once outside, it spreads out and disappears into the pink morning.

"I was trying to make fried rice."

"With an egg and ketchup?"

I shrug.

Bernie stares at the floor and stuffs his hands into his pockets.

There's a scratching sound at the back door. Bernie walks over and opens it to let Marty in. Instead of his usual scramble to the food bowl, he limps slowly inside.

His left leg is crusted with dried blood and clumped fur, and part of his fluffy tail is bald and hangs low, as if it's broken.

My heart stops.

"Oh my God, Marty!" I say, dropping my towel and rushing over to him.

Despite his limp, my sudden movement startles him, and he darts underneath the couch. Bernie and I get down onto the carpet on our stomachs and peer at him. He looks back at us, blinks his golden eyes, and then proceeds to lick his bloody leg, slowly. He seems to be breathing heavily, his eyes unfocused and disoriented.

"Marty." I try to call him to me, gently. He mews weakly.

"Do you think a coyote got him?" Bernie asks me quietly.

"If it was a coyote, I don't think he would've made it."

"Maybe he fought him off."

"I bet it was just another cat, or a dog, or something."

I hope it wasn't a coyote. You can hear them sometimes. They roam the mesas and even the city at night. Joggers have been noticing them more lately, according to the news, because of the drought. Stalking prey.

"What should we do?" Bernie asks.

I'm so tired from not having slept that my skull feels tight around my brain, but the sight of Marty's limp and bloody leg has set my heart pounding, too.

"I'll take him to the emergency vet."

"I want to come," he says.

"Okay, if you want," I say, like it's for him and not for me. "Close the door so he doesn't run out."

I push myself up, run to the garage to try to find Marty's cat carrier.

It's a soft black carrier that we bought on the day we adopted him from the shelter, when he was just a little kitten, eight years ago. He looked like a little orange fluff ball back then. He could fit in the palm of your hand.

I dig through two boxes full of mismatched kneepads and broken Christmas ornaments before I find it. I guess we haven't really taken him to the vet in a while, I realize with a fresh pang of guilt.

When I emerge from the garage, I find Bernie attempting to coax Marty out from under the couch with a limp hot dog.

"Does Marty like hot dogs?" I ask.

"I thought he might. He doesn't seem interested."

"Can you reach him? We might just have to pull him out."

"No, he's all the way in the back by the wall." Bernie bites his lip. "Should we call Dad?"

"There's no time. Okay, maybe you lift the couch up a little bit and when he comes running out, I'll grab him," I say.

"Okay," Bernie says, getting up and walking around to the side of the couch.

I crouch down and try to anticipate where Marty will come out. "Okay, ready? One . . . two . . . three! Lift!"

Bernie lifts up one end of the couch and Marty comes darting out from underneath. I grab him, and he makes a sound I've never heard him make before, a cross between a snarl and a yowl, as he twists and bites my arm.

"Get the carrier!"

Bernie hurries over with the cat carrier as I try to hold on to Marty, gently but firmly, and slip him inside. He scratches at my arms before I can finally get the zipper closed.

"You're bleeding," Bernie says, gesturing to the long red scratches Marty's claws have left on my forearm.

I hadn't felt them. Now they sting.

Marty settles into a crouch in his cat carrier, his eyes droopy and strange. I have a sinking feeling in the pit of my stomach.

"It's okay, buddy," I tell him gently.

I know he didn't mean to hurt me, but it's just that I was right there.

I slide a small yellow blanket inside the carrier with him to keep him warm.

After waiting for fifteen minutes under the bus shelter, we walk the two cold miles to the veterinarian's office, taking turns carrying Marty, who is eerily silent. We don't talk the whole way. The only sounds are our footsteps on the sidewalk and the cars whooshing by us on the busy streets.

The sun is almost overhead by the time we get there, the strip mall with a huge parking lot, a used bookstore, a tattoo shop, and an old-school New Mexican diner. We probably should have called first, but that only just occurred to me.

A little bell rings when we push through the glass door. I place Marty's carrier gently on the reception desk. The woman behind the desk looks to be in her fifties, with glasses, and she's wearing pink medical scrubs. Her pin-straight black hair is streaked with gray, lying in a thick braid over one shoulder. Her round face and scrubs remind me of my mom, so much, so powerfully, and suddenly I'm crumbling.

"I don't have an appointment, but our cat got hurt," I say, trying to control my voice, trying not to make it sound like it does, like a child's.

I feel Bernie standing behind me. I swallow hard and raise my eyebrows in an effort to control my face.

"That's okay, sweetheart," she says, getting up and peering into the mesh lining to look at Marty. "Who's this?"

The way she looks back at me only makes it worse.

"Marty," I say.

"Let me give you some paperwork to fill out, okay? I'll take Marty."

She hands me a clipboard and a ballpoint pen and I shakily begin to fill out the paperwork.

"I'll be right back," she says.

She picks up Marty in his carrier and turns toward a swinging white door, quietly clucking at him.

"I think maybe he got attacked by a coyote or something," I say at her retreating back. "He came home and he was like that. His leg is bleeding and his tail is funny."

"Okay, sweetheart. Make sure to fill out both pages."

I just stand there at the counter and do it. I hate writing in pen because the pressure of not being able to erase anything always makes me mess up. I write my name where Marty's name is supposed to go and I have to cross it out. So then, right there at the top of the paperwork, it says *Marisol* (crossed out) *Marty Martin*. It looks so stupid I almost ask for another form, but then I tell myself it doesn't matter and I just have to finish.

I hurriedly fill in the rest with our address and phone number.

The woman has reappeared without Marty.

I hand her the clipboard with the paperwork.

"You can have a seat," she says. "The vet is examining him now."

Bernie and I sit in a couple of cushy chairs in the waiting area as she begins to type at the computer. It's only then that I notice we're alone, with just one old lady with her really old, really big dog. She smiles at me and I try to smile back.

On the table, there are several very old issues of *Cat Fancy* and *Dog Fancy* magazines stacked up, in addition to a plastic jar full of bone-shaped dog treats.

We both stare blankly ahead. It's so quiet in the office, all we hear is the soft typing of the woman in pink scrubs and the faint hum of traffic out on the street. I almost have a heart attack when Bernie's cell phone goes off.

"Jesus Christ!" I say, taking a deep breath. I feel like I just jumped a mile in the air.

Bernie digs in the pocket of his jeans for his cell phone and pulls it out.

"Oh, crap," he says. "It's Dad."

I'm too exhausted to keep up the lies anymore. "Just answer it."

"Hello?"

I can hear Dad's voice on the other end, though I can't make out what he's saying. The tone comes through, though.

He's definitely not happy.

"I know," Bernie says. "I'm sorry. No. We're at the vet. Marty got hurt. No. We walked here. I'm with Marisol. Yeah."

He hands the phone over to me.

"He wants to talk to you."

I swallow.

"Hi."

"Why didn't you guys call me?" he asks, exasperated.

"Because I'm handling it."

"What if something happened? Nobody knows where you guys are, because you're not where you're *supposed to be.*"

"Like what? What could have happened?"

"Anything can happen, Marisol!" he almost shouts.

"Absolutely anything can happen at any time, and I need to know where you are and what you're doing."

"Don't you even care about Marty?" I explode. "A coyote tried to eat him!"

Before he can respond to that, I hang up on him. I hand the phone back to Bernie and stare at my shoes, fuming, embarrassed that the sweet lady in the pink scrubs and the old lady with her giant dog heard me yelling at my dad.

But *doesn't* he care? That Marty climbs into bed with me when it gets cold out, and warms up my feet, that his eyes close when I scratch him underneath his chin, that I bury my face in his warm fur when he sleeps on my pillow, that he knows when I'm sad?

I swipe at the corners of my eyes as we sit silently for I don't know how long.

"Marisol?" The woman in pink scrubs calls me.

I get up, whacking Bernie accidentally with my bag.

"Sorry," I tell him.

The lady in the pink scrubs beckons me back through the swinging white door. I look over my shoulder.

"Can my brother come?" I ask.

"Of course," she says gently.

Bernie gets up and puts his hands in the pockets of his sweatshirt. His nose is red and he follows me silently down the hallway into a brightly lit room that looks sort of like the doctor's office. There's a table with thin paper on it and there's the veterinarian, a woman in a white coat and glasses, and then, when she turns around, there's Marty lying on the table, lying there still and quiet.

"Did you drug him?" I ask.

"No, honey," the vet says. "He went into shock. I'm sorry."

He's so still.

"There was some internal bleeding, worsening from the time of the impact. You may be right. The injury seems consistent with an animal attack."

He looks like he's asleep, facing away from me, though his tail does not move with dreaming.

"He looks so small," I say, my own voice sounding far away.

He was going to be okay, he just seemed a little out of it, he was just limping a little. He had enough strength to run under the couch, and to bite me.

"He's gone, sweetheart," the woman in scrubs says to me.

Yesterday when dad brought me home after the crash, he was twisted up in a blanket that had fallen on the carpet, purring noisily, safe inside the house. If only I had kept him in. That was only yesterday, just a few hours ago, really. I remember yesterday. I hold yesterday close in my mind, but it's already slipping away, second by second.

"What would you like us to do with him?" the vet is asking.

"What?" I blink.

"I can provide you with a list of options," she says gently.

Should I call Dad? I wonder. But then I look at Bernie, and he looks so sad, and I just want to get him out of here as soon as possible.

"Yes, please," I say, putting my hand on Bernie's back. "That would be good, thank you."

"We can give you a minute," the vet says. A shuffle of feet, and a door clicking.

Bernie and I stand there, alone with Marty, who looks so small. I rub my hand across Bernie's back, his bony shoulder blades tensed together, as he brings his palms to his eyes.

"It's okay," I say, and he starts to cry.

❊ ✳ ❊

About an hour later, Bernie and I are sitting in the diner. The blue vinyl cushion beneath me is torn, with a bit of white fuzz coming out.

Bernie is fussing with the sugar packets, tearing them open and dumping the sugar onto his empty plate, which he has meticulously eaten everything off of in clockwise order. Bernie has eaten two tamales, green chile chicken enchiladas, rice, beans, and a sopapilla with honey. I, for once, am not hungry, and I wrap my fingers around my mug of black coffee.

When Dad walks into the diner, he pauses to search the restaurant before he sees us.

And for a moment, I see him not as my dad, I see him just as a guy, because he doesn't see me yet. He's just a guy in a diner, in a denim button-down shirt and a faded coat.

He looks sad.

Seeing us, he lifts his hand in a small wave and joins us in the booth. He slides in next to Bernie, and the server appears with a menu.

"I'll have a grilled cheese," he says. "And a coffee."

The server jots down Dad's order with a little broken pencil and takes the menu back from him. She asks me if I want more coffee, but I say no, thank you. She smiles at me.

Dad puts his arm around Bernie's shoulders and squeezes him, just a little squeeze.

He folds his hands on the table and sighs. He puts his hand on the back of Bernie's neck and looks down at the smooth blue tabletop. Bernie nods firmly and looks down at his plate of sugar.

My eyes go unfocused and all I see is that blue, smooth and cool, and all I hear is the clink of silverware and the scraping of chairs being pulled across the floor, and I go somewhere deep inside myself.

I'll never have to leave this diner. Won't ever move, won't get into the car and drive home to that house with old feelings imprinted onto the furniture, into doorframes, won't even think of going in there, where Marty's fur is still clinging to blankets and my mother's scent has entirely faded from her sweater that I keep hidden in the back of my closet.

But then I remember there was something that I wanted to do.

"We can pick up the ashes in a couple of days," I say.

"Oh?" my dad says, surprised.

That I handled something? That Marty's been cremated?

"Maybe we could scatter them by Mom's roses," I say.

Dad doesn't say anything while the waitress pours his coffee.

"He liked being there," I say.

The server brings over the grilled cheese and coffee.

Saying nothing, Dad slides the plate over to our side of the table and picks up his coffee. When neither of us moves, Dad pushes the plate a little closer to us.

I take one half of the greasy sandwich and Bernie takes the other half. The hot cheese stretches out between us.

＊ ✳ ＊

When we get home, I shut the door to my room and lean against it. In the dim light, I grasp my elbows, holding myself. The streetlight filters through the blinds, and it's too easy to see it, all of it—Marty jumping cleanly through the window from outside. Marty pawing at my feet beneath a blanket. Marty weaving between Mom's ankles while she waters the roses in the pink dusk, *so they won't get scorched by the sun*. Bernie and I, stomping in the slushy snow while Dad assembles the telescope. The car with the tree in it, its yellow leaves rippling like water. The records falling from Bernie's jacket onto the floor at Charlie's. Joel and Lila sitting on the steps of the basement while Miriam sings the saddest song I've ever heard. The steering wheel turning beneath my hands. The dog that wasn't Cash. Elizabeth's car sliding in the fine dirt. The bell chiming as Dad pushes Bernie through the door. The bamboo thwacking the gymnasium floor. Yvonne doubled over with laughter as Nick's arm circles her shoulders. Nick taking my pencil from my hand, *here, M, let me show you*.

I climb into bed with my clothes on.

It's cold at first and I'm shivering. Gathering my blankets up to my chin, I close my eyes.

I don't want to sleep.

But all I want to do is sleep.

So, finally, I sleep, and sleep, and sleep.

Chapter Twenty-Two

NOW

When I wake, it's dark. And I feel like I was just dream-ing, but I don't remember it. My body doesn't feel like it does when I've had the nightmare, though. It feels like I've been severed abruptly from something that I'm still reaching for. I pat around the top of my comforter for Marty, searching for his warm, sleeping form, until I remember, and then that empty spot makes me feel so, so alone. It's so quiet and everything is so unfair.

There's a faint knock on my door.

"What?" I choke out.

My door opens slowly, and I just barely see the outline of Bernie in the dark. My hand reaches for my glasses and my cell phone—it's midnight.

"What?" I ask him again.

He comes to sit on the edge of my bed, holding a Tupperware full of cold mashed potatoes with two spoons in it. I wrinkle my nose, but then I soften a little at this odd attempt to comfort me.

"I'm not hungry," I say.

He sets the Tupperware in front of me anyway.

I stare at the cold mashed potatoes, which were made from a box. In the box they were a powder, but now they are this. They have little green flecks in them. Are the little green flecks supposed to be herbs, and if so, what kind? Are the little green flecks real? Was the tree I hit real? Is anything?

"Let's go on the roof," he says.

"Why?"

"There's a meteor shower tonight," he says. "And, according to my phone, Jupiter is at its closest point to Earth in thirty years."

"What?"

"Just come."

All the lights are off in the house, so we creep down the hall in the dark with two blankets, the Tupperware of mashed potatoes, and Mom's telescope from the garage. The Christmas lights are still on, twinkling in the window, little chile peppers, alternating red and green. The faint outlines of cars pass on the road, their headlights piercing the sheer curtain. In the kitchen, the frying pan I was using this morning now sits in the kitchen sink, burnt grains of rice still clinging to it.

Bernie has the telescope, still in its box, resting by the back door.

The air outside is cold.

He noiselessly props up the metal ladder against the side of the garage. When we scramble up onto the roof, the sky is thick with clouds. Bernie sticks the telescope on its tripod into the gravel, and I sit down, leaning against the boxy metal swamp cooler, which is quiet now. It's not summer. If it were summer, we'd hear its steady rattle, and we'd hear cicadas, but there's almost nothing, just the occasional car rolling down our street.

I pull my blanket tighter around myself. A swath of light lurks behind the clouds. The moon.

"We won't be able to see anything," I say, squinting at the silent wall of clouds.

Bernie leans on the swamp cooler next to me, tilting his head toward the sky.

"You never know."

It's true. The clouds could decide to clear out any minute, and then they'll be over in Arizona within a half-hour. You never know.

My eyes burn. I close them and breathe in the cold, clean air.

"Oh man," Bernie says.

He rubs his nose with the palm of his hand.

"What?"

"I think I felt a raindrop or something."

The air has changed. I stand. It smells like rain, but not. The sounds are muffled. I tilt my face upward, and I see it now. Snow. Big white flakes drift and swirl all around us. Eyes up and it's like I'm flying forward. I turn around to face my brother, the blanket grazing the gravel at my feet.

"Where do you go?" I ask him.

Bernie keeps looking up into the sky. "What do you mean?"

"When you're not in school."

The snow falls silently, covering everything.

"Who told you about that, anyway?" he asks.

"Janelle and Karina Parker."

"Oh," he says, shrugging. "I just go wherever, the mall. But I don't have money, so I would just sit in the food court.

But I started seeing more cops there, so I stopped. Different parks, sometimes. But that's not always the best company either."

I try not to move or breathe loudly or anything, because this feels like the most Bernie's said to me, like really said to me, in a long time.

"One time," he says, "I got on a bus and took it to the end of the route. The driver almost left me in the bus. He didn't know I was there."

Jupiter's pull is lurking, beyond the clouds. The snow is starting to stick, all around us, in patches. It's so quiet. The first snow.

"I'm sorry," he says. "About your job at Charlie's."

I nod, studying him for a second.

"Why do you do it? Steal stuff."

Crossing his arms, he's a reflection of me.

"I don't know," he says.

I nod again. It's the truth, of course, but not all of it. Sometimes you can know something and not know it at the same time, because you shove it away so hard.

"I'm sorry I was so . . . ," I say, my throat thickening. "You know. When she died."

Bernie looks at his knees as I wipe my eyes with the back of my hand.

"I'm sorry, too," he says.

"For what?"

I sit down next to him, shoulder to shoulder.

"I don't know. I didn't know what I was supposed to say or do, so I just didn't say or do anything."

"I still don't know what I'm supposed to do. And I feel like I know less and less the more time goes on."

"You're not drinking anymore, though," he says. "Not like you were."

I wince. I had abandoned him when he needed me. The snowflakes are gathering slowly, a thin film of crystals coating the gravel, my shoelaces, Bernie's hair.

"No," I say. "And I won't ever be like that again."

I fish out the big Tupperware of mashed potatoes and offer Bernie the other spoon.

He takes it.

We eat the cold mashed potatoes and listen to the silence for a while.

Bernie leans his head against the stucco wall.

"Can't you just, like, *tell*," Bernie asks, "that Jupiter is at its closest point to Earth in thirty years?"

"Definitely," I say.

The King of the Planets. Its giant body swings toward us, straining against its own massive weight. Its face is an ever-churning storm that rages and rages forever and forever. I wanted to stop feeling, to be numb, but it didn't work. Sometimes I could delay it, but the storm always came roaring back, stronger than before. I feel both that I am the storm, and that the storm is crushing me. I imagine my body, sucked into the middle of its evil red eye, crushed into stardust. Sucked out the other side, into another universe, where Mom unwraps the telescope, under the tree. The telescope is smooth and perfect in her hands, and it isn't too late, because we still have plenty of time to become the people we were meant to be.

The plastic eyepiece is cold on my fingertips, and I feel Jupiter's presence, skulking just beyond the clouds.

I look into the telescope, but all I see is white.

"Do you want me to pretend to be sick tomorrow?" Bernie asks. "I can stay home with you. We could play video games. Did Mom ever do that with you?"

My heart clenches.

"Mom let you stay home sick from school and she played video games with you?"

He pulls at a thread on the cuff of his sleeve. I can't believe it. I never saw her play a video game, not even once. I can't even picture that.

"Do you want to see?" he asks.

In the living room, it's as if he's showing me some secret garden, some hidden passageway, the way he opens the drawer underneath the TV and pulls out the video game console. He carefully untangles the wires wrapped around the plastic controllers.

"We were actually getting pretty far. She said her friend at work gave this to her to help her relax. She said she was playing it to try to quit smoking or something. So yeah, one day she showed me when I was home sick, and then it kind of just, became a thing."

He means it became their thing. They had a thing. Of course they did, they probably had lots of things. Bernie probably knows things about her that I didn't. He remembers things that I don't. He holds pieces of her that I'm missing.

He hands me the controller.

The room is dark, but he's all lit up in the blue from the

screen. The music is down way low, electronic and repetitive and soothing.

There is one saved game called *Flubs and Mommy*.

"Let's start from the beginning," he says, creating a new game. "I'll show you how."

Chapter Twenty-Three

Long after Bernie goes to bed, around 1:30, I pace back and forth across my bedroom floor, which is covered in dirty clothes. And I think about what it could look like. Homeschooling with Dad. Watching Bernie leave with his violin case for LMHS every day. Waiting until I can take the GED. It's only a year and a half.

But each second of each minute of each one of those days weighs heavy. Every day with Dad. Just me and Dad, in this house, with his rules, and his way, and there's no room for mine. No room for me. And I know that I won't go there— because what could possibly be there for me?—but I do think about Tucson, Arizona, the place stamped on the envelopes from my grandfather. And say I did board the Amtrak train that leaves at dawn, say I did leave, what might I say to him, when I got there?

So, Grandpa, I've been thinking about getting crushed inside Jupiter's Great Red Spot.

I've been dreaming of my mother. And in the dream I can't speak, and then I leave her behind.

What do you think that means?

Say I did go. Somewhere. Outside the city grid that binds my life. What then?

I dump the contents of my backpack onto the top of my bed,

books and pencil stubs and torn notebook pages tumbling out. I shove some cash I've been saving into my empty backpack. Then I wrap my arms around a pile of clothes on the floor and stuff them in, pull my jean jacket from the back of my closet and put it on.

When I jam my hands into my pockets, my fingers close around cool metal.

A delicate chain. I pull it out slowly.

Chapter Twenty-Four
THEN

Mom's cold fingers fumble with the clasp at the nape of my neck. I touch the charm, a single teardrop that catches the light. It's her necklace, the one she wears to church and to non-church, anytime she's not at work, like when she's leaning over an open textbook from night school, when she's studying to get a certificate for—I forget the word for it, but it will mean she gets paid more money by the hour than she gets paid now. Leaning forward, highlighting something, and the teardrop sways forward.

She's always working her first job, or her second job, or studying to get a new job, or feeding the neighbors or yelling at me.

And this necklace is always resting at the base of her throat. And it's not fair at all, her life, how much of her time on earth is taking care of people who treat her like dirt, and she never complains about it, she's never mad at the world, just me.

When she finally gets the necklace closed, she looks at me, at my reflection in the mirror, and says it looks perfect with the confirmation dress, as if she could *make* everything perfect by just making it look that way. I know that during the ceremony, she'll be holding up her phone with both hands, recording the entire thing, but she'll be looking at me through the camera lens, layers of glass and plastic and microchips between us, processing the image of me and turning me upside down until I look like the daughter in her mind, the daughter she can send an image of back overseas, with a caption that says, *We're doing so well, see, it was worth leaving, in the end.*

Chapter Twenty-Five

The chain is warm in my palm. The teardrop charm is smooth. The corner of my sketchbook peeks out from underneath a stack of haphazard papers—fake driving logs, worksheets that I'll never finish. I put the necklace on and it rests right on that tender spot at the base of my throat.

With a click, I turn on my desk lamp, and my workspace is illuminated.

I brush aside the stack of paper.

Pull the sketchbook toward me, open the cover.

All these pages I did. Pages and pages of panels and words and faces, but the central focus is always the same: what I said, what I didn't say. What I did, what I didn't do. Compulsively returning to the page, to the same moments in time, trying to find it, the exact moment where I went wrong. The shading, the focus, the placement: me. Me, at the center of every panel. What did *I* do? What did *I* say?

I flip through until I find a crisp, blank page.

Pencil scratches out the kitchen tiles, and a soft-faced Bernie, a toddler, crying, really hard. Screaming, his face all red. He is rolling around on the linoleum, pulling at his shirt, pounding his fist against himself.

"What, Bern?" Dad asks, frustrated.

He's tried everything, but nothing is working. He has papers to grade. He has dinner to make.

"What do you want?" he begs. "Come on, Mommy's trying to sleep."

He's pleading with him, begging him, but the harder he begs, the more Bernie cries.

Then Mom enters the frame, looking exhausted, her hands cupped together, cradling something precious. She bends down, and she takes Bernie's hands, and she puts something in them.

"Can you fix this for me?" she says.

I shade his chubby little fists, the fat tears rolling down his face, his chest still heaving. He looks down at it, the necklace from her jewelry box. A gold chain, tangled up in a million tight little knots.

"Can you untangle it?" she asks.

And he takes a big breath in. This takes up a whole panel, the big intake of breath.

His little chest rising, filling.

He wipes his nose on his sleeve and sets to work with his long little fingers. He pulls himself up and sits cross-legged, loosening the chain. Knot by knot. And when one knot comes undone, another forms. And then he undoes that one. And the next.

Mom and Dad watch his breathing until it slows, calms.

"I was handling it," Dad says.

"It's fine," she says.

Mom's long, dark hair falls over her shoulder as she closes her eyes to listen to the silence. I don't appear on this page at all, but I was there, watching. I was always watching, trying to learn what I was supposed to do, and not do, so that Dad could grade papers, and make dinner, and so that Mommy could sleep.

Chapter Twenty-Six

NOW

My phone screen lights up at my elbow. It's 2:30 a.m.

When I straighten up, my neck is stiff from being hunched over my sketchbook.

I can't believe whose name I see on my phone screen. Of all people. And at this time of night.

"What's wrong?" I ask.

I adjust the rearview mirror again, still dissatisfied. The seat still feels uncomfortably upright. My dad's driver settings are all wrong for me. As I pull away from a beige house on a beige block, the sounds of a house party recede into the distance.

Yvonne Morales is slumped in the passenger seat next to me, her eye makeup running down her face.

She draws the seat belt down and clicks it into place, hiccuping softly. She's drunk, and I've never seen her drunk before. Not at any of the parties we'd been to together at Jasmine Padilla's house. At each one of those, I watched her drink just enough. Just enough to be seen as fun, and part of the group, by Nick and whoever else. Just enough so that when she asked Tes to drive her home it would seem reasonable, and then Tes would have to stay as long as Yvonne wanted to stay, and therefore I'd have to stay, and none of us would be lying to our parents when I said we'd been together all night.

But not enough to lose *control*. Not enough to ever be caught looking like this, so blurred around the edges. Rumpled, and hiccuping, and weepy.

"So, what? Tes didn't pick up the phone?" I can't help asking.

She glares at me, and then she's more like Yvonne again.

"Shut up," she says.

The streets are empty. It's just us, headlights illuminating the dotted yellow line. The cell towers on Sandia Crest blinking against the dark.

"Are you okay?" I ask after a while.

She shrugs.

"I'll be okay."

She does not elaborate on what she already told me over the phone, which was that she needed a ride home and from where. She did not seem to think I wouldn't come. Because of course I would. She called, and she needed me, and so I came.

"When did you get your learner's permit?" she asks.

"I didn't," I say, laughing.

"Well, you seem like you know what you're doing," she says.

"The last time I drove, I crashed into a tree, so hang on tight."

I can feel her peering at me in the dark.

"What?" I ask.

"You're wearing your mom's necklace."

My fingers touch it lightly.

"Seriously, though. Thanks for coming," she says, looking out the window. "You didn't have to. I know you hate me."

"No, I don't," I say.

"Of course you do," she says. "You've hated me for a long time. I could tell. I just couldn't figure out why. I thought, for a while, it was because you liked Nick. But that's not it, is it?"

I chew the inside of my cheek.

"Did you guys get into a fight?"

"Maybe. Do any of your new punk rock friends know where I can get my tattoo removed?" she asks.

That dumb barn tattoo on her hip. How do they even remove tattoos? I imagine a big pencil eraser. A tattoo gun, going in reverse, sucking the ink from skin.

If only it were possible. To go backward. To undo. My heart aches. To be with my mom again. For just one minute. If only I could have pulled her close that night instead of pushing her away. *If only, if only.*

"I just wish I could take it all back," I say to the dark, winding road ahead. "Yvonne, it was all my fault."

Chapter Twenty-Seven

THEN

Mom's late for work already. I know that. But she's the one choosing to make herself later by screaming at me in my bedroom over a dumb shirt.

"You're not wearing it," Mom screams. "End of story."

It's my very favorite shirt. It's soft and it's a nice color on me and Yvonne even borrows it, without asking. But she doesn't want me to wear it to the youth group tonight, the youth group meeting that I don't even want to go to, and where no one cares what I wear anyway.

"This shirt has *holes* in it," she says.

"You don't get it! What is *wrong* with you?" I scream.

I scream not just because of this moment, not just because of the shirt, but because of all the other times, and most of all, I scream because I want her to understand, or at least *try*, and I'm starting to think that she never will. That she'll never understand that I'm *not* Yvonne. I'm not. I need her to know. I need her to see. Right now. Even though she looks really, really tired. Even though I feel like shit.

It's like I'm screaming at myself sometimes. I think it's like this for her, too. Sometimes when she screams at me I think she is screaming at herself.

She thinks that if she just wears the right thing and says the right thing and does the right thing, every single time, then life will get easier. And people will respect her. And she wants the same for me, so that's why she is pushing it so hard. But I know, deep down, that she's wrong about this. And I'm mad that the world is like this. But I can't scream at the world, so I scream at her.

"You don't understand *anything*!"

"Why do you talk to me like that?" she asks.

And I hate myself.

When Dad tells her to calm down, like he always does, I kind of feel vindicated, but I also kind of resent it, because nobody asked him, and he doesn't understand any of this, and it's like this intrusion.

"We gotta go!" Dad calls out.

"You know what, I'm *done*," Mom says.

I snatch my shirt back and it's supposed to feel like winning, so why doesn't it?

"Do whatever you want," she says.

"Great. I will," I say.

And she throws her hands up in the air and walks out of my room.

"I'm driving myself tonight," she tells Dad.

He has been waiting there by the door to take her to work. In the morning, he'd return to pick her up, leaving the car radio off so she could close her eyes against the rising sun in peace, shutting out all she'd seen while we slept.

"I need to clear my head," she says, and takes the car keys.

And I go to the stupid youth group and Yvonne is there in some boring shirt and asks to borrow mine, she actually point-blank asks if we can trade shirts in the bathroom, and I let her,

I actually pull it off and give it to her because I feel like I have to do it, and I always do things I feel like I have to do except when Mom asks me. And when we face the mirror, she's wearing my own shirt better than me, shining and happy and fixing her hair, and when I look at myself, I look desperate and confused, and it scares me to think that it shows on my face.

And in the morning, I wake up early and get on the bus, like always, but then, as soon as I walk into homeroom I get called into the principal's office and my neighbor Mrs. Trujillo is there. And Principal Peña is looking at me in a way that freaks me out. And Mrs. Trujillo is wearing a bathrobe and saying there was an accident and we need to go to the hospital right now.

And it's the same hospital where she works, that she had just been driving away from, with the same break room where I sat with worksheets on Take Your Child to Work Day. And it's weird, walking past that room, because it's like I can see myself in there, with my legs dangling, sitting on the chair, coloring.

There are all the same sounds, the same machines beeping, and Bernie and Dad are in the room already with her, because they came together from Mesa Middle, and she has all these tubes in her, and she's wearing socks that aren't hers, her eyes are closed, and if I could only just go back to being that little girl sitting in that room over there, coloring, I would do every single thing different. Every single thing. To not be looking at her like this. Anything.

Chapter Twenty-Eight

NOW

"If only I hadn't fought her about the shirt—"

"Marisol," Yvonne says, forcing me to look at her.

We're at a stoplight. I'm crying. Her face is bathed in red light.

Behind her, across the street, a line of giant satellite dishes at the radio station point up at the stars.

"She was probably just exhausted," Yvonne says. "People fall asleep at the wheel all the time. It happens."

"Exactly. She was overworked. That's why my dad was going to drive her, but she wanted to be alone because *I'd* pissed her off so much—"

"But look at all the times she *didn't* crash," Yvonne says. "He didn't always drive her. She'd made that same drive lots of times. It could have happened any time."

"But that night, he *was* going to," I say, my breath catching. "He was standing right there, he had the keys in his hand—"

"You didn't know what was going to happen," she says. "How could you possibly have known?"

The light turns green.

"Sometimes bad things happen," Yvonne says. "Nobody has any control over it. No matter how much we wish it weren't true."

We're the only car on the road. Everything is silent except the sound of my own breathing.

"I really didn't hate you," I say.

"I see that now," Yvonne says, tilting her face toward the green light. "You can go."

Chapter Twenty-Nine

NOW

I wait, across the street with the headlights off, until Yvonne gets inside her house. All the windows are dark. She turns to look over her shoulder at me before disappearing silently inside her house, and I picture her taking off her shoes, and walking down the hall, and somehow I know, I just know, that I'll never be inside Yvonne's house, ever again.

But then she turns the light on in her bedroom. And I'm not sure anymore.

It's the strangest night ever. It's the strangest thing.

I've got my dad's car. A full tank of gas. My bag is resting in the back seat. The roads are empty, unending. I could go, just to see where they lead. I could go anywhere. I could leave forever, like Dad did when Grandpa kicked him out.

I could drive and drive and drive and never look back.

The car radio, volume turned all the way down, is glowing silently in the dark. I reach for my phone, and I put on Miriam's song. The one she played in the basement that night.

My heart pounds as I listen to the whole thing, the guitar chords, now familiar, and her yearning voice, and then play it again, because the song is like a time machine. It brings me back to that night in the basement, yes, but also to the crackle of the fire in Tara's backyard, and the twinkling lights, the furniture pushed to the side, the music turned up to the highest volume.

The photos of Tara and Joel's grandmother in the hallway. The way we danced. The way we sang with Elizabeth and Tara. The way Joel said, *The veil is thin right now. The veil between realms.*

Before I can think about it too much, I'm opening a text message to Joel Duran.

> did you know that the word for mom in tagalog comes from nahuatl?

I chew on my thumbnail. It's the middle of the night, he's probably asleep.

Then my phone lights up with a reply.

> late night fun fact that is amazing. how?

The cursor blinks. I chew on my lip, take a deep breath, and type.

> i learned a bunch of stuff. what are you doing right now?

I'm waiting in the car, across the street from Elizabeth's house, clutching my phone to my chest, hoping for something, wanting something.

Afraid to be, but doing it anyway.

My heart jumps when Joel rolls into view on his bike, beneath the streetlight.

One rolled-up pant leg. I swallow hard and step out of the

car as he comes to a stop in front of me, placing one foot to the pavement.

I look up at him as he removes his helmet, pulling my coat around myself more tightly.

"Thank you for coming," I say.

"I love a good mystery mission," he says.

"Did you have everything?" I ask.

He swings his backpack around and gives it a good pat.

"I got the goods," he says.

He's looking at me curiously, like he's not sure what he's doing here, exactly, beyond the obvious.

"What is it?" I ask him.

"To be honest," he says, "I kind of thought you hated me."

"What?" I blink. "What do you mean? Since when?"

"Well, since always," he says. "But then I thought maybe you didn't, at Tara's party. But then it changed again."

"Joel, I—"

With a click, the porch light of Elizabeth's house comes on.

"Oh shit!" Joel says. "It's Mrs. Parker. Quick, jump on my handlebars."

"What?"

"Now, now!" he says as I scramble up and we glide into the darkness.

The front door to Elizabeth's house opens, but we're already disappearing down the block, out of sight. The tips of my ears have frozen instantly in the wind, my arms are bent behind me, gripping the handlebars.

We barrel downhill, away from the mountains, the city lights shimmering in the valley below, the whirring mechanical sounds giving way to the white noise of the wind rattling against my ears as we pick up more and more speed.

"Okay," I shout. "I think we're in the clear now!"

"I know," he says, laughing. "Now it's just for fun!"

He swerves into the middle of the street, and I yelp.

"For who?!" I ask.

"You good?" Joel shouts.

His words tickle the nape of my neck.

I'm laughing now.

I can't stop laughing, actually.

"Yeah, I'm good!"

We cut through the night, down side roads, passing quiet houses with shriveled pumpkins covered in a thin layer of snow, little white crystals dusting the clumps of desert weeds and the cracks in the sidewalks. Dead center in the street, with no one around, nothing but empty road, it's a new way of taking up space, a new way of looking at old places. It kind of feels like flying in a dream, which is weird, because how do I know what flying feels like?

We've done a loop already and now we're coming up to Elizabeth's house from the other side.

"Okay, hop off in three . . . two . . . one!"

I hop off onto the concrete, pulled back down to earth, not flying anymore. But my heart pounds with the memory of it, and as I look up into the sky, at the big moon threatening to break through the clouds, I just want to scream, to do *something*.

I want to make something happen. Something good.

Gravel crunches as Joel emerges from stowing his bike away

in a shadow in Elizabeth's side yard. The street lamp coming through the neighbor's chain-link fence casts a pattern of light and dark across his face.

I could just kiss him.

Pull him toward me by his jacket collar. I could do it.

So when he walks right up to me, I do.

Our cold noses touch as he wraps his arms around me, and his lips are warm, soft. And as the world falls away, instead of feeling numb, I feel alive. My hands are in his hair and his are in mine, fingertips and lips and breath.

When the kiss breaks, we look at each other.

"Oh," he says, surprised.

His eyes search mine.

"What?" I ask, catching my breath.

He smiles that Joel Duran smile, the one that goes up a little farther on the right than on the left.

"Just, oh," he says, and moves a stray curl out of my eyes.

Tara's truck pulls up behind my dad's car.

"Hey!" she whispers from her driver's-side window, grinning. "Get a room!"

❖ ✳ ❖

We climb into the back seat of Tara's truck to wait for Elizabeth to emerge from her bedroom window. My knee is bouncing up and down as I check my phone again.

What if she doesn't come?

And I begin to panic a little, about the whole thing, because it's kind of an intense thing to do, to ask them to come with me to my mother's grave, for a kind of belated Undras, but maybe I'm kind of an intense person, and maybe, if I let them in on it, just a little, they won't turn away.

Even though Tara is sitting there, Joel leans forward from the back seat and reaches for the key, still in the ignition. As the key turns, the radio comes on, and the truck's headlights illuminate the empty street. He clicks them off, and the darkness swallows up the scenery again. I put my hands over the heating vent to warm my fingers.

Joel's shoulder brushes mine and a shock goes through me.

He spins the radio dial, in search of something in the static. A few snatches of words, chords, come through here and there, but every time he passes something and tries to go back, it's gone.

I always thought that if only I could kiss Joel Duran, he would seem like less of a mystery to me. That the space between us would disappear. Kissing him is something I have been thinking about for so long, I was sure that my life would be completely different afterward. But now I'm just sitting here, watching him attempt to find a song in the static, a look of concentration on his face, and he remains a complete and total mystery. And he probably always will. He may as well live on a distant planet, with its own moon and nights and days.

Joel glances at me, catches me looking at him.

"You okay?" he asks, smiling.

I want to kiss him again. Just then, the tuning dial catches something in the static, between two radio stations. We're in between, too, right now. We can barely hear the in-between song. I lean forward. It sounds like it's coming from very far away. Maybe it's coming from outer space. Just a few guitar chords falling down from the stars.

Joel settles into the back seat, shoving his hands into his pockets, and to my surprise begins to sing along. I lean against the headrest and close my eyes, listening to him sing the fuzzy song from space. Tara joins in, her voice like smoke. And I don't know what is going to happen next. There are infinite possibilities. But in the song, we're in the middle, and on the outside of the timeline, all at once.

When Elizabeth appears in the shadows, I sit up. I push the door open and hop down, running to meet her. She sees me and starts running, too.

"I'm sorry!"

"I'm sorry!"

We both whisper it at the same time as I grab her and pull her into a hug.

"My mom's a dick," she whispers. "I was a dick."

"No, she's not," I say into her hair. "Well, she kind of is, but who isn't?"

She squeezes me a little harder.

"I was the biggest dick of all," I say over her shoulder. "I mean . . . You know what I mean."

"I know."

"I know you were trying to help," I say. "I think I was just really intimidated."

"No, I was being overbearing. And I was intimidated by *you*. You obviously always do what you want, and you don't care what people think and you don't need my advice."

"No, I *never* do what I want, and I care a lot about what people think! But also, I kissed Joel."

She squeaks and pulls away, holding me at arm's length.

"Finally! Oh my *God*," she says. "Okay, so I hope what I brought is okay . . ."

She links her arm with mine as we head to the truck. It won't take long to reach our destination. Tara drives, weaving her fingers together with Elizabeth's at the gearshift. Joel sits at my left, his hat in his hands and his hands at his knees. The radio is blasting along with the heater as Joel takes my hand in his.

When we finally reach the cemetery, it's the deepest part of the night. The clouds have rolled away, revealing all the stars that are always there, whether or not we can see them, whether or not we know to look. I spin around slowly beneath them when I step down from Tara's truck into the cool night air.

We leave the truck outside the gate and navigate between the trees by the light of the moon, which is a warm, almost copper color. When we reach my mom's grave, I almost lose my nerve. A thin film of snow clings to everything. I grab Elizabeth's arm, just for a moment, before moving forward.

Even though I've only been here once, I still know exactly where she is.

We gather around her stone in the ground. It's obscured by frozen pine needles and leaves, and I feel a surge of guilt and shame. I kneel down, clearing everything away, knowing that we need to come back here, me and Bernie and Dad, soon, and never let it get like this again. The leaves come away easily, revealing her name.

ANITA CELEBRADO MARTIN. MUCH LOVED.

I place my palm against the stone and close my eyes. Elizabeth puts her hand on my shoulder. Then she's kneeling beside me, placing the candles she's brought on the stone—*sorry, I only had scented ones*—and then Joel produces a plastic bowl of microwaved rice covered in plastic wrap from his backpack. He situates it between the two candles. Next to the rice, Tara places a pack of cigarettes. My mom's brand.

Joel produces four little cups and Tara pours rum from a flask into each one, passing them around. It was something my mom drank.

"Thank you for inviting us to your belated Undras," Joel says. "That article you sent was cool."

"How does it look?" Tara asks.

Elizabeth's scented candles from her bedroom, microwaved rice, and a pack of cigarettes. I think Mom would be mad about the cigarettes, and she never microwaved rice, and one candle is apple scented and the other looks like a devotional candle, but when you look closely it's actually Dolly Parton.

"It's perfect," I say.

We raise our little cups and touch them to each other, sitting back to take a sip, and I'm so moved that they're here and they're not looking at me like I'm weird for doing this, that each one of them is acting like this is a totally normal thing to do in the middle of the night.

"Classic brand of smokes," Tara says.

I wipe my nose with my sleeve and laugh.

"She pretended she didn't even smoke," I say. "She wasn't fooling us, but we just let her pretend."

Joel nudges me with his shoulder, gently. I push back with mine.

Elizabeth waggles her eyebrows at me and Tara snorts into her cup.

"Wow," Joel says to them.

"Yeah, really, wow," I say.

"Hey, why didn't I see you at school today?" Joel asks.

I look up into the trees.

"I have to be homeschooled now," I say. "Because my dad doesn't trust me. It's a long story that involves me not going to driver's ed and lying about it."

I look at my mom's name in the stone in the ground and remember seeing it for the first time, and thinking, *Why is her name there?* How surreal everything was. How abrupt. Everything was happening so fast. It wasn't supposed to be like this.

We were supposed to get past this.

We were supposed to have more time.

"But now I think I just couldn't go because if I did, that means I'm moving on. It means I'm going on without her, or something. And I don't want to."

"Have you told any of that to your dad?" Joel asks.

"No, but—" I look up into the sky, full of stars. "He wouldn't understand."

"Feelings like that, they always go somewhere," Joel says. "Even when I try to tamp them down or pretend they aren't there. They come out anyway, you know?"

My hand goes to the base of my throat, to the place that aches, where my mom's necklace now rests, and I think about everything that I've been trying to tamp down.

A chorus of coyote howls floats through the cemetery.

The sound of their collective call chills me.

I place my hand on the cool stone and think about what still scares me.

When Tara turns the keys to the truck, the headlights flood the darkness and a sea of glassy eyes stare back—the coyote pack.

Elizabeth gasps.

Tara flashes the headlights at them. Blink. Blink.

The coyotes scatter into the brush, silently, a blur of gray against the trees and the headstones.

Chapter Thirty

NOW

It's so dizzyingly and frighteningly effortless to just leave everything, everyone, in the dust.

The car cuts through the night, putting distance between me and what's behind me so easily. Elizabeth and Tara, sitting in the bed of Tara's truck, looking up at the stars in front of Elizabeth's house. Joel Duran, unlocking his bike beneath the streetlight. They all disappear quickly as I point the car west and drive, and drive, and drive.

I punch my dad's number into my cell phone, taking a deep breath. When I hear the line connect, I hit speaker and then toss the phone into the empty passenger seat.

"Hi, Dad."

"Marisol?" he asks, angry, and maybe scared. "Where the hell are you?"

"Well . . ."

Glancing in the rearview mirror, I can see the city lights flicker in the distance. In front of me, a long, dark stretch of night, and the twinkle of one single set of red brake lights, somewhere far down the highway.

"Dad, we need to talk."

"Where are you?" he asks. "I'll come get you. Just tell me where you are."

"Dad. I need you to listen to me. Can you just fucking do that for me, please?"

There's a silence that fills the car.

"Thank you," I say. "Remember when Mom wanted you to go to that grief group?"

"Yeah . . ."

"Why didn't you go?"

"Why are you asking me that now?"

"I'm asking because you never talk about it, you never talk about anything, and you never let Mom talk about anything either. It was always just like, 'Why talk about the past? Everything is fine now.' Well, as you've probably noticed, it's really not fine right now."

I hear him shifting on the other end of the line. Clicking on a lamp.

"I know that, but—"

"Dad, I took the car. I'm driving. I'm driving away from Albuquerque and I'm thinking about never coming back. And I'm thinking about how Grandpa kicked you out and how I can't imagine what that was like for you. And that I don't want us to be like that. But I feel like it's getting there."

All I hear is the wind combing over the mesa. The yellow line on the highway goes and goes forever and ever.

"I would *never*," he says, "kick you out of the house. There's nothing that you could ever do that would make me do that. How could you think that?"

I wish I believed him, I want to. But I can't.

"But Grandpa kicked *you* out," I say. "What did you do?"

I think maybe the call got dropped, because he's silent for so long.

"We didn't get along. You know that. There's really nothing more to say."

"You just didn't 'get along'? And that's why you won't say his name, or go to church?"

"Oh, you know how I feel about church," he says. "They make me sing in front of people there. I hate that."

Tears spring into my eyes. I *knew* he'd try to brush this all off with some dumb joke, like it was nothing.

"No you *don't*," I say.

He doesn't hate to sing. I know the story of how Mom and Dad met at the karaoke party. I know how it was between them. I know that Dad was always trying to protect her from her own feelings. To distract her. From her sadness. Her isolation. He bought her a karaoke machine for our living room. She'd sway in front of the TV, holding the microphone too close to her mouth, Dad leaning into it when it was his turn.

Every year, Mom had to work either Thanksgiving or Christmas, so whichever one she had off was an extra-big night, with enough food for a hundred people, as if she only knew how to cook in portions for a large extended family, but it was just us. Bernie and I were overstuffed and groaning on the couch as they subjected us to their terrible, off-key duets.

"You *hated* me asking questions about Mom's beliefs," I say. "Because of *your* own shit with *your* dad, which has nothing to do with her, and you're obviously fucked-up from Grandma dying, and you're not dealing with it, and I'm fucked-up from Mom dying and I need your help to deal with it. I really do. Because I feel like I'm losing her all over again, every day that goes by, because I'm nothing like her."

"Short Stack, you're exactly like her. In every way that matters."

He can say that, but I don't see it. I don't see it at all. I shake my head back and forth and back and forth and then I remember he can't see me, but I still can't force out any more words. I don't know where to go from here, what more I can say.

The radio static crackles quietly.

"He liked cats," he says.

"What?" I ask. "Who did?"

"Your grandpa."

All of a sudden, Marty wasn't just our cat, he is one cat in a long line of cats.

"He was a gruff dude, really serious. Not very touchy-feely, you know? But he liked cats. We had a black cat with big yellow eyes named Rosebud. He called her Rosey. He never said he loved me, but sometimes he would tell me that Rosey loved me."

Jesus.

"Did *you* tell him that you loved *him*?" I ask.

"No, I just said, 'Rosey loves you, too.'"

"Dad, that's really a lot to process."

I feel the ghost of Rosey and the ghost of Marty curling up together in the passenger seat, a shadow and an orange flame.

"I saw your drawings," he says.

"What?"

"You left them on your desk. They're really good."

My eyes blur and I wipe away angry tears. Focus on the road. They are *not* good. And they aren't supposed to be, either. They're angry scrawls and half-formed shapes. I imagine him turning the pages under my desk lamp, illuminating those pencil-smudged attempts at untangling myself.

"Those are really personal."

"Sorry," he says. "But I'm glad you're drawing again. You always liked to draw when you were younger."

"What are you talking about? When?"

"You know, it seemed like you had a hard time talking, sometimes," he says. "When you maybe got a little over-whelmed. You didn't want to talk, but you'd let me sit next to you while you drew pictures."

I don't remember that at all.

The light has changed, just slightly, into that thin, predawn gray.

"That's why I got you that notebook when your mom died."

Un. Believable.

"Oh my God," I scream. "Jesus Christ, Dad! You said some-body left it for me. Somebody?! That's so weird! Why didn't you just *say* it was from you?"

"I don't know!" he screams back at me. "My wife has never died before. I've never been a single dad before. I don't know the etiquette."

He's so unbelievably dumb, I realize, and I don't hate him, I also realize. He's dumb in the way that I'm also dumb.

He's a person.

"But I *am* sorry," he says. "About everything."

The headlights illuminate the next sign at the side of the highway.

"Are you really driving right now?" he asks.

ARIZONA
THE GRAND CANYON STATE WELCOMES YOU

"Holy shit, you'll never guess where I am!"

"Wait. Where?"

If only he could see. If only he could see where I've come, hugging highway turns against massive rock jutting out from the earth.

"Okay, I'm on my way home," I say. "Sorry, I took the car. But I'll be back in a few hours."

"Where *are* you?" he asks.

"Arizona," I say smugly.

"Marisol, what the fu—"

I hang up on him. Take the exit and loop back around.

Punch the radio. Turn it up, loud. The song rises, swells, as the sign comes into view:

WELCOME TO NEW MEXICO
THE LAND OF ENCHANTMENT

The ancient tabletop rocks glow red in the thin dawn light. For a moment there's just me, the steady hum of the engine, and the wheels turning over and over.

The sun is coming up, and it's a bright cold morning.

Epilogue

Perspective is a concept in European art where the artist basically shows you how to view the painting. I learned this in art therapy. You think you're just looking at what you want to look at, but the way the light falls and the length of the shadows and the placement of the subject are all telling you, *Look at this. I want you to look at this part and only this part.* You can look at the same piece over and over and miss the other parts, if you're not looking carefully.

And when you're the one making the art, there are a lot of things you might forget. Because you might be focusing on just one part. Now I'm trying to include all the pieces that I forgot. Pieces that I didn't know were there. Pieces that I pick up from viewing someone else's perspective.

There's a lot to look at in the parking lot outside the library, for example. There's the hand-painted mural splashed across the door of the community fridge, and the word *gratis*. There's the volcanoes in the west, dormant, waiting. The mountains in the east, smooth, then jagged, then smooth again. The folding table that Bernie and Dad open together, its legs clicking into place.

The tote bags full of groceries in the bed of Tara's truck, which she hands to Elizabeth, who hands them to Joel, who hands them to me, and I place them onto the table. There's the space she left. The space she filled. The space she never left. My drawings include all these things now.

I've stopped asking the page what I could have done. It wasn't the right question.

ACKNOWLEDGMENTS

I owe a huge debt of gratitude to the many people who helped me, directly and indirectly, in the publication of this book, which is my first book—unless you count the one the generous librarian at McCollum Elementary School in Albuquerque, New Mexico, put on the shelf to humor me. Thank you, first, to her, and to all the librarians like her. Thank you to all of my English teachers over the years, many of whom allowed me (nay, encouraged me) to subject my classmates to a number of very emo-, and to be honest, anime-inspired stories, scripts, and half-baked essays during school hours, including a one-act play entitled *EMPTY* (oh the drama). Thank you especially to Mrs. Gordon, who in seventh grade talked me out of the pen name I was fixated on at the time. I'm glad my name is on this book, and I assure you, reader, that any missteps in it are mine only, and that just about everything good is because of someone else.

Thank you to my literary agent, Serene Hakim, for your thoughtful edit letters, phone calls, and lunches filled with gentle encouragement and cheese in all its glorious forms. Serene once asked the question that every writer needs to hear: "Do we need all these paragraphs about coyotes?" and no, we did not. But seriously, Serene, thank you for everything you do. You saw and believed in what I was trying to do before I even did.

To my editor, Kat Brzozowski, whose keen insight and warm affirmations were always spot-on, thank you for helping me bring Marisol's story into focus and balance. I'm in awe of what you do and how you do it—working with you is making me a better writer. What more could I ask for? Thank you to the entire team at Feiwel & Friends, where my book has found its perfect home: Jean Feiwel, Liz Szabla, Rich Deas, Holly West, Anna Roberto, Dawn Ryan, Celeste Cass, Emily Settle, Rachel Diebel, Foyinsi Adegbonmire, Lelia Mander, Brittany Groves, Veronica Mang, and Meg Sayre. Thank you to Katty Huertas for this gorgeous cover art: It's perfect, right down to the nopales.

I am forever grateful to all the wonderful writers who read this book and discussed it with me, in its many pieces and permutations, each generously lending me their time and perspectives and impacting this story in indelible ways, including: Megan Vasquez, Tina Ehsanipour, Lalita Abhyankar, Blake McKay, and Elizabeth Dwyer, who has been there since the beginning. Thank you to my cousin, Elé Rogers, who, in addition to lending me her valuable "mom" perspective on the manuscript, informed me of the critical differences between gophers and prairie dogs.

Thank you to everyone in my MFA workshop groups at Antioch University Los Angeles, especially Erica Colón, Ariel Lawrence, Regan Humphrey, and Aldo Puicon. A special shout-out to Debbie Wright, who once picked up the phone to call me (!) after I'd responded to her *how's the writing going?* text with a dire update: *well, I'm lying on the floor.*

Words fail to describe my gratitude for the world's most iconic critique group: Randi Burdette, Sara Lord, Phoebe Low, Rosemary Melchior, Elishia Merricks, Gigi Rodriguez, Theresa Soonyoung Park, Carolyn Tara O'Neil, Samantha Panepinto, Jennifer Poe, and a special thank you to Kacen Callender, who founded YA Writers Unite. I literally could not have done this without you all.

To my amazing MFA program mentors and workshop leaders at Antioch University Los Angeles: Lilliam Rivera, Gayle Brandeis, Francesca Lia Block, and especially to Naima Coster, Aminah Mae Safi, and Aditi Khorana for your indispensable help with this manuscript. Aditi, your guidance was a gift at a moment when this story was extremely tender and finding its footing, thank you especially for showing me just who I am writing for, and why it matters. I'm so thankful to the entire MFA program team, especially Victoria Chang, Lisa Locascio Nighthawk, Daisy Salas, and Natalie Truhan, for everything you did to make the experience impactful for and accessible to writers like me.

Thank you to the incredible writer Ream Shukairy for your comraderie and support. I'm so glad we're on this debut journey together. Thank you to Kelli Trapnell and Sarah Kennedy for everything you do to bring creative people together no matter where you are.

I have so much gratitude to the artists and mentors at Tricklock Company, and to Dr. Ted Jojola and Dr. Adelamar Alcántara, for the Manoa Project, which changed my life when I was a teen. Tita Dely, rest in peace.

I'm grateful to my therapist, Miriam, who has helped me navigate grief, wrap my mind around trauma, and begin the work of understanding myself so that I can (endeavor to) be a better daughter, sister, partner, and friend.

To my dad, Tim, who took me to the library whenever I asked, and wrote in the margins of all his books, I wish I knew what you would have written in mine. Thank you to my mom, Erlinda, my sister, Sarah, and my brother, Matt, and to all my family and friends who have shown up for me in ways that are steady and breathtaking and that I frankly don't feel like I deserve, thank you. This book is obviously inspired by you.

Adam, I owe you a lot of sandwiches (my favorite food), and it will take years and years to pay you back, but I can think of no better way to spend them.

Lastly, I must mention the cats. My beloved furry companion, Nina, did nothing in support of this book. In fact, she did everything in her power to keep me from writing it so that I would cuddle with her in a sunbeam instead. Perhaps that's why it took me so long. We miss you, girl.

Thank you for reading this
Feiwel & Friends book.
The friends who made

*I'd Rather
Burn Than
Bloom*

possible are:

JEAN FEIWEL, *Publisher*
LIZ SZABLA, VP, *Associate Publisher*
RICH DEAS, *Senior Creative Director*
HOLLY WEST, *Senior Editor*
ANNA ROBERTO, *Senior Editor*
KAT BRZOZOWSKI, *Senior Editor*
DAWN RYAN, *Executive Managing Editor*
CELESTE CASS, *Production Manager*
EMILY SETTLE, *Editor*
RACHEL DIEBEL, *Editor*
FOYINSI ADEGBONMIRE, *Associate Editor*
BRITTANY GROVES, *Assistant Editor*
LELIA MANDER, *Production Editor*
VERONICA MANG, *Associate Designer*
MEG SAYRE, *Junior Designer*

Follow us on Facebook or visit us online at mackids.com.
Our books are friends for life.